≠ 37
7/92

Naked to the Waist

Naked to the Waist

ALICE ELLIOTT DARK

Houghton Mifflin Company

BOSTON

1991

For information about permission to reproduce selections
from this book, write to Permissions, Houghton Mifflin
Company, 2 Park Street, Boston, Massachusetts 02108.

Library of Congress Cataloging-in-Publication Data

Dark, Alice Elliott.
Naked to the waist / Alice Elliott Dark.
p.   cm.
ISBN 0-395-57818-3
I. Title.
PS3554.A714N35   1991
813'.54—dc20   91-4761
CIP

Printed in the United States of America

AGM   10   9   8   7   6   5   4   3   2   1

"The Comfortable Apartment" previously
appeared in *The Pacific Review*.

FOR

Adrienne Adam Bachrach

AND

Larry Dark

.

Contents

The Interior Studio

FOR MANY YEARS, just before she began to bleed each month, Lela slept all afternoon wrapped up in the old flowered quilts she'd rescued from her mother's attic. The quilts had been a wedding present to Lela's parents, twin-bed quilts, just the thing for a nice fifties couple. Lela had no interest in sewing; nevertheless, she tried to preserve the quilts by patching the rips as they occurred. It was a hopeless project. The quilts were destined to disintegrate, with or without her. Eventually she accepted the fact that when she napped on them they would tear, and she would awake to find tufts of down pressed into her legs and forearms, as if it were her own stuffing that was leaking away.

On those afternoons she dreamed of her father, who had died when she was ten. She was no longer afraid to dream about him the way she had been when she was younger. On the contrary, she welcomed the opportunity to see him again in any form. The unbearable part was to wake up and discover that he was not alive. Even twenty-seven years later, it was still a shock. She carried him away from her naps and into her day, wondering about him. What would he think of my apartment? Would he like Lewis? Would he think my paintings are good, or would they be too quirky for him, too intense?

On days when she was walking around with her father so heavy inside of her, she could barely get any work done. She ached — her arms ached — to pick up her brushes, but she had learned that painting under those circumstances only made her doubt her past accomplishments and her talent in general. It was smarter not to try. As much as she believed in sticking to a schedule, it was sometimes more productive to stay out of her own way. If that meant skipping a day, so be it.

"Be sure to tell everyone that you played hooky today," her husband, Lewis, advised her whenever she lost time to a foggy mood. "That's what everyone wants to think you do anyway. Don't waste an opportunity to enhance your indolent image."

"Maybe I should wash the kitchen floor," she would say thoughtfully, not yet free of the guilt engendered by willfully taking a studio day off. Everyone she knew who worked in an office all week thought she had an easy life because she had only a part-time job. From her perspective, her free time had been claimed by something other, something bigger. From the moment she decided to paint seriously, she devoted herself wholly to that pursuit, and rarely ever felt at leisure. She was too busy monitoring her thoughts, trying to figure out what was true, or at least how to honestly transfigure her own experience into something that worked on canvas, and that was not easy, not for her, not if she did it right. She could not explain what exactly the difficult aspects of her work were to anyone not involved in a similar process. Most of her old friends seemed to be constructing increasingly elaborate strategies to justify the choices they had made in their lives, while she was busy peeling away the layers of false explanations and spurious connections she had invented to help her survive the shocks of growing up.

"Everyone is in denial at some level," a psychiatrist told her at a dinner party. "Anyone who sees the world too clearly goes insane."

"That implies that the real world is utterly irrational, that there is no grand design," said Lela.

The psychiatrist stared at her blankly.

"Science suggests a rational network of principles and relationships in the natural world," she went on. "But you're contending that when someone sees the natural world for what it is, what they see drives them crazy, so I'm saying that in that case, the natural world could not be based on the type of grand design that science, or religion, for that matter, purports."

"That doesn't make sense," the psychiatrist said, smiling fiercely.

"What doesn't?" she smiled back.

"What you said."

"How not?"

"We need our defenses to protect us from the harsh realities."

"Or perhaps," Lela said, "if we see the harsh realities for what they are, we'll behave accordingly."

The psychiatrist narrowed his eyes at her. "What do you mean?"

"Your steak, for instance. We can either defend ourselves against the reality that this piece of meat was cut from a mammal who died in pain and proceed with our meal based on the illusion that all's well that ends up tasting good, or we can go back to the origins of the food and face the possibility that, all things considered, perhaps we should become vegetarians."

The table grew quiet. Lewis shot her a look of concern.

"It has been my observation that people who sentimentalize the fate of domestic animals have not yet come to terms with their unhappy childhoods," the psychiatrist said. He smiled at several other people around the table, effectively isolating Lela from the group.

"Are you saying that carnivorism is a sign of mental health?" she asked in a high, watery voice.

"I'm saying that I'll have to charge you if we continue this conversation any further."

Everyone laughed and resumed eating. Lela burned with embarrassment and rage. She was more sensitive than she had been as a teenager, more and more grieved by the injustices and injuries that her friends dismissed as "reality." She did not go out of her way to offend people, but she found herself offending them anyway, simply by the way she lived. She was no longer a relativist. She believed that certain kinds of behavior were unequivocally wrong. She was not interested in the mind of the serial murderer, or the childhoods of people who hurt other people. She recognized that abuse was liable to create an abuser; so what? Lela had no patience with mitigating circumstances. Her opinions were strict and absolute, and she was less and less able to keep them to herself.

"I said too much, didn't I?" she asked Lewis anxiously on their way home from the dinner party. "But why can't I feel free to say what I believe? I'm not trying to be outrageous." She shook her head. "I need new friends."

Lewis took her side completely until he sensed she was calm enough to scrutinize her own behavior with a measure of objectivity.

"I will develop a lighter touch," she vowed.

"Think of how Jesus told parables," Lewis said.

"You're right. It was when he deserted storytelling for action that he really got into trouble."

"You have to admit, it's easier to buy a nice story about a good Samaritan than it would be to have your money-lending table flipped over in the temple."

"I would never have a money-lending table!" Lela said automatically. Lewis raised his eyebrows.

"Well, I wouldn't," she said stubbornly, trying not to laugh. "If I wouldn't have a money-lending table, or eat an animal, or cheat on my taxes, why should I, under the rubric of sophistication and maturity, let it go when other people do those things?"

"There's no reason why you should. Your problem is, you want people to like you for pointing out the error of their ways. Instead of wasting your energy at a dinner party, why don't you reserve your observations for your work?"

When the dreams of her father became too pervasive, Lewis suggested she paint about him. She did sketches of every story she'd ever heard, and then she painted the ones that most compelled her. When she started the project, she wrote it off as time apart from her showable work, assuming that nothing serious would come of it. In her private symbology, she conceived of it as a room in her interior castle that had to be painted before she could move on to the next. She had borrowed the metaphor of the castle from Saint Teresa of Avila, who used it to describe the soul in its quest for union with God. Lela, too, was on a quest to an inner room of her own, and she had learned that there was no way to get there without coloring the outer rooms first. There was no real way to cheat.

She had resisted this part of the process for a long time, hating to waste materials and effort on work she knew had no value, but when she was in such a room, if she didn't give herself up to it, she found that the doors would shut on her and she could not paint at all. To avoid that, she had learned to obey her subconscious impulses, even if they were too private to amount to much. However, as she worked on the paintings about her father over a period of months, they became less about her psychological preoccupations and more about her artistic convictions. When she was finished, she took Lewis up to her studio in Harlem to ask for his opinion.

"Wow," he said as soon as he stepped into the room. "I didn't expect so much color."

"Is it too much?" Lela asked nervously.

Lewis put a finger to his lips. "Let me look."

He moved quickly from canvas to canvas, circling the room several times rather than staring pensively at each one as most people would have. Lewis did things his own way, so much so that he had no idea what Lela was talking about when she said he was a person of true originality and integrity. He always argued that he would happily sell out and write for the movies or television, if only he could figure out how to do it.

When he had seen enough, he joined her by the battered old school desk where she drew.

"It's good work, Leel. Sad, but good."

"You really think so?"

"I think you were brave to do it."

She crossed her arms. "I don't feel brave. I only did it because I had to."

"I know."

"I was actually the opposite of brave. It wasn't even my idea. You were the one who suggested I go ahead."

"That hardly matters."

"I was afraid to paint him because I knew that if I did, I would push him out of my system forever. I was right, but it turns out that pushing him out of my system wasn't a bad thing to do. Strange how all this works."

"So what are you going to do now?" he asked.

"I don't know. I don't even feel a need to keep them. For a while I thought we'd have them all over the apartment. But now they're done, it's over, and I don't feel attached to them as objects at all. I could even paint over them."

"Paint over them? This is your best work, Leel. People should see this."

"You really think so?"

"Definitely. You have to get some really good slides made this time and send them around. I'll bet you a hundred dollars something will happen."

Lela frowned. Her commercial success, or lack of it, was an uneasy subject about which she had contradictory sentiments, made worse because she had had a show of her own soon after she moved to New York and assumed that it was the first of many, one a year in New York and others elsewhere for as long as she could pick up a brush. That was many years earlier and it had never happened again. The best she had done was to place individual pieces in group shows. Lewis empathized with her frustration, but she didn't think he really understood. How could he? He was ten years younger than Lela, still in his twenties. He had gone to graduate school for creative writing, but had yet to complete a novel that he thought worthy of publication, so he didn't feel rejected on that score. He'd sold several stories and poems and articles and had a book of interviews with young immigrant writers due out soon. He felt both successful and hopeful. The world was meting out validation to him in doses strong enough to keep him going. In spite of the example of the way things had happened for Lela, he believed it would all work out for both of them.

"All right," she agreed. "I'll get slides."

"I think this could be your breakthrough," he said.

"You mean my comeback," Lela corrected.

Before doing anything, however, or making any decisions, she decided to take a week off from painting. For days she stayed busy from early morning until late at night in an effort to stave off the sense of purposelessness that followed the completion of a major chunk of work. When she wasn't at her part-time job at the magazine, she was running through the list of gallery openings and movies and friends she wanted to catch up on after the isolation of the last few months.

One afternoon, she was dressing up to spend a few woman-of-leisure hours browsing the uptown galleries when she found herself pulling the old flowered quilts out of the closet instead. Her period arrived accompanied by a new kind of pain that rendered her nonfunctional until it passed. She took an Empirin and wrapped herself for her customary sleep. For the first time in two years, she woke up without an image of her father haunting her. She thought that for once she had dreamed of nothing, perhaps due to the influence of the drug, but as the day wore on, sights surfaced from a new dream world altogether. By dinner, she had pieced together the outlines of a curly-haired child, male or female, she did not know. At bedtime, as she laid her head on her pillow, the breadth of the afternoon's dreams returned to her all at once, and she knew she had been overly optimistic to think her recent paintings had set her free.

Lela gave her name to the receptionist. "Will it be long?"

"Not too long." The woman placed Lela's folder behind a row of at least twenty other folders.

"I hope you have some good magazines today," Lela said, calculating an extended wait.

"Why don't you go for a walk?" the receptionist suggested.

"Really?"

"Just be back by three."

Lela stood still, considering. She did not want to miss her turn. She had been to three doctors since the pain had gotten worse; this was her second appointment with a specialist who had asked her to keep track of her symptoms for a month. She had little to report except for pain, and the feelings of powerlessness and distractions that went with it. The thought of waiting for even another few hours to get relief was almost unbearable.

The receptionist glanced up from her appointment book. "You have time. Go ahead if you like."

"All right," Lela said finally. "I won't miss my appointment?"

"Just be back by three."

In the spirit of killing time, truly obliterating it, she headed for the Ralph Lauren mansion on a corner of Seventy-second and Madison. She had not been there since her first marriage ended, but when the heavy door was opened for her by the actor who played the role of a dignified doorman or footman or butler or some combination of the three — the generic imaginary loyal retainer, she supposed — she found herself adapting with alarming ease to the lure of a carefree parallel universe. Her demeanor shifted to match her surroundings. Her back became stiff and straight. She casually examined dresses that cost more than her monthly budget and clicked them back on the rack with a frown, as if there was something wrong with the clothes. When saleswomen approached her, she kept up the pretense of being a live customer by accepting their help. No one had to know she was just looking; she knew how to act as though she were a discriminating buyer who carried a wad of credit cards in her bag.

She had grown up with money. Her parents had had money, enough so that Lela never really had to think about it. Her parents' money was quiet, so hushed that facts about where it came from or what one had to do to get it were not an acceptable topic of conversation in the house. Lela had not thought they were particularly rich. They did not buy fancy cars or stereos or television sets. They had none of the spending habits of people with easy money. Instead, they lived in a simply furnished house on a wild piece of land in an old-money suburb, and provided their children with private schools, tennis lessons, camp, and trips to Europe, all of which had seemed natural at the time.

Her first husband had perpetuated the dream, allowing her to float along in a secure world that included trips to stores like Ralph Lauren. Then, after her divorce, she suddenly had very little money: no one was silently paying her way. During the breakup of her marriage, she imagined that the worst part would be to lose the emotional security of having a husband, but it actually came as a greater shock to lose the money he had provided. Her place in the world vanished overnight. She moved to a crumbling apartment and learned to think about whether she could afford items like candles, hardcover books, and tinned asparagus, not to mention winter coats and vacations. She was good at economizing, and it was almost gratifying for a while to see what she could do on a few hundred a month until the reality of her situation sank in, and she realized that the condition of always counting pennies might be permanent. Then she felt as though she had died young and lived on in spite of it.

She remembered becoming dizzy when it occurred to her that she might never again see a live palm tree. It had taken a while to let go of the anger that came with her discovery of having been lulled by her former circumstances into a luxurious myopia. She wanted to blame somebody. She wanted someone to recognize she had not gotten a fair deal. It was when she gave up the assumption that someone would come along and fix things for her that she began to make the necessary accommodations to the new facts of her life.

She wandered from the top to the bottom of the Lauren store as if it were an old family house, which, of course, was the intended effect. In a corner, she found a red cashmere cardigan sweater at a nearly reasonable price. Lela wanted the sweater. She tried it on and mentally ran through her wardrobe, checking off how many things she could wear it with, convincing herself what a practical purchase it would be. She took it to the counter and was about to pull out her credit card when she reminded herself of the upcoming doctor bills, the cost of the slides, the new paints she needed. She laid the sweater on a nearby chair, too unnerved to take it back to where it belonged. Yet when she returned to the doctor's office and found she still had over an hour to wait, a vestige of the sense of entitlement imparted by the Ralph Lauren mystique remained with her and she would not stand for it.

"Twenty minutes is the outside limit for waiting for anyone," she said at a level designed to be overheard. "Please reschedule my appointment."

She saw the women in the waiting room cock their heads, curious to discover how her demand would be treated.

"Doctor had a delivery today," the receptionist said.

"Then you should have called and told me he was running late."

The receptionist glanced uneasily toward the waiting room where the other women were listening. She stood up and leaned forward, her hair accidentally touching Lela's.

"I'll put you in next," she said in a hushed voice.

So that's how it works around here, Lela thought. She wanted to insist on a new appointment to demonstrate that women's passivity couldn't always be counted on, but the pains in her abdomen and legs rendered her passive in a different way, a captive of her own desperation.

"No, I'll wait my turn," she said pointedly.

By the time she walked the few steps to the waiting room, the other women had trained their eyes on their magazines, her rebellion having drawn to an undramatic close. She imagined describing the incident to Lewis, picturing how amused he would be by her hopes that the other women in the waiting room would commend her for her fairness. In fact, she thought, they probably considered her a fool for not pressing her advantage when she had the chance.

She read the advertisements for miraculous weight loss and mismatched bikinis in the backs of magazines until a nurse led her to an examining room, where she changed into a paper robe and placed her folded clothes in a neat pile on the chair. She began to wait again. She gazed curiously at the chart on the wall of the female reproductive system. There were two drawings of torsos exposed from waist to mid-thigh, the organs pictured from both a front and a side view. Lela looked at them as if they were maps of formations on another planet. She realized as she read the anatomical labels that she rarely thought of the scientific words for what existed inside her body. It seemed enough that she faithfully went to the gynecologist for the requisite checkups and Pap smears. She might have let that go, too, if she hadn't heard stories about the advanced diseases often seen in women who thought a doctor's visit was unnecessary because nothing hurt. Older women were particularly susceptible, she had been told, owing to their incorrect notion that they no longer had to be concerned with their reproductive systems after the onset of menopause. They turned up in emergency rooms with cancers eaten all the way through their backs.

Tired of waiting, she lay down on the examining table. As she settled her head on the rather demeaning slip of sanitary paper that covered every surface she was likely to touch, she immediately had a vision of the curly-haired baby pointing with a cocked finger at the alluring spectacle of paper and wood burning in a fireplace. Then a larger hand loomed into the picture and pushed the smaller hand away. She sat up again and returned to the dressing room, where she took her hairbrush from her handbag and began to smooth her hair. There was a shock of silver at each temple that made her look like a stranger to herself. She removed her clothes from the chair where she had folded them into a pile and sat down. The longer she waited, the more witless she felt for doing so. She was on the verge of getting dressed and leaving in spite of the pain when the doctor arrived in the room and bellowed for her.

"Where are you, Mrs. Frame?"

"In here," Lela called out. She quickly returned to the examining table. "Hello, Dr. Dumas." She held out her hand but he didn't see it. Embarrassed, she pulled it back.

"How are you? Is everything all right?" he asked, his back to her. He was a big, blond, Swiss man whose energy further enlarged him. His white jacket pulled across his shoulders. She listened to his instruments click as he arranged them on the table. He turned toward her. "How have you been physically?" he asked as he motioned for her to lie down.

She described her symptoms. He examined her quickly and efficiently. His work was finished while she was still recounting her pain.

"It's endometriosis," he said. "I will schedule you for a laparoscopy at the end of the month so we can see exactly what the situation is. Have you been trying to get pregnant?"

"Not really." ·

"What have you been using for birth control?"

"Usually a sponge. Sometimes nothing."

He palpated her breasts. "It is so hard to get pregnant after thirty, much harder than anyone thinks. But there are things we can do if you want."

"Oh." She had forgotten that fertility was a big part of his practice. His waiting room was full of middle-aged women.

He pressed her abdomen. She moaned.

"You have a cyst on your ovary. That will come out. Come into my office when you are ready."

She dressed slowly and reapplied her lipstick, assuming he would see other patients before he saw her again. When she could no longer bear to groom herself in the confines of the stark changing room, she went to wait for him. To her surprise, he was already there.

"How is the twenty-eighth?"

"Fine, I think."

"I will send you a letter to confirm. It is an easy procedure. You will experience only minor discomfort afterward. I think the operation will give you great relief."

He had a thick, clipped accent. She had to concentrate to understand what he was saying.

"Is there any chance this could be cancer?" she asked calmly.

"There is always that chance with any growth, but it is awfully large for you not to have exhibited any other symptoms. My educated guess would be that it is not."

"And what exactly is endometriosis?"

He explained quickly, drawing diagrams in the air of errant tissue attaching itself to abdominal organs and the uterine wall.

"What about children?" Lela asked.

Another woman stuck her head in the door and said good-bye. The doctor smiled and waved.

"Children? You know endometriosis is a major cause of in-fertility . . ."

She hadn't known, in fact.

"But there is a good drug, the Danocrine, that can shrink it away, and after that people have a chance. This is interesting — after the Danocrine, eighty percent of the people have a girl."

She wasn't interested in drugs she could take in the future. She wanted to be clear on what was going on now.

"Can I have a baby?" she asked again.

"Not right away. Maybe after the laparoscopy."

He stood up. She did not move.

He shook his head slightly. "We will go one step at a time, Mrs. Frame. First the operation." He picked up a copy of one of his books. "I explain everything in here, and I give a very good diet to help you shrink the tissue. I think it should answer all your questions." He put it back on the desk. "You can buy it at any large bookstore."

He beckoned her toward the door. She stood up and adjusted the strap of her bag on her shoulder as she tried to think of what else to ask. There were too many questions to know where to begin, and she was thinking slowly.

"One more time," she said. "What are my real chances of being able to have a baby?"

"I have seen miracles."

Finally she understood. If she wanted a baby, a miracle is what it would take.

She headed away from the doctor's office on foot, up Madison Avenue, past all the beautiful stores. In her old fantasy about having children, it was always Christmas, and she had an apartment facing Central Park. Every year she and her husband would order two Christmas trees, one for the children that went up early and one for the adults to contend with on Christmas Eve. The children would watch from the doorway as the adults decorated their tree, their drinks pasting thin cocktail napkins to the top of the piano. Her husband's parents and her mother would remark on the obscene quantity of presents under the tree. She would laugh and say that things didn't spoil children, people did.

At Ninety-fourth Street, she tried to call Lewis. "I'll be home soon," she said to the machine. Then, without stopping to think whether or not it was the smart thing to do, she called her mother.

"What's wrong?"

"I'm calling from a phone booth." Lela stalled. She knew she would start crying as soon as she explained. "How's everything up there?" Claire lived in Maine.

"It's been raining for the last four days, so the house smells like dog fur and all the towels are damp."

"Please buy a clothes dryer."

"Everything smells so much better on the line."

"That's fine, but what about when you can't use the line? If you had a dryer, you'd have options."

Her mother laughed. "Spoken like a true New Yorker."

Lela sighed. "Is that what I am?"

"What's wrong?" her mother asked again.

Lela described her doctor's appointment. She had very few answers to her mother's questions.

"He has a book on the subject. I'll buy it and read it and then I'll know more."

They both allowed the absurdity of that to sink in. When it did, they laughed.

"Lewis isn't suddenly pressuring you for children, is he?" Claire asked when the laughter had drifted off.

The tears Lela had held back all morning began to come. "How am I going to tell him?"

"I thought you said he didn't care about children."

Her mother couldn't remember major events in her own life, but she never had any trouble remembering Lela's confidences.

"It's one thing to think you're making a choice," Lela said. "It's another thing to be told you can't have something."

"It's your body."

"Yes, but it's his life. He's only twenty-eight. What if he changes his mind later?"

"What if he does?"

"Hopefully I'll have my career together by then. Then if he leaves me, at least I'll have a life."

"Exactly. You'll have a good life. You'll be free."

"Mom, are you sorry you had us?"

There was a pause. "I like my children more than I like anybody else, but there are a lot of things I could have done with my life if I hadn't had you all. You have real talent, Lela. Children would use up all of your creativity and your time. Let the others have the children. The world is overpopulated, anyway."

A man tapped Lela on the shoulder and pointed to his watch. She nodded at him, holding up a finger to indicate she'd be done soon. "I have to go," she said into the phone.

"I'll come down for the operation."

"No, you don't need to. It was enough to talk. I feel better now."

Lela said good-bye and gathered her bags. She'd barely stepped away from the phone when the man who had been waiting rudely pushed into her spot and began screaming into the instrument, but she was protected from him by her mother's affection, which had settled over her like a shield, rendering her as remote from the world's ugliness as she had been in her parents' large, safe house.

Lela and her mother were close in a fierce, essential way that wasn't always friendly or even kind. Claire was not a strong person. It took very little for her to turn her back on her friendships and responsibilities and retreat into a narrow range of demands that left her untouched. The only events she could be counted on to respond to with the full extent of her concern were her children's illnesses. Lela often thought it perverse that something had to go wrong with her body for her to be able to attract her mother's full attention, while Claire saw sickness as an occasion when everything was as it should be between mother and daughter. Daughter needed mother, and they were both still alive.

As Lela thought about how she would tell Lewis what the doctor had said, she automatically began to clean the apartment as a way of reassuring herself that everything was still in place. She was aimlessly rubbing at a spot on the table when Lewis came in carrying two bags full of groceries. He hoisted the bags onto the kitchen counter.

"Guess what I bought, among other things?"

"Diet Coke?"

"Better than that. Creamed spinach and Cameo cookies." He held up the packages. "Your favorites."

He had baby skin on his neck. Sometimes he behaved like a little brother. She helped him unpack the bags as he told her all the little incidents that had happened to him during the course of his errands. As she set the dining room table, she watched him as he bounced around in the kitchen, popping plastic-wrapped blocks of creamed spinach and potatoes into the microwave. Then his shape was obscured by a sudden vision of the curly-haired child teetering around the kitchen, reaching up, its chubby fingers flexing back and forth. Unbidden, her eyes filled and her arms quivered as though she'd carried the heavy baby a long distance. She was relieved when Lewis came in with the food.

"So what did the doctor say?" he asked as they ate.

Like her mother, he had a lot of questions that she couldn't answer. He was angry with the doctor for not taking more time to explain things to her. Her ex-husband would have said she hadn't been assertive enough.

After dinner, they lay down on their bed.

"What if we can't have a baby? Will you mind?"

Lewis laced his fingers behind his head. "I don't really want children."

"We certainly can't afford it."

"No."

"Although no one believes us when we say that," Lela said. "I'm so tired of people telling me that we could afford it if we really wanted to. Don't they think we know how much money we have?"

"I could always get a real job," said Lewis.

"Exactly. So could I. Then neither of us would be artists anymore. We wouldn't be ourselves. We'd be other people, with a baby."

"I'm not sure that giving up everything we've worked for would be the right thing to do, even if we were dying to have children."

"I would definitely resent giving up my time," Lela said.

"I'd have the opposite problem. I'd be so obsessed with the baby that it would completely overshadow everything else. You would end up resenting me for not spending enough time with you."

"True."

"You would?" Lewis still became nervous when he sensed any threat to their solidarity.

"Yes." In her second marriage Lela had chosen to forgo whatever tendencies she had toward mollification. "Wouldn't you?"

He turned toward her, propping his head on his palm. "When I was growing up, I always assumed I would have children. I never considered any alternative. But that was before I became a writer, when my father wanted me to follow in his footsteps and be a salesman and my mother wanted me to be a lawyer. I assumed I would end up doing one of those things, and that I would marry a nice domestic girl, and that we would have children. Now I'm happy with my writing and you. I don't need anything else."

"Are you sure?"

"Yes. How about you?"

"I'd like to have a baby, but I don't want to stop painting for anything, and without money . . ."

"I know."

"But I really want you to think about it," Lela said. "I don't want you coming to me fifteen years from now saying you wish you had children. Or at least not to the degree where you plan to do something about it."

"The same goes for you," Lewis said. "If you really want one, I'll go along with it. But get through the laparoscopy first, and then we'll see."

He lay on his back. She stared at his profile. Sometimes she thought that perhaps the reason she didn't feel as crazy to have a baby as some of the women she knew was because she never tired of looking at Lewis. It was difficult for her to say exactly what it was that made him different from all the rest, if he even was different. All she knew for certain was that as she learned about him layer by layer, bit by bit, she began to love him in a way that made her think she'd never really loved anyone before, not even — she guiltily admitted to herself — her ex-husband. She wasn't obsessed with him as she had been with some of her old boyfriends. Her obsessions had been shattering, her jealousy unpredictable and intense. She'd had a penchant for men who were destined to make her unhappy. She threw herself into love as though she were diving under water in an attempt to make herself disappear from the surface of the planet. There were many ways of justifying and explaining what she was doing. Sometimes she claimed she was submerging her ego, as in an Eastern religion. At other moments she believed she was on a mission to make her men great. No matter how she put it, it didn't work. It was all an excuse not to do what she really wanted to do. She wanted to paint, but it was easier to go out with a painter.

It was different with Lewis. She was able to see his separate self shimmering beside her without giving up her own edges. Sometimes she felt swallowed up and made hurtful remarks to regain her own ground, but there were certain lines she was careful never to cross. She knew how possible it was to destroy one person's innocent enthusiasm for another with a single wrong phrase. What she had with Lewis was a fabric of the most refined quality, a woven silk. She treated it as if it were a holy icon with fragile material properties. She was as honest as she knew how to be, but at the same time she did everything she could to avoid tearing their delicate fabric.

As always, on the mornings of the days that Lela went to the office, the apartment loomed large and full of minutiae that needed attending to while time spun off, wild and out of reach. When she woke up, her first thoughts were of her current painting, but by the time she dressed and ate and made the bed, the ideas that had seemed so clear in the first quiet minutes of the morning had broken up, fragmenting into dozens of irregular bits, and the old self-doubts seeped in between the cracks. As she moved five items in the refrigerator to get at a sixth or got doused with water from the leaky shower head as she washed a stain on a throw rug under the faucet, everything seemed a conspiracy to drain her time.

When she arrived at her office building and melded into the rushing crowd, her mood shifted. She felt a sense of peacefulness come over her as she bought a coffee and took the elevator to the twenty-eighth floor. It was relaxing to work at a job in which she didn't have to generate any ideas, and the only pressure was speed. It made her feel almost normal.

Tony, her boss, was still at lunch when she arrived at the office, but her coworkers were at their desks. Her best work friend, Anne, had a chapter of her novel spread out in front of her and was busy marking it up. Lela waved at her, then asked everyone else how their weekend had been as she looked over the list of stories that were due in at the copy desk that day. It looked like a reasonable work load, but that didn't necessarily mean her boss would be in a good mood. He was the human equivalent of the capricious Old Testament God who bestowed favors unpredictably, depending on his own unfathomable agenda.

Anne spun around in her chair. Lela jerked her head, the signal to take a walk to the ladies' room.

"How is he today?" Lela asked as they headed down the corridor.

Anne wiggled her hand. "So-so."

Lela sighed. "I need some time off. Is he going to kill me?"

"Yes. What's wrong?"

Lela gave the short version of her visit to the doctor.

"So are you going to have a baby?"

"I don't know yet. I'm not sure we can. We'll decide after we get the results, I guess."

"My sister is going to a good fertility specialist."

Lela laughed. "That term always makes me think of women dancing around a fire, shaking gourds."

"It makes me think of triplets, quadruplets, quintuplets."

"That too."

Anne pulled her hair over one shoulder and held it to the side as she bent over to drink from the water fountain. Lela smiled at the higher-ups who walked by.

"It's a hard decision. It took me a long time to decide not to have a baby," said Anne. She carefully wiped her mouth with the heel of her hand.

"What made you decide?"

"Money."

Lela nodded. "That's the major factor for us, too."

"Mainly I was afraid that if I had children, I would never be able to become a writer, or if I insisted on devoting the kind of time to my writing that I know I need, I wouldn't be a good mother."

Lela nodded. "The thing is, I know I'll regret it if I don't have a child. I already regret not having had one when I was younger. But I suspect that if I gave up everything I would have to in order to have a baby, I would regret that even more."

"Exactly," Anne said.

Their eyes met and they smiled shyly at each other. They had both been brought up to take their places among the legions of good wives and mothers, and it still surprised them that they had ended up so differently.

"We'd better get back," Anne said.

Tony was in his swivel chair and raised an eyebrow at them when they returned to their office. Lela thought she might as well get it over with.

"May I speak to you?" she asked.

Tony laced his fingers behind his head and crossed his ankles on the desk. He was very handsome, although Lela had become immune to it over time. "Go ahead," he said, frowning.

Her coworkers were occupied with various tasks, official and not. They were politely pretending not to listen, a skill they had all acquired as a result of the boss's habit of opening his most private conversations to a public forum. Everyone in the company knew the most intimate details of his life. Lela had not planned on discussing her health with the group, but she realized that, in this instance, a public announcement would lead to public support, and Tony wouldn't be able to give her a hard time.

"I have to have an operation. I'm afraid I'm going to need a week off."

"What kind of operation?" Tony asked.

"Female," she heard herself say, to her shame. She saw everyone trying very hard to concentrate on their newspapers and their computer screens.

"Are you going to be all right?"

"Yes. I'll just need a couple of days to recover."

"Do you want to take this as sick days or vacation?"

"I would assume an operation would qualify as a sickness."

"Suit yourself," Tony said.

"So I'll be out the week of the twenty-eighth, but I'll be back the following week if everything goes well."

"Fine." He wouldn't look at her. "Do you have someone in mind to cover for you?"

"No," Lela said evenly. If she just called in sick, they would have to make do without her.

"Maybe one of the proofreaders could do it." He leaped from his chair. "I'll go try to find someone."

He left the office in a flurry of self-important injury. Lela took small steps to her desk.

"You understand this is about him, not you," said Anne.

"That's right," said one of the other men. "It's about his inconvenience."

"Naturally," said Lela.

They all exchanged helpless glances, then returned to their work.

Lewis was offered a word-processing job for two weeks, including the day of Lela's operation, but Lela told him to go ahead and accept it. There wouldn't be anything he could do for her, and they needed the money badly. As she sat in the doctor's waiting room filling out her pre-op papers, however, she wished she'd asked him to come. The doctor suspended regular office hours three days a month in order to perform surgeries in the operating rooms upstairs, so there was only one other woman in the waiting room with Lela. The office seemed strange and threatening without the usual throng of impatient families milling back and forth. She read a disclaimer concerning the risks of anesthesia, which included death, and she signed it, feeling reckless and brave as she did so. She read a disclaimer about the risks of surgery. In the blanks provided for the type of procedure to be performed, the doctor had written "exploratory laparoscopy" on one line, and "D and C" on the next. He hadn't said anything to her about a D and C. She wasn't even sure what it was; something they did after a miscarriage, or for an abortion, she thought. Was it scraping the cervix? At any rate, she didn't see what it had to do with endometriosis, unless the doctor thought he could reduce the risk of the endometriosis spreading by scraping her clean. She winced at the thought of it, then realized she was wincing at something she had just made up. She thought she should ask the doctor if she really needed a D and C and what it was before she signed the form, but when the nurse came to lead her upstairs she found herself being pleasant and cooperative, the habits of a lifetime defeating her intelligence.

She was shown to a cubicle with a gurney in it, where she changed into a paper shift and lay down. Someone wheeled her into another, brightly lit room, where a woman anesthesiologist younger than she asked her if she had any allergies and how much she weighed. When the doctor appeared, she reminded herself about the D and C, but he touched her forehead reassuringly and she stifled the impulse, not wanting to annoy him when he was about to operate on her. She took several deep breaths to relax as they pushed her into the operating room.

"Any questions?" the anesthesiologist asked.

Lela glanced up at her. "What made you want to be a doctor?"

The anesthesiologist and the nurse both laughed.

"That's not the usual question we get," she said, but before she had a chance to elaborate, the drug they'd injected into her IV line traveled from Lela's vein to her brain, and she drifted away, unconscious before she even knew she was falling asleep.

Heavy. Heavy. Stiff-limbed and gutted like a fish. Pain suddenly, strange pain, as if her private hair had gotten caught in a trap and was being ripped and pulled every time she breathed. She moved her hand toward the source of pain in slow awkward stages, her arm still rubbery from the anesthesia. Her fingers located a large lump on top of her pubic bone.

"Hello?" she called out. "Is anyone here?"

She opened her eyes. She was in the same tiny cubicle where she'd exchanged her own clothes for paper some time earlier, still on the gurney, with curtains pulled around her on all four sides.

"Are you awake, honey?" A young Puerto Rican woman zipped the curtains back.

"What time is it?"

"Twelve-thirty. You woke up fast. How do you feel?"

"It hurts down here."

The woman picked up the sheet and looked underneath. "That's where they make the puncture to put the gas in. He had to take a few stitches. They didn't shave you?"

Lela struggled to look. "I don't know. Were they supposed to?"

The woman dropped the sheet and took a step backward, her expression becoming more professional and removed. "Not necessarily. It's up to the doctor. How are you getting home?"

"My husband."

"Should I call him?"

"Am I ready? Shouldn't I wait and talk to Dr. Dumas?"

"He'll call you tomorrow."

"Then I would like to go home," Lela said.

A few minutes later she heard the woman speaking to Lewis over the phone. "No, she really insists on leaving now." She made it sound as though Lela was being difficult.

She defended herself when the woman returned. "I'm not in a hurry."

"You just rest until your husband gets here."

Lela obeyed. When Lewis arrived, he led her outside, where it had begun to rain. He held an umbrella protectively over her, allowing himself to be soaked as they walked the few slow steps to the curb. In the cab, she held Lewis's hand and laid her head back on the seat as she tried to absorb the pain. At the apartment, she lay as motionless as possible on the bed while Lewis went to get her prescriptions filled.

"You're sure you don't mind if I go back to the office?" he asked when he returned.

"I'll be asleep anyway."

"You're sure?"

He didn't want to leave and she didn't want him to go, but he left and she took a Percocet, which knit her day dreams to her sleep dreams as she drifted off.

"I can't believe that women put up with this," Lewis said.

They'd been sitting in Dr. Dumas's waiting room for over two hours.

"I know. It's absurd, isn't it?"

"What about the pregnant women? They must be suffering."

"Yes."

Lewis looked at her. "I don't want you to suffer, Lela. I want you more than I want some baby."

"Let's hear what's going on inside of me. Then we'll decide."

They talked quietly until it was her turn. The nurse led her to an examining room she'd never been in before. She sat freezing on the angled table until the doctor arrived, all smiles.

"I tried to call you," she said before she lost her sense of purpose to his authority.

He furrowed his brows. "Any problem?"

"Not really," Lela heard herself say. She became mute in the face of his abundant energy. "I had some gauze inside of me."

He brandished a pair of scissors and a tweezers and went to work on her stitches. In less than thirty seconds — one sharp jerk — he was done.

"You should have some relief now," he said. "We took out a lot of material that was giving you pain. We also cut out the cyst. One of your fallopian tubes is blocked, but the other one is all right. Any questions?"

She was lying spread-eagled on the table, naked from the waist down. "So I'm all right?" she managed to say.

"I am going to give you a course of Danocrine to shrink the

tissue, but it might grow a little hair on your face and make you gain some weight, so I think we'll wait until winter when you do not have to go to the beach, right?"

He edged toward the door.

"What about cancer?" Lela asked.

"You do not have to worry about that."

"And what about children?"

"It is possible. It is possible," he repeated.

She struggled to sit up. Her stomach muscles were weak from a postoperative lack of exercise. She had to prop herself up on her elbows and push from there.

"You're in good shape," he said. "You did very well. You do have rather large fibroid tumors, but I think we'll let them go for a while. Now you must tell your husband he is going to have to be a superman to get you pregnant. With one fallopian tube out of commission, you only have six chances a year. You can have fun trying, okay?"

He smiled and winked at her. Before she had a chance to collect her wits, he was gone, and she realized she was still shivering. She probably had been all along.

Lewis jumped up when she returned to the waiting room.

"Let's go," she whispered wearily.

"I thought we were going to see the doctor together." He had dropped his voice to match hers.

She shrugged and turned away from him before he could ask her anything more. She felt guilty that he'd waited for nothing, but she could not explain to him while she was still in the office how easily the doctor overpowered her. She pulled out her checkbook and went to the receptionist's desk, only to learn that the fee for the follow-up appointment was covered by the cost of the surgery. She felt shocked by this bit of luck.

"Are you sure?" she asked.

The receptionist nodded. She was on the phone.

Lela headed toward the door, beckoning Lewis to follow. Before they were safely out of the office, the doctor walked by. He patted her briefly on the back as he eyed Lewis. She saw him size up the situation, realizing in an instant that while this must be

Mrs. Frame's husband, he was not a husband who required too much of his attention, no one particularly rich or important or demanding. When he'd calculated that he didn't have much to fear from Lewis, he held out his hand.

"How do you do? She's going to be fine."

Lewis shook his hand and mumbled a garbled reply. He was no braver in the face of the doctor's successful rush than Lela had been. They stepped from the seasonless cool office into the heat of Park Avenue, too defeated even to speak to each other for an entire block.

"I should have demanded that he tell me what was going on," Lewis said finally. "I didn't protect you."

"I should have insisted he treat me like a human being," Lela said. "I hate myself." She glanced at him. "But we can have a baby."

"Really?"

"If you can tap into the superman aspect of your being, to quote the good doctor."

"Do you want a baby?"

"I don't want to take Danocrine and grow a beard, that's for sure."

"I'm willing to let nature take its course," Lewis said.

"It would be nice not to think about birth control."

"Don't, then. If we get pregnant, we'll deal with it. Other people do."

"Settled," Lela said, sensing that this was best left as a short, seemingly inconsequential conversation. "Now what?"

They stopped in the island in the middle of Park Avenue to discuss the possibility of a restaurant or a movie or a walk through the park.

"What do you really want to do?" Lewis asked.

Lela looked at the sidewalk. "I really want to go to the studio."

"I'd like to go write."

Lela held him. "Good," she said, inexpressibly grateful to have found someone she loved and trusted enough to feel free to spend time, when they could be together, apart.

•   •   •

One afternoon, after a particularly grueling day in the studio, Lela stopped in a drugstore for some toothpaste and found herself automatically heading for the shelf that held the birth control supplies. She was reaching for a box of contraceptive sponges when she realized she didn't need them anymore. In the course of her lifetime, Lela had used a variety of forms of birth control: the Pill, vaginal suppositories, foam, an IUD, a diaphragm, sponges, condoms, and, more than once, luck. She had for the most part been extremely careful about birth control because she never wanted to be faced with the decision of whether or not to have an abortion. Now, when she didn't have to worry about keeping the babies away anymore, she found that birth control was a difficult habit to reverse. Lela always knew when she ovulated, and was surprised to find herself automatically avoiding Lewis on those days. She had guarded against the possibility of conception for too long to simply change overnight. For his part, Lewis never asked whether or not the time was right, and she knew he was as tentative as she was about actually *trying*.

When she arrived home she found a message on her answering machine from the owner of a gallery in Soho. He wanted to arrange a time to come up to her studio. He liked her slides.

She went out and bought a pack of cigarettes, fortification for her return telephone call to the dealer. He had left for the day. She was anxious all evening, her hopes alternating with advance defenses against disappointment as she asked Lewis over and over if her work was good. Finally she fell asleep, taking her fears with her. This time the curly-haired baby was trying to climb up a wooden slatted fence until someone lifted her onto the ground again. She woke up in the middle of the night and reached out to Lewis, telling him about her dream.

"Have you got your period?"

"It usually starts right after I have one of these dreams."

"Come here," he said.

They made love with tenderness, bound by the bittersweet knowledge that nothing would come of it.

•   •   •

John Brandt, the gallery owner, loved Lela's paintings. After his studio visit, he took a day to think it over, then called her to schedule a show for the following fall.

"I can't believe it," said Lela.

"Why are you so surprised?" Lewis asked. "You've been working toward this for years."

"I know, but I'm so used to the idea of a show being somewhere in the future that I can't believe it's going to happen soon."

"Get used to it." Lewis was happier for her than she was capable of being for herself.

"I can't believe I'm going to be a real painter," Lela said.

"You already are a real painter."

"Maybe," Lela said thoughtfully.

When she was a child, Lela had created illustrated books. She loved to make up stories. Heavily influenced by Pooh and Paddington, she invented a character called Bear-o, who was able to manage his human family in a happy style contrary to that of her own fretful parents. She could hardly stand to reread the Bear-o books for what they revealed about her longings for normalcy. It amazed her to discover how early she'd developed the habit of art as an escape. She counted herself lucky to have found a way out, and she often thought that all the sorrow in the world was created by people who hadn't.

At school, she was not the most precocious painter in her class. One day she saw a girl draw a tree with real branches, a technique she recognized immediately as an advance over her own practice of making a green swirl on top of a brown line. When she tried it herself, the girl complained to the teacher that Lela was a copycat. Lela was shocked. The teacher looked at her work.

"Imitation is the highest form of flattery," the teacher said to the other girl.

Lela intuitively understood what the teacher meant, although the expression was complicated and unfamiliar to her. She knew she had not done anything wrong, yet her whole body was on fire with shame as she tacked her picture on the wall to dry.

She often thought about that episode when she considered why she kept returning to art when other children who seemed more naturally gifted lost interest and gave their attention to other things. Her path to becoming a painter hadn't been direct. There were years when she hadn't produced much at all. It became more than a hobby only when her first husband liked her work and gave her some encouragement. She painted for six solid months in the spare bedroom of the large apartment he owned on Seventy-eighth Street, and then she had a show — instant success. It was a time of great excitement, when she and her husband thought they were on their way to conquering New York, but it all fell apart as quickly as it had come together when she arrived at her opening and saw all her paintings hung on the walls of the gallery being stared at by other people and, as if seeing them for the first time, she realized how unequivocally bad they were. They consisted mainly of stationery supplies she had pasted to her canvases, with weighty words written around them in a graffiti pastiche. She hated them, yet people wanted to buy them. She was embarrassed for those people, and acutely ashamed of herself. She wondered why she hadn't been suspicious when it had all happened so easily. After the party was over, she asked the dealer to take the show down and not go through with the sales of anything. He asked her what she was talking about.

"These paintings are bad. I want them destroyed."

"Are you questioning my taste?" the dealer asked lightly, yet with clear menace.

"She's not." Her husband spoke for her. He laid a heavy hand on her arm. "Let's get some sleep. You're exhausted. Everything will look better tomorrow."

"I know a bad painting when I see one," Lela said. "I don't think anyone should have to pay for these."

"That's not for you to judge," said her husband. "Your job is to create the work. Let other people decide if it's good or not."

He exchanged concerned glances with the dealer.

"If I didn't think I knew what was good," Lela said, shaking with rage, "do you think I would be doing this?"

"It's a little early in your career to be pulling the temperamental artist bit," her husband said.

Her husband's having taken a hard line with her left the dealer free to play the good cop. "You're terrific, honey. You're just having first-show jitters. It happens to everyone."

Her husband was right, she was exhausted. She didn't have the energy to fight both of them. The early bad paintings went out into the world against her will. It gave her chills every time she thought of their being out among innocent people.

Slowly she began to work again, this time starting from scratch, promising herself no compromises or distractions. She rented a studio uptown. It was good to have a place to go where she had nothing to do but work, yet it didn't automatically make her work any better. Goodness seemed universes away, yet the more she looked at great work and read the biographies of the artists who created it, the more she became convinced that developing the self had as much to do with genius as did any special talent with color or line. Those who painted with great refinement were themselves refined, regardless of their appearance or behavior. There was a part of them that was hammered gold. Realizing this, there was nothing for Lela to do but to hammer away at herself, which she did in a variety of ways ranging from yoga to keeping a journal to sitting alone in the dark, searching deeper and deeper into her memory, pushing back toward her early consciousness when she had a past as a creature floating in a watery world.

She tried to see things clearly, convinced that seeing things clearly had everything to do with good painting. She tried to keep the obscuring operations of her mind away from what she saw. Again and again she despaired of ever being able to simply look at what was in front of her and see it for itself without thinking about it when, one afternoon, it happened. She had arrived early for a dental appointment. She flipped through several magazines, studied the postures of her fellow patients with a mind to how she might draw them, and restlessly tried to occupy herself until her gaze settled on the fish tank. She stared at it passively as she thought about all she had to do that afternoon and other busy ideas. The fish flicked their tails rhythmically back and forth. Every few minutes she had a memory of an incident she regretted. Her body grumbled angrily as she reprimanded herself for not handling this situation or that one better, more wisely, with greater aplomb. The fish glanced at one another as they angled across the tank, paying no attention to the ceramic models of treasure chests and mermaids that lay in the brightly colored stones at the bottom of their small sea. She didn't blame them. The decor was silly. From time to time they shifted to avoid a wave of water created by the motion of their companions. Vibrations filled the water. The water buzzed when the bubbles broke.

She entered the world of the tank through a blip in the time line that allowed her to exist only in the moment and nowhere else. Her mind stopped spinning, becoming instead a sensitive magnetic surface that registered the tiniest sensations. Colors overlapped sounds overlapped tactile impressions. Somehow, she knew what the fish were thinking. Their thoughts were quite unlike her own, nevertheless they were highly organized and intelligent. She came into contact with their minds, an experience somewhat akin to running her fingers over a curve of smooth marble. It was a perfect, pleasant connection, remarkable in the sense of satisfaction it provided, awesome in its rarity, yet also oddly ordinary. It was an ordinary experience in the best of all possible worlds. Astonishing, she thought, and then she was outside the tank again, ripped away from the experience as soon as she put it into words. Words had a time value that separated her from the present. She accepted that. It was enough to have had a glimpse of the parallel universe that was there to be seen when the veil of preoccupation was pulled away.

After that day she rededicated herself to her work, determined to become more than a housewife who painted in her spare time. That she was no more than that was the truth she discovered when she stopped tricking herself about her level of seriousness. She had assumed that because she believed in the equality of women and because she'd lived a relatively free life in a relatively free country she was therefore liberated herself. It was a mistaken assumption. She began to fight herself for her own liberation. Act by act, idea by idea, belief by belief, she reexamined her life. She learned to say *no* without feeling mean-spirited, to make her own plans and stick to them regardless of what anyone else wanted her to do. She spent long, silent hours thinking through all the obstacles that existed between her current abilities and what she wanted. What she had been doing was avoiding the painful issues of her own ambition, her drive for exhilaration, triumph, accomplishment.

In order to do her work, she had to change some of the assumptions on which her marriage had been predicated; without those assumptions, the marriage quickly fell apart. Her ex-husband met someone else almost immediately. She had her work. With something for each of them to turn to, they were able to conduct a civilized divorce and to part with their dignity intact. It was such a decent ending that Lela, not wanting to risk ruining a perfect record, had never dared speak to him again. She supposed he felt the same way, because he'd never called. He remarried and she chose to be alone, which was perhaps, she thought, the way it should have been all along.

For three years after her divorce Lela stayed single. Occasionally she had an affair or even some sort of relationship, but men in their early thirties, her age, were either looking for a wife or for fun, and she didn't fulfill the requirements for either role. Her inadequacies were fine with her; she was too busy to feel she was missing an important ride on someone else's boat. To her surprise, as she stripped away the layers of taboo surrounding doing what she wanted, she found that she didn't evolve into a monster after all. She was still nice. She still did things for other people. She still remembered everyone's birthday. She also painted, left her records out of their jackets, stayed up late, ate coconut cake for dinner, painted some more, learned to speak French well, watched exceptionally uneducational television, and felt content to live alone. She saw this existence going on indefinitely and had no intention of changing when she made the mistake of going to a party she didn't even care about and came face to face with the unforeseen element destined to change her carefully contrived plans. There, standing by some stranger's fireplace, was the funny, happy-go-lucky boy who became her second husband, Lewis Frame.

ॐ

Lewis always said that Claire was the world's best mother-in-law because she essentially left them alone. When she came to New York she refused to impose on them, staying instead with one friend or another in a large apartment on Central Park West or Park Avenue, where Lewis and Lela would be invited to come pay their respects over drinks or dinner. These were invariably light, pleasant evenings, full of topical, impersonal talk. Lewis was always impressed that Claire's friends intuitively understood that he would not be interested in stories about their children. Claire agreed with whatever Lela said to the group, as if she were an exciting new person whom Claire had just met. Often, as they were leaving, Claire would casually hand them a bag containing a present.

"I like your mother," Lewis always said in a slightly surprised tone.

"She's great if she's not your mother. I just wish she would spend some time alone with me. I'm the only person I know who has to beg her mother to pencil her in," Lela said.

During the week before Christmas, at Lela's insistence, her mother agreed to meet her for lunch. Lela had no trouble spotting Claire among the crowds in the great entry hall of the Metropolitan Museum of Art; she was the one in the beret and Birkenstocks, her eyes closed in contemplation of whatever was coming through the earphones of her Walkman. She looked eccentric among all the furred and jeweled ladies, yet effortlessly aristocratic. She had never worn makeup or skirts or jewelry, and therefore had had to make no concessions to her age in her appearance. She didn't really look younger than any other sixty-year-old woman, yet she gave the impression of youth. Perhaps it was Maine, Lela thought, the preservative powers of fresh air and cold weather; Claire climbed a mountain every day.

Claire wanted to see the Chinese garden again, but they found it packed with a school group of jiggling teenagers. Claire glanced around nervously. She panicked when faced with a crowd. If anything, she needed more privacy than Lela did. They gave up their hope of a contemplative interlude in the garden and went back downstairs to American furniture. Lela led her mother through the strange galleries where the furniture was warehoused on shelves, row upon row of antiques sadly out of use. Claire occasionally pointed to familiar pieces, but the quantity of items in the museum defeated her.

"I'm getting rid of everything I own," she said. "I don't want anything anymore. You children can have my furniture. If I wasn't married, I'd be in a Zen monastery right now."

Lela made no comment, although she could think of several pieces of her mother's furniture she would love to have. She'd learned from experience that if she expressed an interest in material objects, her mother labeled her covetous, and if she didn't lay claim to what she wanted, Claire gave whatever it was to her sister. There was no way Lela could win with Claire. She had stopped trying. She led her mother to the Frank Lloyd Wright room.

"This is nearly perfect," Claire said. "I'd move that piece six inches farther from the wall and use a little more color over there, but otherwise . . . Wouldn't you love to have a room like this?"

Lela didn't trust herself to answer. She inhaled deeply and pressed her fingers into her cheeks. "We did have a room like this, Ma."

"Not with this furniture."

Lela shrugged. Her mother had had three husbands and had never had to work. She'd had summer houses, club memberships, whimsical expensive vacations, endless dinners with famous people, five well-educated, well-clothed children, a tennis court, a swimming pool, a seventy-five-foot living room, and the freedom to do what she wanted all day long. Now she lived in a small house in Maine on the interest of investments her second husband had left to be divided between her and his children from his first marriage. She was more at home in her current modest circumstances with her third husband than she had been with the advantages and opportunities afforded by her former marriages.

For years, Lela had felt that the damage Claire had done to her was the central fact of her life. She could not shake her resentment; it dogged her step for step, contained in an ethereal body that mirrored the dimensions of her own. It accompanied her wherever she went and made the acquaintance of everyone she met. She knew she ran the risk of repeating her mother's pattern of squandering the moments of her life by imposing her own unhappiness on them, but for a long time the knowledge of what she was doing was not enough to prevent her from doing it. She envied her mother, and she judged her, thinking of all she would have done with Claire's financial security.

They settled at a table in the members' dining room and ordered a substantial winter lunch. As soon as the wine arrived, Lela announced her intention to consider becoming a mother.

"Now?" Claire said. "Just when you're about to become famous?"

"I doubt that." Lela blushed involuntarily.

"You don't need a baby. Everyone has a baby. Do you know how far it would set you back?"

"You've always said that. Now I'm not so sure it's true. I'm beginning to think I could handle it."

Claire lowered her eyes, effectively cutting herself off from Lela's difference of opinion.

"Listen, Ma. I'm beginning to have a little confidence in myself, enough to believe it might be possible for me to do a few of the things that everyone else does without thinking."

"You cannot be a great painter and take care of children."

"Is that true, or did I learn it from you?"

"I had talent, too, you know. But I had you children to care for. There was no time for me to be an artist."

"You have time to be an artist now," Lela said pointedly.

"It's too late. I don't have the ability to concentrate anymore."

"You had help. You could have rented a studio and gone there and painted every day, like a job."

"Yes, I could have."

Lela felt a sudden fluttering beneath her ribs as she noticed Claire's sloped shoulders, the deep lines leading from her nose to her mouth. She was getting old.

"I'm sorry, Ma. I know it was hard for you. It just looks as though it should have been easy."

"I suppose." Claire glanced around the room.

"We women have to stick together," Lela said lamely. Claire always made her feel awkward. Lela masked her uneasiness with a sudden stream of opinion on the subject of women's second-class status while Claire ate. She asked questions and answered them herself. She made small jokes. At first her mother smiled at her, but gradually Lela saw her expression change. Claire laid down her knife and fork and clasped her hands in her lap. Lela kept up her patter until it became undeniably obvious that her mother wasn't listening to her anymore.

"What's wrong?" she asked finally.

"You're not making sense," Claire said.

"What do you mean? I'm just being funny, or trying to."

"You're talking too fast. How have your thoughts been lately?"

"Fine, thanks. And yours?"

"You know what I mean, Lela. You can't afford to let things go, if you're not feeling well."

"I'm feeling fine." She forced herself to smile. "I'm just excited, that's all."

"About the show?"

Lela glanced away. The truth was, she was excited to see Claire. She found herself aiming to please her in a way she never did with any other person. She flirted with her mother and tried to make her laugh. Claire, in turn, because of her own tendencies toward self-erasure, found Lela's behavior alarming, too urgent. "Yes," said Lela. "I'm excited about the show, and Christmas, too. Lots of things."

This was a dangerous conversation. Lela wondered if she would ever be allowed to forget that once a psychiatrist — a friend of Claire's — had diagnosed her as a manic-depressive. Since then, every time Lela said or did anything even slightly animated or sad, Claire thought she should go back on lithium. She would not. On lithium, there was no Lela, there was no painting; there was only lithium. There was the memory of emotion but no real emotion, no authentic experience. The only thing the drug had done for her was to make her want to learn how to take care of herself so she would not have to live her life at the whim of misinformed friends and relatives and mental health professionals.

After going off the drug, the first thing she had to give up was the idea that feeling good was normal. She charted her thoughts during the period when she was not feeling good, and found that they were either faster or slower than they were during less volatile periods. Over the years, she developed strategies to cope with this. When her thoughts came too fast, she did her best to keep them to herself. She stayed home as much as possible, restricted her entertainments to repeated listenings to Broadway musicals, watched no television, read no new books, ate a macro-biotic diet, and meditated until she fell asleep. When her thoughts became too slow, she jumped out of bed the second she awoke, even if it was two-thirty in the morning. This technique alone was enough to save her life, or at least to save her hours, days, months, of obsessing on all the sadness in the world. She also made it a point to avoid sugar and alcohol, and to paint even if it meant buying a paint-by-number kit and working to stay inside the lines.

Her methods carried her through until she met Lewis. He was a calming influence in and of himself. In the new atmosphere of safety that he imparted to her life, she began to discover all the anger that lay beneath her disrupted thinking. It rose to the surface in discrete bubbles that broke every time she heard about an instance of unfairness or saw an example of cruelty. Even when she meditated, her rage was with her, making her blood rush to bother her heart.

There was no point discussing her rage with Claire, though. Claire would take it personally.

"I don't know what to get for anyone for Christmas," Claire said. "Do you think they'd notice if I didn't send much this year?" Lela picked up her wine with relief. The subject of her artistic personality had been dropped.

Claire had always had a strict Presbyterian suspicion of the excesses of the American way of Christmas. She had grown up on her father's stories of finding a lump of coal and an orange in his stocking and being grateful for it.

"You're the grandmother. Yes, I think they'd notice."

"I can't face the stores. You probably have all your presents already, don't you?"

"Wrapped and ribboned."

"Everyone always says you give the best presents."

"They do?" Lela felt her neck flush. She had never heard this before. She spent hours choosing presents, trying to find exactly the right thing for each of her nieces and nephews. Her wrappings were equally careful and creative, incorporating photographs and tiny toys and cut-out words. In return she received, at best, perfunctory thank-you notes, at worst, nothing. Sometimes she felt as if she might as well drop her presents down a sewer hole. Lewis told her her efforts were pathetic more than once. He was teasing, but it was the kind of tease that was painfully close to the truth.

"They do, really?" Lela repeated. "Maybe it's because I remember what it's like to be a child."

"You do, don't you?" Claire chewed at the edges of her thumb, a habit acquired since she'd quit smoking. "You really are an artist. I can't believe it's all actually working out."

"Let's not be too optimistic. There are a lot of things that could go wrong between now and the show."

"They could, but they won't. It's time for things to happen for you. There's a place in the world for your work. I've always known that."

"I hope you're right." Lela struggled to sound calm and sensible. "I do feel like a different person already, even though the show is a long way off. I feel the way men must feel when it's taken for granted that their work takes precedence over all other considerations. It's nice to feel one's efforts have value, even if you don't particularly agree with the current value system."

"I'm so relieved I don't have to worry about you anymore."

"Well, I'm not sure I'd go that far."

The waiter cleared their plates. They held on to their glasses of wine and ordered coffee.

"So what are the paintings about?" Claire asked.

Lela shifted uneasily. She had lived with the paintings for so long that she'd forgotten she hadn't discussed their content with anyone except Lewis and her dealer.

"They're about Dad, actually."

"Michael?"

Lela nodded.

"I didn't realize you still thought about him. You can't remember him, can you?"

"I do."

Claire opened her purse, then her wallet. She looked at her credit card, then put it away and laid the purse back down on the floor.

"You were so young when he died. I can barely remember him," Claire said finally.

"I was ten. That's not young."

"I never think about the past, you know. At least I wouldn't if you children weren't around to remind me all the time."

"You really never think about him?" Lela asked tensely.

"No."

"I can't understand that. Do you at least think about us, when we were children?"

Claire folded her napkin carefully. "You were a good baby, except that you had no interest in learning how to walk. I had to carry you everywhere. Duncan was on his feet at six months."

"I remember he used to climb up on top of the piano to drink his bottle."

"My friends always thought I was too permissive."

They looked at each other and laughed again. Lela wondered if Claire felt as touchingly awkward with her as she did with Claire.

"Tell me something, Ma. Are you glad you had children?"

Claire considered. "Glad is not the right word for it," she said finally. "I was too ambivalent for too long to ever say I was glad. Motherhood had its moments . . . such as when I had you alone, before all the others were born. Such as now, when you're an adult I can have lunch with in New York."

Lela's eyes blurred.

"Anyway," Claire said, "there's really no point in going into all that. The point is — "

"Let me guess." Lela smiled. "Your children are the only people you really like."

Claire smiled back, and signaled for the check.

Lela always took Claire's preference for her children as a compliment, but when she thought about it further during the bus ride home, it occurred to her that what Claire was really saying was that she didn't like anyone she hadn't had a heavy hand in shaping to her specifications. Claire was like Dr. Frankenstein, she thought. In a sense, all mothers were like Dr. Frankenstein. They formed a creature with what they thought were the best of intentions, but secretly, they always wanted it to be their monster.

In January, after paying off the credit card charges for all her Christmas purchases, Lela realized that her savings were almost depleted. Since Lewis had finished graduate school, they'd been living off a combination of the advance he received for his book of interviews, her salary, his freelance work, and the lump-sum settlement from her ex-husband. While it had lasted, the settlement had allowed them to postpone the inevitable moment when they had to make real financial plans. Now the small cushion of money they had dipped into whenever there was an emergency was gone, and Lewis's predictions of imminent success seemed dreamy rather than optimistic.

"I think you're going to have to get a job," she said to Lewis. She brought it up at night, when they were in bed.

"Can we talk about this tomorrow?" Lewis said, immediately tense.

"No, we can't talk about this tomorrow. If we keep putting this off, we're going to end up with no money."

"I'm working on a lot of things. I've got all these proposals out, and we'll get royalties from my book."

"We can't count on any of that. Those are all maybes. We need some real financial security in our lives. I can't live this way. I'm too old to live this way."

"Everything will work out. Trust me. I want to take care of you," Lewis said.

"You don't have to take care of me. Just take care of yourself."

"You don't have faith in me."

She refused to play to his hurt tone. "I have faith in your future, complete faith. It's the present I'm worried about. We need money coming in right now."

"What do you expect me to do about it in the middle of the night?"

"You could at least talk to me," Lela said, an edge in her voice.

"About what? You've already told me you want me to get a job."

"I don't care if you get a job or not. You can do anything you want, as long as you bring in some legal income. I can't support you anymore."

"You have no confidence in me at all."

"I have confidence in you. I'm just worried about money."

"Can we please talk about this tomorrow?"

"No."

Lewis groaned. "It's not that I don't want a steady income," he said. "It's just that I don't want to change to get it."

"And I don't want to change you. Maybe we should break up. If you were on your own, you could live a lot more inexpensively and you wouldn't have to work at all, aside from your writing. Maybe this marriage was a mistake," Lela said matter-of-factly.

"I hate it when you say that."

"I feel like I have to say something shocking to get through to you. You just act as though money is going to appear out of nowhere. I think your problem is that you spent too much time with your mother when you were growing up. You imprinted on her. You would be perfectly happy puttering around the house and reading for the rest of your life."

"I hate it when you say I'm like my mother."

"Well, then don't act like her."

"I'm not acting like my mother!" Lewis snapped.

Lela lay still, afraid she'd gone too far. It was all confusing. She had grown up having an expectation in the back of her mind that a husband would support her, and the ghost of that expectation still haunted her, in spite of the fact that she knew living under those conditions bore no real relation to the facts or goals of her life. On the other hand, because Lewis was younger and because of his talent and potential, she wanted to protect and promote him, to create an atmosphere in which he had the chance he deserved.

"Let me work it out," he said. "You just concentrate on what you have to do."

"Maybe it's the winter that's making me feel so claustrophobic about my bank account," she said.

"It's a little late in the conversation to start being nice, Lela."

"Fear makes me mean," she said defensively.

"Maybe you should figure out another way of being afraid. It doesn't make me exactly want to run out and do what you say."

"What do you want me to do? Manipulate you? Trick you? You married the wrong person, if that's what you want."

Lewis sat up. "I'm going to go read in the other room for a while."

"You can't leave like this."

He pulled his jeans over his thin legs. "I'm your friend, Lela," he said. "I got your message, and I'll do something about it, I promise. I just can't talk anymore right now." He brushed her forehead with his thumb in a mute benediction.

"I'm sorry," she said.

"Don't," he warned, and walked out.

She willed herself not to follow him, knowing she wanted to do so only to push for reassurance or at least for the last word. I love you, she thought, hoping he could feel it, missing the days when she had naively believed that love was all she would ever need.

•   •   •

The gallery wanted three additional pieces for her show, so she stretched and prepared canvases larger than any she'd ever before attempted. These were to be paintings of her father as she still saw him in her mind's eye: gazing up at the church as if he could see the bells ringing in the steeple; standing with his hand on the record player as if to hold the music; clenching his jaw as he drove. These were snapshot images, yet she had no pictures to go on to check the clothes or background for period accuracy. She was painting neither from life nor from imagination, but from her own memory. It was painful work. Her sketchbooks were crammed with ideas for angles and perspectives, color and line. Oddly, an unplanned figure appeared and reappeared in her sketches. It took some time for her to realize that it was her dream child, the curly-haired baby. She began to incorporate this figure into the paintings in a variety of forms until finally it congealed into an angel, a putto delivering messages from her unconscious to her memory. As she worked, she waited for those messages to become clear to her.

Lela looked at the clock. In a few more minutes she would have to get ready to meet Patsy Thorpe for lunch. She was looking forward to going out. For so many years, she had not allowed herself to see anyone on days when she was at the studio, but since she'd gotten the show, she'd found that having a real deadline to work against gave her more free time than had her own self-imposed goals. She had even begun to putter around the apartment, taking care of repairs and reorganizations that she had been putting off. She cooked real dinners, setting the table with candles and their wedding china, and found herself laughing gleefully at Lewis's descriptions of his job interviews.

It came as something of a surprise to her finally to articulate to herself what was going on; she was allowing pleasure to seep into her life. The previous day, she'd been walking down West End Avenue when she heard an odd warbling coming out of an old brick building. Rather than walking on, she stopped and watched as a cricket crawled out of a crack in the wall. It was a small thing, but it made her unaccountably happy. She felt the same way as she walked through the rain to the restaurant where Patsy had suggested they meet. The cold rain stung her skin and soaked through the worn soles of her shoes. She purposely left her umbrella at the studio, arriving at the restaurant with sopping hair.

"What happened to you?" Patsy asked.

Lela shrugged. "Isn't it obvious?" She folded her raincoat in thirds and secreted it under the table, then squeezed the ends of her hair with a napkin. Patsy waved for the waiter.

"I've got to get back, so do you mind if we order?" Patsy said.

Lela asked for a spinach salad without the bacon. Patsy lit a cigarette.

"Since when do you smoke?" Lela asked.

"It's my tribute to motherhood. I took it up again when I started having it all."

"How is the heir?"

"He's teething, which is yet another of nature's ways of torturing parent and child at the same time. Aside from that, he's adorable."

"My offer stands to come baby-sit for an evening."

"The thing is, I don't see him all day, and when I go home at night, that's all I want to do. It's wild. When you're a mother, you really miss your kid when you're away from him."

"I'm sure," Lela said.

Until she turned thirty-five, Patsy had vowed she would never have children. Then she changed her mind. When she did, her desire for a baby always struck Lela as being more acquisitive than emotional, an impression borne out by Patsy's bafflement when her baby turned out to be a human being. "He doesn't like me," Patsy would say when the baby cried. It didn't occur to her to read a book about child rearing until someone described Dr. Spock as an owner's manual. When she had finished the book, motherhood seemed more wild to her than ever. Lela joked to Lewis that Patsy was a perfect example of a little knowledge being a dangerous thing.

"He's mad at me for going back to work."

"Oh, come now," Lela said. Patsy's son was five months old.

"He won't smile at me when I come home. How would you explain that behavior?" Patsy challenged her.

"He's a baby, that's how. Don't take it personally."

"Maybe you're right. Anyway, I promised myself I wouldn't talk about the baby too much. I remember how boring it is when you don't have one."

"It's not boring to me."

"You're just being polite." Patsy waved smoke away from her eyes. "So how's Lewis's job hunt going?"

"Fine."

Patsy looked at her expectantly. Work was her area of expertise.

"Actually, I'm worried about him," Lela said. "He's used to having his days to himself. This is a real shock to his system."

"Welcome to the real world," Patsy said. "Everyone else has to work. Why shouldn't Lewis? Don't you dare feel guilty about it."

"I don't feel guilty, I feel sorry for him. I'm afraid he's going to stop writing. That happens, you know. It's like exercise. You skip a day, then two, then three, and it's hard to get it back."

"Look," Patsy said, "everyone would like to stay home and do what they want, but that's not how the world works. Maybe he'll learn how to be more directed. At least he'll learn what it's like to have to pay a little more attention to the bottom line."

"Patsy, he has a book coming out," Lela said hotly. "He has an M.A. He knows how to finish things."

"Then he'll figure out a way to finish a novel. He can work at night and on weekends."

"Can he? Can you?"

"The world doesn't owe Lewis a living."

Lela stared at her. Patsy barely knew Lewis, yet he bothered her so much that the vein in her forehead throbbed.

"Lewis doesn't stay home to practice his golf swing. He's writing."

"Fine." Patsy was flushed.

"You're mad," Lela said.

Patsy pointed to her mouth, stalling for time by using the excuse of chewing her food. She'd gained fourteen pounds during her pregnancy and it was already long gone. She and Lela had become friends during Lela's first marriage, when Patsy was one of Lela's ex-husband's account executives. When she visited the office and waited for him to emerge from one meeting or another, Patsy kept her company. She was one of the few of their mutual friends who'd stuck by Lela after the divorce; after the fact, Patsy told Lela that she thought her ex-husband was an asshole and a skirt-chaser anyway.

Their circumstances had changed so much since then. Lela had gone from being the boss's wife to a struggling artist, and Patsy had become a successful account manager in charge of her own staff. They still saw each other a few times a year, and although neither had said it out loud yet, they had less and less in common. For one thing, they hadn't taken to each other's husbands, nor did the husbands have much to say to each other. The four of them had gone to dinner once; by tacit agreement, never again. Yet Lela maintained the friendship out of loyalty and, when Patsy's son was born, sent a present for him, the extravagance of which was in inverse proportion to her feeling about the event.

"I think everyone has a responsibility to contribute to society," said Patsy.

"Are you implying that you don't think artists contribute to society?"

"He's not an artist yet."

"But he could become one, if given the chance."

All of a sudden, Patsy seemed to deflate. "I'm being a bitch, aren't I?"

"Kind of."

Patsy leaned her forehead on her fingertips. "It's just that I'm so exhausted. I'm working as hard as ever, then I have to go home and take care of the baby. It's like I have not only two jobs, but two careers."

"Does it really seem like a job?"

"The way I do it, it does. You have no idea what this does to your life."

Of course I do, Lela thought. I wouldn't be an artist if I didn't think I could imagine what it was like.

"Nothing is the same," Patsy continued. "Nothing. Of course, I don't have any regrets about doing it. I just had no idea what it would be like. But everyone says it gets easier. You'll see what I mean when you have one."

"I don't think we have enough money to have a baby," Lela said, figuring that Patsy would understand money.

"You'd work it out. You could work days and Lewis could work nights, or you could stay home for a couple of years and take in proofreading, or something like that."

"And then what?"

"Maybe you'd have more money by then."

"How? And what about my painting in the meantime?"

"So you'd miss a couple of years," Patsy said matter-of-factly.

"So I'd miss a couple of years. What would happen to your career if you missed a couple of years at this point?"

"I can afford to keep my job and have my baby. I've worked toward that. You have to decide what you really need most, and then you have to make sacrifices to get it. What's more important to you, painting or a baby?"

"My painting," Lela said automatically.

"Then don't have a baby," Patsy said.

"Oh, that's fair."

"Life isn't fair." Patsy lit another cigarette. Lela reached for one, too.

"We're not having fun, are we?" Lela said.

"No, we're not."

"What are we going to do about it?"

"We could try not to be so judgmental of each other, but that's kind of impossible, isn't it?" Patsy blew her smoke to the side. A woman at the next table waved it away.

"I guess I'm fairly judgmental these days," Lela said.

"Me too."

"Maybe we should get the check and try again some other time?"

"It's not that I don't appreciate your predicament, Lela."

"Yes it is. You don't. You can't. I mean —" Lela stopped herself before making matters worse. "Let's talk about it later. I'm under a lot of pressure because of my show."

Patsy signaled for the waiter. She paid for the meal with her corporate credit card. They went outside and stood beneath the awning to say good-bye.

"Have you heard the latest about your ex?" Patsy asked.

Lela had heard that he'd remarried and was busy fixing up a seventeenth-century farmhouse on ten acres in Connecticut. Co-incidentally, the name of the road he lived on was the same as his last name, which seemed to legitimate the image he had of himself as a country squire.

"He's so pompous!" Patsy said.

"He has a few good points."

After the divorce, Lela had promised herself never to speak badly of her ex-husband, on the theory that it was their relation-ship that had gone wrong, and it was possible he could get along with someone else perfectly well — as apparently he could.

Patsy lowered her eyes. "Maybe I shouldn't tell you this."

Lela's stomach dropped. She instinctively knew what the news was going to be, but she asked to hear it anyway.

"Don't get upset. She's pregnant."

"Why would I be upset?" Lela said defensively.

"I shouldn't have told you."

"I mean it. Just because he didn't want a baby when he was with me . . ."

Lela turned away until she could control herself. When she was more composed, she hugged Patsy and they promised to do this again soon, but Lela doubted they ever would and she suspected Patsy felt the same. Spontaneously, they hugged again, as if to re-capture whatever feeling they'd had for each other at one time, but the feeling was gone — they both recognized it — and they broke apart with embarrassed smiles. Lela watched Patsy turn the corner, then headed back uptown. All the way home she thought about Carl and his new wife and baby. Irrationally, she felt she had some claim to it; it was all that sperm he had left in her, she supposed.

•　　　•　　　•

"I'm the opposite of most people," Lela told Lewis. "I could love a child with a physical problem just as easily as I could love a healthy child. But I would like it to be a girl. And I'm beginning to think I wouldn't be completely horrible as a mother, either."

Lewis laid his hand on the back of her neck. "You'd be very patient."

"It also has to do with love. It has to do with the way I feel about you. I'm curious to know what a baby of ours would be like."

"That interests me, too."

"What about our work?" she asked.

"Other people manage it. We would, too."

"So you would feel okay if we have one?"

"I'd have nine months to get used to the idea." He looked at her thoughtfully. "It could be a very strange creature, you know."

"I'm ready to take that risk."

"Risk? I'm saying strangeness is a good thing."

She never thought she would feel such unabashed longing to have a child, but once it began, there was nothing she could do to stop it. Her eyes began to fill whenever she saw a baby, even if it was only on television, flogging a product she would never buy. More shocking still was the distance she began to feel between herself and women her age who were mothers. They seemed like another species to her, and she understood why motherhood was regarded with such a combination of fear and awe in societies throughout history. How did they do it? she wondered.

She went to a large bookstore in Times Square where she was not likely to run into anyone she knew and spent an hour flipping through books on pregnancy, trying to pick up a few tricks. She and Lewis had not used any form of birth control except ambivalence since her laparoscopy, with no results. If she really wanted a baby, she would have to try harder. She was already thirty-eight years old.

Never before, on any subject, had she felt herself to be such an absolute beginner, or so willing to humble herself to learn from people whose opinions she would not seek on any other subject.

She discovered that there existed a hearty body of new old wives' tales peculiar to postfeminist motherhood. You could not drink even while you were trying to become pregnant or your baby could be irreparably damaged. You should stay home from work on days when it was likely for you to conceive. If you did not go back to work within six months after the birth of your baby, you would never go back. This last one in particular caught her fancy. The woman who gave her the information appeared to have no idea that most women worked for reasons quite unrelated to the gravid presence of a growing baby in the house. Lela would have to work after she had a baby whether she fell prey to the lures of domestic life or not. She would need the money.

Even to become pregnant cost money. Her friends gave her the names and telephone numbers of their doctors, each of whom was guaranteed to be a miracle worker who could produce a healthy baby for anyone. Lela smugly replied that her own doctor was the fertility expert who had written the books that everyone kept somewhere in their house, usually next to the cookbooks in the kitchen. As the months slipped by, however, and nothing happened, she decided it wouldn't hurt to get a second opinion.

"It's possible for you to become pregnant," said this new doctor, who had come recommended by a friend who had urged Lela to see a woman. The doctor was extremely overweight, smoked during the consultation, and wore bright blue eyeshadow on her heavy lids. Lela saw that the effect she was trying to create was that of being nonclinical and down to earth; Lela found it condescending and tacky. Still, the doctor was telling her what she wanted to hear, so she tried to like her.

"My regular doctor told me I need to take a course of Danocrine."

The doctor rolled her eyes. "Do you want to grow a beard?"

Lela laughed. "That's how I felt about it."

"It's easy for these male doctors to prescribe disfiguring drugs. I myself don't recommend it. There's a new drug you could take that is just as effective without any of the side effects, but you have to take it by injection and it is expensive. And" — she peered out at Lela over the top of her half-moon glasses — "I don't think you need any of it."

"You don't?"

"I think you should continue trying to become pregnant, and if nothing happens and the endometriosis comes back, you should have a partial hysterectomy and not be bothered anymore."

The doctor smiled. Lela did not.

"What exactly are my chances of getting pregnant?"

"Let me tell you something," the doctor said. "The body isn't meant to have babies at age thirty-eight. Two hundred years ago, women died at your age, and their adult children carried their coffins to the grave. Evolution doesn't happen fast enough to make the kind of adaptation that women want to make these days. It's not natural. Women used to have twenty or thirty menstrual periods in their whole lives. Now they have hundreds. It takes its toll."

The doctor shook her head. Behind her on the wall hung photographs of her adult children. This woman hates me, Lela thought.

"You're welcome to become a regular patient of mine," the doctor said. "If you want to try the shots, we can do that. Insurance usually covers most of it."

"What if I just try to get pregnant the old-fashioned way?" Lela tried to joke. She was an awful joke teller.

"It's possible," the doctor said dismissively.

When the bill for the consultation arrived, Lela paid it quickly, before she could develop the gnawing feeling of having been ripped off.

"If you hate them, please don't say anything," she told John, her dealer, knowing how unprofessional it sounded even as she made her request.

She watched him anxiously as he circled the room. The curly-haired baby had become a prominent feature of the work, a guardian spirit with tiny, diaphanous wings and calves and forearms plump as melons. Her favorite painting was of her father in a business suit flying the baby like a kite.

John spun around, his left hand on his hip, his right index finger pressed thoughtfully to his lips. "I love them."

"You do?"

His eyes roamed acquisitively around the room. "They are unlike anything I've ever seen. I think we can get whatever we ask for these. You don't have a problem with selling them, do you?"

"My reputation precedes me," Lela said, knowing that asking the dealer at her first show to give back her paintings had made her a minor celebrity in a certain small circle.

John smiled. Both hands were on his hips, holding his soft, tea-colored jacket away from his body. His postures were relentlessly suggestive, yet he did not seem to be trying to attract her. His posing was second nature, and solely for his own benefit. "The art world is a small one, in case you hadn't noticed."

Lela wanted to change the subject. "So you think they're okay?" She was pressing. Once she showed her work, she could not get enough reassurance.

"They're terrific. I'm a genius to have discovered you." He gave a short, self-mocking laugh, indicating that he knew he should be joking, even if he wasn't.

"I thought I discovered myself, or at least was on the way toward doing so." She smiled back at him. He looked at her uncertainly.

"Let's just say it's a mutual discovery," he said.

"All right." She extended her hand.

"All right." He shook with her, squeezing her hand between both of his. "I think we'll get some important reviews on this. Not to mention making some money."

"That would be nice."

After he left, Lela stared at her paintings, trying to see them as a stranger would. She decided that the most accomplished aspect of her work was her use of color. She had invented a way of making black have the feel of green or red or blue that lent a different mood to a scene. A stranger probably would not see that, however. She struggled again to see her work with a fresh eye, but she could not even focus on each one as a whole. Instead, her gaze traveled from brush stroke to brush stroke, leaping back and forth between the paintings in remembrance of how they had gathered force. She saw the last few months of her life pass before her eyes. Here were the three final portraits of her father and the odd, hovering presence of the curly-haired baby, the coupling of whom was evocative enough to require no further meaning. Yet buried within the images were all her own recent thoughts: her ambivalence about having a baby, her new consciousness of the correlation between money and freedom, her frustration at the low status of unsuccessful artists. The struggle to come to livable conclusions about all these issues, she decided, was what made the work good.

She walked home through Riverside Park. It was a balmy early-summer day. Everywhere she looked there were children in various stages of growth. Her favorite of the day was a small girl with thick glasses who was playing tag with her father. Whenever she pointed out this type of child to Lewis, saying she'd love to have a kid who looked like that, Lewis would frown.

"Don't you want our kid to at least have a chance at having some friends?" he would ask.

He worried about what kind of father he would be. He was afraid that either he would overwhelm the baby, or the baby would overwhelm him. She wished he wanted it more. She had to laugh at the position in which she found herself, where neither her mother nor her husband cared if she had children. They wanted her to paint. A hundred years ago, fifty years ago, ten years ago, even now, in another part of town, she would have found herself with the opposite problem; she would be alone with her need to make art. Instead, she felt alone with her body's need to create a variation of itself, of her arms to hold a baby, of her lips to kiss new hands and pristine new feet. It amazed her how much she suddenly wanted this, but then again, all her life her body had surprised her. She never quite felt that she was it or that it was she except during moments of pain or pleasure, moments that got the better of her. Even then, she had strategies for making those feelings go away.

Essentially, she had ignored her body, yet it was the one material constant in her life. At best, she took it for granted. More often, she and her body were at war. Yet what did she know except what she had learned from it? When she was young, she had modified her behavior to weave in and out of the expressions she saw on other people's faces without realizing that by doing so she was molding herself to their judgments and prejudices; by trying to garner a smile from them, she was creating the emptiness she felt. She cast her memory in terms of emotion, but behind those abstract complexes of thought and feeling were the bruised senses that engendered them. When she reached out for her first husband, for example, it was her fingers that discovered how his flesh turned goosey when she touched him, how it shrank away. And when she had an idea for a painting, the urgency to make it real came not from any picture she had in her head, but from a heaviness in her arms that pulled at her until she picked up her brush.

Her legs ached as she walked up the steps to her apartment, and she realized that her period was almost two weeks late.

"Are you tired?" Lewis stirred a pot on the stove. "Go take a bath first, if you like."

"I'm hot."

"That's a first."

"I'm not complaining, but it is hot out there."

She poured lavender bubble bath under a stream of hot water. Sometimes she became so exhausted or distracted that she got into the shower or tub without remembering to remove her underwear. Such episodes had amused her at one time, but lately they seemed a portent of a confused future, the kind of shameful incidents that would one day annoy nursing home attendants rather than amuse anybody. With that in mind, she placed her towel and slippers in readiness for her exit from the tub.

Lewis came to the door.

"You're pretty," he said.

"I'm bloated. My period is late." She paused. "I think I'm pregnant."

He leaned forward slightly. "Are you sure?"

She sighed. "I just have that feeling. You know why? For once I didn't get weepy when I saw the children in the park."

He sat on the edge of the tub and took her hand. "I didn't mind you doing that."

"Good, because I think I might start crying now."

"Me too."

Lewis pulled her from the tub and wrapped her in the towel. They lay on the bed in each other's arms, crying quietly.

"I'm not sad," he told her.

"Neither am I."

They made love carefully, afraid of hurting the baby. Afterward, they tried to picture what it looked like just then, the entire creature smaller than either of their eyes.

She did not feel tired. She did not feel sick, at least not inordinately so. She wondered if it was because she'd heard so many horrible stories about pregnancy that the reality seemed to be a snap in comparison; then again, perhaps she was one of the lucky ones. It seemed more and more that the latter was the case as the summer unfolded and she floated easily through the city. When the days of queasiness had passed, she began to visit bakeries and pâtisseries to buy the éclairs and Napoleons that she'd denied herself during all her adult life — and she ate them without getting fat. Her body seemed finally to be working for her rather than against her. She swam whenever she had the chance, performing a slow but powerful crawl to make her arms strong in preparation for carrying the baby. As she moved quietly through the water, she imagined the baby swimming inside of her, already preoccupied with its own liquid dreams. Sometimes, after a session in the pool, she ended up in such a different conceptual world that she had trouble understanding what people were saying. She gazed at them vaguely, not really caring whether or not she cracked the code of everyday English, and they stared back at her as if she were a mad woman.

It *was* a sort of madness, she supposed. Who could make sense of actually creating another person from the perishable materials that comprised one's own body? She understood why pregnant women often seemed so self-satisfied; what could compare to what they were doing? She pitied men for their lack of this particular creative capability. Hearing their conversations in the elevator, at the office, conversations that once filled her with boredom or rage, now drew on her sense of compassion. No matter what they did, they could not have a baby. She felt an irrational urge to protect them from the truth about what they were missing, and her tenderness, in turn, inspired their protection when she needed it most. It occurred to her that perhaps it was this exchange of consideration that kept women from seizing power on the basis of their very real biological power. What would happen if women joined together to shepherd their reproductive capabilities as the world's most powerful resource, and controlled it as if it were oil or diamonds or wheat? What if they simply refused to have children until men agreed not to send those children to war, or to mind-deadening schools where they would learn to respect authority and not much else, or to let anyone lead a life of poverty? The vision of Lysistrata had yet to be tested properly.

Chances were, she thought ruefully, that women wouldn't be much better at wielding power than men were, at least not as power was currently conceived. Then again, they might be noble and fair. It was certainly worth a try. But who would give up her chance to have a baby for the sake of an experiment?

Not Lela. Not anymore.

She was content in her waking life, and therefore could not understand why her dreams continued to be disturbing. The curly-haired baby was learning to crawl, and every move forward was agonizing to watch. She could feel the baby's frustration as it was pulled this way and that, unable to pursue its natural impulses. It could not control its muscles, nor could it do anything to prevent the large hands from latching on to its waist and pointing it in another direction. She saw glimpses in her dreams of life through the baby's eyes as it grew older. She watched it suffer the small humiliations and disappointments that it would carry with it into adulthood as bad memories, wayposts that would make it difficult to approach certain situations without fear, impossible to approach others at all. Lela ached for the baby. She tried consciously to program her mind to give the dreams happy endings, but she could not control what happened once she laid her head on the pillow.

"Why don't you paint what you see?" Lewis said. "That helped you when you were having these types of dreams about your father."

"Those dreams weren't this bad."

"Yes they were. You were in mourning."

"I was, wasn't I?"

"Buy a new fan for your studio. I think you need to spend more time up there, baby or no baby."

"I'm afraid to go up there now."

"Work here, then," Lewis said.

So she began a series of small paintings based on her dreams that she worked on at an easel by the window. She went at the project with great energy, hoping that she could arrange a happy future for the small soul developing in her abdomen if only she painted well. She tried to paint the happy endings she wanted for the baby, but her sketches seemed false and forced. Finally she relented and painted only the most frightening moments of her dreams, finding relief, if not solace, in her efforts.

No, Lela thought, not here. Please not here.

She placed her hands on the desk and breathed deeply, concentrating on the hard surface beneath her fingers. Behind her, she heard her boss crackling his newspaper while the rest of the people in her department occupied themselves with reading or telephone calls as they waited for the day's stories to come in. She had a pile of bills to pay and letters to write, but the pain that had suddenly gathered around her middle rendered her afraid to move. She sat quietly at her desk, staring at the picture of Lewis she had hung from a magnetic clip beneath her bookshelf. In the photograph, taken on their honeymoon, he was standing in front of a country church. His hair was long, not as long as he wore it now, but longer than anyone in his family had ever worn it. His family looked at her as having been the instigator behind his decisions to grow his hair, become a vegetarian, and move to New York, but she didn't think she'd really changed him as much as she'd encouraged him to do what he wanted. The baby was the first thing she'd pushed for that would change him against his will; it was the one change she'd made that his family was happy about.

She moved her hand slowly across the desk toward the telephone. When the motion seemed to have no effect on the pain one way or the other, she pushed their number.

"Good timing," he said. "I just got home. The interview went really well; I think this might be it."

She stared at his honeymoon face and could not speak.

"What's wrong?" he asked, automatically concerned. "Lela, say something."

"I can't."

"Did something happen?"

"No."

"Are you obsessing about the show?"

"No. I feel a little sick, that's all."

Suddenly a pair of invisible hands took hold of the muscles in Lela's abdomen and ripped them downward all at once. A nearly imperceptible moan vibrated in her teeth as she stubbornly refused to groan aloud. No one noticed except Lewis.

"Maybe you should come home," he said.

"I can't," she said.

"They know you're pregnant. Everyone will understand."

She moaned aloud.

"I'm coming over there," Lewis said.

"Are you all right?" Anne asked from across the room.

Lela leaned back in her chair and closed her eyes. When her boss called an ambulance, she heard his voice bellowing into the telephone from far away as she turned all her concentration to the painful struggle to hold her body together even as it irrevocably tore apart.

"I had no idea."

"About what?" Lela said.

"That this is what your studio is like."

"Well, it is."

Her mother walked to the window. "It's so big. You've got such a wonderful view."

Lela smiled. "Most mothers would be more concerned with the ancient wiring and the bad neighborhood."

"It doesn't look bad from here." Claire laid her palms on the sill and leaned out. From the rear she looked as lean and taut as a young girl. "I always wanted a view like this, over the trees. A good, solid, tenth-floor view."

"I would like to live in a house," Lela said.

"You wouldn't, really. There's always something that needs to be fixed, and you find yourself wasting all your creative energy making it look nice. You're better off living in an apartment. You might not have become a painter if you'd lived in a house."

"I think I would have." Lela felt the stirrings of a particular variety of distress peculiar to her relationship with her mother. Claire had a way of belittling Lela's accomplishments that tore through all the defenses she'd built up against rejections from gallery owners, reviewers, teachers, friends, her ex-husband, herself. What Claire said implied two things to Lela: one, she believed she could have been an artist — a better artist, perhaps? — if only she hadn't had the burden of a family and a house to contend with, and two, that Lela's artistry depended on the minimal responsibilities of her living arrangements.

"Why don't you want me to have a house, Mother?"

Claire appeared confused by Lela's sudden anger. "I do, if that's what you want. But you want to be an artist, don't you?"

"I want both."

"I hope you get both. Most people don't, that's all, and I can tell you from my vantage point that being able to paint is ultimately much more valuable than owning a house."

Claire had on her summer outfit of a T-shirt and loose, clownlike pants. Her Birkenstocks were smooth with wear, and she had recently cut her hair as short as a man's, which she did periodically when she was feeling lighter, less depressed. Lela suddenly had the dark thought that perhaps Claire had felt relieved after Lewis called her with the news of Lela's miscarriage. Claire had immediately flown down from Maine to help with the meals and cleaning so Lela could do nothing but rest after her ordeal. Her concern was welcome, but Lela wondered if she'd actually produced a healthy baby whether Claire would have come at all.

"The point is, Mother," Lela said, "that I would like to live in a house. You may be completely right that I can't be a painter and live in a house, but I'd like to find out for myself."

"Fine." Claire gazed blankly at a painting. She pressed her fingers against her lips as if to physically enforce a promise she must have made to herself not to fight with Lela while she was still recuperating. Her sudden ability to control her pronouncements struck Lela as smug.

"I don't think it *is* fine with you, Mother. You've always said you don't want me to have a house, or children, or anything regular in my life. You didn't even want me to get married. If it were up to you, I'd be living alone and friendless in some garret, slowly poisoning myself to death on turpentine fumes."

"Because I wanted you to be an artist! You wanted to be an artist! You can't paint and take care of a house and children, not without a lot of help. You know that as well as I do. And the fact that that's the way the world currently works is not my fault. I was just trying to support you."

"What support? I don't see you giving me the kind of support I really need. You give money to the rest of your children so your grandchildren live in decent places and have nice clothes. If you really want to support me, put your money where your mouth is, so I won't have to lie awake at night calculating how I'm going to pay my telephone bill."

"You didn't want to be an artist?" Claire demanded.

Lela shook her head. Her abdomen still ached. "I didn't know what I wanted. I was a child. I liked to draw, I liked to write, I liked to climb trees and play house. You encouraged my painting. You made me afraid to have anything else in my life except for my work."

"I can't believe you took my opinion of what you should do so seriously."

"You're my mother! How am I supposed to take what you say?"

"Lela, you're almost forty years old. At this point, I think you should take what I say any way you want."

They faced each other, their arms wrapped tightly around their ribs. Lela's fear of the pain her mother was effortlessly capable of inflicting was mirrored not only in Claire's eyes, but in her entire body. On the surface, they did not really resemble each other; Lela looked like her father. Her physical similarity to Claire was a trick of shared mannerisms and expressions. The mirror that reflected them back at each other was a trick mirror, costly and unreliable.

Claire shook her head. "I can't talk to you when you're like this. You're being irrational."

"Is it rational to be happy when your own daughter has a miscarriage?"

"If you think that, you're crazier than I thought."

Unbidden, Lela's foot shot out and caught the underside of her battered school chair, hurling it across the room. A fresh pain flowed upward from her toes. "Fine," she screeched. "So I'm crazy. If you say so, that's what I am. If you want me to be an artist, I am. If you don't want me to have a baby, guess what? I don't have it. I want you to be happy. I'm glad you're happy. I suppose that if I were a really good daughter, it would make me happy that you're so happy, but it doesn't, because I'm too sad."

Lela's voice rose as she began to weep. At some point she felt her mother's arm arc around her in a tentative gesture of comfort. Lela struggled for control. It embarrassed her deeply to cry in front of her mother. There seemed to be nothing she could do, however, to stay the grief that rolled over her in cold, bleak waves. Claire stood by, patting her timidly on the back. Lela wiped her sticky hands on her jeans.

"I'm sorry," she gasped.

Claire stroked her.

"Do you have a Kleenex?" Lela sniffled.

"No."

Lela gave a small, rueful smile. "Of course not. Why do I keep trying to make you into a normal mother?"

"Probably for the same reason that I keep trying to make you into an irregular daughter."

Lela nodded. "The thing is, Ma, I'm not being greedy. I'm not asking for everything in the world, but I would like to have a family and I would like to paint. I want you to think that's possible."

"You're right."

Lela blinked. "What?"

"You're right. Just because I couldn't do it doesn't mean you can't." She reached out and touched the canvas where Lela had painted her father's hand hanging loosely at his side. "For years, I thought he betrayed me. But I betrayed myself."

"It's not too late, Ma. You could still do something."

"I could, but I probably won't. It would be yet another betrayal of myself to pretend I'm going to change. Now may I use your bathroom?"

Lela pointed across the loft. "It's awfully basic. We could leave."

"You know I don't care about things like that."

While Claire was gone, Lela went through her supply cabinet drawer by drawer, taking inventory. After her show was over, she wanted to be ready to go right back to work. She had to throw herself into it again, to remember why she'd stubbornly worked over and over many of the same canvases while her eggs died month after month as she lay wrapped in the old flowered quilts dreaming of her father. She had to stop blaming herself, or at least to figure out how to go on living while blaming herself. She had to discover a bridge she could walk across to find Lewis again, to be able to absorb his sorrow, too. She had to go back to the office and see if she could convince her boss to scrounge up a few extra days of work for her, to help cover the emergency room and ambulance bills.

When she'd finished the list, Lela walked over to the window and looked at the sight that had so appealed to Claire. It felt good to have yelled at her mother. It was the only thing that had felt good all week. Even the throbbing in her foot was a relief after the kind of pain she'd gone through. She leaned her shoulders out the window and recklessly dreamed of how good it would feel to jump. She could fly through the air for a few seconds, fly free with no future, no obligations to be brave or recover or valiantly push on. She would not have to make any more lists or diaries full of resolutions or write thank-you notes or plan budgets. She had not been very good at life. She should be like Claire, she thought, and stop pretending she would become any better.

"Lela?" Claire interrupted. "Come here for a moment, will you?"

Lela crossed the loft. As she moved toward her mother, she pictured the window at her back, casting lights and shadows in poignant shapes on the floor. Claire stood before the closet.

"What are these?"

Claire held in her arms the stack of small paintings that Lela had done of the curly-haired baby. Lewis had mentioned to her that he'd moved them up to the studio while she was in the hospital. She hadn't thought about them since.

"Oh, those. Those are dreams, really. I was dreaming about the baby even before I got pregnant."

Claire flipped through the work. "These aren't dreams." She put her hand on her brow as if she had a headache.

"I think I had to get this material out of my system before the baby came, so I would know how to treat her." Suddenly Lela realized that, although it had never been clear in her dreams, she had always assumed the curly-haired baby was a girl. "That's how I work. I try to dig out all my impressions about a particular subject so I'm sure of what I want to paint."

She peered over Claire's shoulder. Part of her ached to see the paintings. Part of her was gratified to see that they were good.

"No," Claire said. "These aren't dreams, Lela. *I* made sure you didn't walk too close to the fireplace. *I* made you watch from a distance when I cooked on the stove. *I* grabbed you — I think I even spanked you, I'm ashamed to say — when you tried to crawl toward the street. You always wanted to do everything before you were ready, and then you were so frustrated when I tried to protect you. Don't you see? That's my hand in every picture."

In the paintings the hand had long nails and healthy cuticles, but Lela saw that it was indeed Claire's, down to the knobby wristbone and the knuckles that looked like elephants' knees. She remembered Claire had had beautiful nails, when she was young.

"I can't believe you don't recognize yourself," Claire said. "Lela, this is you."

Claire turned to her, her face transfigured, young. Lela met her eyes for a moment, then closed her own. It was a hot summer day. She was lying on the flowered quilts in the backyard, wearing only a diaper, with her parents' prone bodies forming a solid fence on either side of her. Lela gazed into the distance and saw the leaves on the tops of the trees shimmering in the hazy sun. She grabbed two large fistfuls of her father's shirt and heaved herself up. Awkwardly she worked her way down his body, holding on to his side. When she reached his feet she let go, lurching onto the grass. She traveled swiftly, her thick legs pumping hard against the unfamiliar sensation of the earth beneath her. When the momentum of her awkward gait finally caused her to topple over, she began to cry, furious that she hadn't been able to reach the trees, and frightened to find herself in the middle of the lawn, utterly alone. She turned around and saw odd, twisted expressions on her parents' faces, a painful combination of excitement and loss. She hurried back to the quilt on her hands and knees and settled among the warm flesh of her family until she was ready to try to walk again.

The Good Listener

"THERE IS only one piece of advice I have to give you about writing," Alex Quinn told his class. "Sit still and be honest. If you can learn to do those two things, you can learn to write, and it shouldn't take you more than ten years to get good at it. Aside from a few technical tricks, that's the sum total of everything I know."

Relieved laughter fluttered through the lounge where his class was held. Alex was equally relieved. The first few minutes were over and he hadn't lost anyone yet. Fifteen hopeful faces were turned to him, full of mute pleas for him to transform their inchoate manuscripts into hardcover books, perhaps even literary celebrity. He lit a cigarette. No fewer than six of his students immediately did the same. He read the first and last few pages of his latest novel and everyone applauded. He wondered why he hadn't taught all along. For years he'd turned down all offers of teaching positions and lectureships until he was invited to give a summer workshop at a small college in New England, and his wife, Anne, talked him into going. He'd always suspected that teaching would take too much energy away from his writing, but what he hadn't considered was the energy it would give him. By the end of class he was vibrating with it, so much so that before lunch he went for a run, then spent half an hour playing Frisbee with his young sons, ages seven and eight.

"It was incredible," he told Anne as he changed out of his

sweat clothes. "They were interested in everything I had to say."

"I'm not surprised," Anne said loyally.

He studied her as she stood by the window, keeping an eye on the boys. He had never written about her. The idea of confining her within the bounds of characterization seemed like a violation of what they had between them, and slightly dangerous.

"You're happy here, aren't you?" he said. "Maybe I made a mistake all these years, thinking I needed to be so alone."

"It's fun to see you having fun."

That afternoon, at his desk, he tried to record his reactions to his first teaching experience, but he was too excited to get it down right.

A few days later he had lunch at a diner in town with several of his colleagues, two of whom were single women. He drank three beers and laughed freely, trading stories about agents and editors, grateful to be among people who automatically understood his perspective on various glitches in the publishing process. By the time he looked at his watch, he found he was going to be late for the scheduled conferences with his students. He pushed himself away from the table.

"Good luck," said another novelist. "Try to stay awake."

Everyone laughed. Alex obliged them with a scowl of dread, though he was actually looking forward to the afternoon.

"Can I catch a ride with you?" asked a poet named Polly Larson.

Alex glanced at his watch again.

"You don't have to take me out of your way," she said. "You can just let me off wherever you park."

"Sure," he said.

"You're sure?"

Alex grinned. "I'm not usually such a fuddy-duddy. No, that's not true. I *am* a fuddy-duddy, and you're just going to have to put up with it if you want a ride from me."

She slung a heavy sack full of papers over her shoulder and waved good-bye to the others. "I think I can handle it," she said.

"Good. Let's go."

Polly chatted easily as they walked to the car. Physically, she was the same type as the heroine in his second book: boyishly thin, fox-faced, on the scruffy side. She'd been married twice — in spite of his reclusion, Alex kept up with literary gossip — yet she gave the impression of being a solitary soul, cozily at home with herself. He found himself assuming she would behave as predictably as one of his characters. The women he wrote about were all relentlessly independent, no matter what their domestic arrangements. Therefore he was surprised when there was an awkward moment as they got into the car. Before she ducked beneath the hood, she looked at him questioningly, causing him to wonder whether she'd expected him to open the door for her. When he dared to look at her again, though, after he'd maneuvered the tricky left turn out of the parking lot, she was smiling serenely, and he supposed he had read her wrong.

"That was quite a boisterous group," he said.

She rolled her eyes. "One of the biggest misconceptions about the lives of the poets is that they get together and talk about art. In my experience, they usually get together for far less lofty purposes, not the least of which is to make money teaching people something that can't be taught. They feel free to get drunk around each other and to behave quite badly because of the unwritten rule that no one except rat finks will tell tales outside the group. But, of course, you find that sort of complicity in every industry."

Alex frowned slightly. As he looked back over the past week, he realized it was true that he hadn't had any really substantive discussions with his colleagues. Mostly the talk was of advances and deals; mostly everyone joked. He'd been so happy to have people to hang out with, people who knew what it was like to sit alone all day, that he hadn't noticed he was missing anything.

"You sound bitter," he said, thinking of what a relief it was not to feel slightly bitter, for once.

"Sometimes I wish I were still a student, so I could actually talk about my work."

The road was lined with outlets and chain stores beyond which rose low, ancient mountains. Alex looked at his watch, angry at himself for being late.

"So what are you working on?" he asked perfunctorily. He could feel her stiffen.

"I'm sorry," she said. "I really wasn't fishing for a literary conversation. Sometimes I talk too much."

"No, I'd like to hear about what you're doing," he reassured her. "I don't suppose a really large group is conducive to that kind of discussion, though, do you think? Don't you find it easier to talk about really serious things one on one?"

She gave him a startled glance. "What are you getting at?"

"Nothing, really." Everything he said seemed to upset her. "I guess I was trying to offer you an explanation for why everyone behaves the way they do."

"Oh." She folded her hands primly in her lap. Although she was probably a good ten years older than he, in her early forties at least, she hadn't yet abandoned the uniform of T-shirts and faded jeans. "Well, if you're really interested, I suppose we could meet one afternoon and I could show you what I'm up to. I could use some advice. How's Thursday, at four?"

He made a right turn into the entrance of the college. Lately Anne had been teaching the boys the names of all the wildflowers along the drive, and helping them iron choice specimens between sheets of waxed paper to make place mats to give as Christmas presents. He knew Polly had seen him with Anne. She knew he was married. "That sounds fine," he said.

He pulled up in front of the faculty office building and parked the car, but she didn't move.

"One question," she said.

"Shoot." He was anxious to get upstairs.

"I wonder why you didn't become an actor."

She jumped out of the car and shut the door as he sat, stunned, in the driver's seat. He shook his head slightly, as if to clear it, when her small, pointy face appeared in the passenger window.

"Why an actor?" he asked.

"Why not?" She shrugged. "With your looks."

After she walked away, he automatically looked in the rearview mirror. He was blushing, but other than that, it was the same old face.

His first appointment was leaning impatiently against the door when he arrived. His second appointment was sitting in a chair, her head in a book. They both stared at him as he unlocked the door.

"I had a meeting," he said. They both looked away. He knew he had given them the impression that he'd been talking to someone more important than they, about work more important than theirs. He felt Polly's strict judgments hovering around him, accusing him of perpetuating a lie. "Actually, I was out to lunch, both literally and figuratively."

His students smiled shyly. He was pleased with himself for having told the truth. He had seven appointments in a row, twenty minutes each, although twice he let the time run to half an hour. It was hard for him to cut them off when they were in the middle of explaining something they cared about, especially when he thought of how much they'd paid to talk to him. Although he'd never done this sort of thing before, he thought he handled each of them rather well. Anne had advised him ahead of time to be kind above all, because you never knew how much someone could improve with encouragement. Her advice seemed to work. Every time he was tempted to tell his students exactly what mistakes they'd made, he held back, concentrating instead on sentences that he liked, images that moved him. As each one of them left the room, he had the feeling they were running straight back to their desks to work harder, with deepened purpose. By the end of the afternoon, when the beers had worn off, he was left with a light sensation in his body, a kind of floating, which he supposed was the physical equivalent of feeling above it all. He allowed himself the small vanity of believing he had been inspiring. He knew how to help his students, and he could explain what he knew in a way that made a difference in their lives. As he packed his briefcase, he prayed an atheist's undirected prayer that he would continue to be one of the lucky ones whom fate allows to do exactly what they want. He was truly, rarely happy.

There was a knock on the door.

"Come in," he called. His voice was hoarse with feeling and exhaustion. The sun streamed through the windows at an angle that filled him with an amorphous nostalgia. At home, he always took this light as a signal to turn off his computer and return to dailyness.

"Mr. Quinn?"

The voice startled him. He'd been expecting Anne or one of his colleagues, not another student.

"I'm sorry I'm late," she said. "I came earlier, but you were running behind, so I went downstairs to the bookstore and I kind of lost track of the time."

Alex glanced at his appointment book, which was still lying open on the table that served as a desk. Rachel Morse was indeed listed as his last appointment of the day. He asked her to come in as he quickly rifled his briefcase for her story.

"Would you rather do this another time?" she asked.

He was on the point of saying yes, if she didn't mind, another time would be better — he wanted to play catch with the boys before dinner — when he saw that two of the books that she held to her chest were novels of his, hardcover.

"No, no." He motioned to her to sit down, yet she still seemed as though she was about to run back out the door. "I was just waiting for you."

"Oh." She sat down and laid her books on the floor. She was the youngest member of his class, perhaps eighteen, yet she was far more out of shape than many of the older, intensely purpose-ful women. Still, she was not unattractive. Her hair was thick, brown, and immaculate, and her eyes, also brown, were thought-ful and deep. She was the type of girl that boys instinctively knew they would be smart to marry, if they weren't so stupidly infatu-ated with aspects of womanhood that had nothing to do with character. As this observation passed through his mind, he real-ized that Rachel Morse was exactly the kind of girl who'd been his friend in college. He ached when he thought how lonely and full of self-doubt those girls had been.

"So what can I do for you today?" Alex asked.

"I have a confession to make." Rachel leaned forward, but lowered her eyes. "I signed up for the last conference period on purpose, because I thought perhaps you might have more time at the end of the day."

Her voice trailed off giddily, as though she'd accomplished something far more daring than a rather routine bit of maneuvering. He told himself to look at her kindly. She was sitting on her hands. For the first time all afternoon, he felt resentful at having his time taken up with student problems. This girl in particular vibrated with need, so much so that he suddenly was afraid she was about to tell him she was pregnant or something like that; he was afraid she would tell him a secret, and ask his advice.

"I've been wanting to meet you for years," she said at last.

Relieved, he leaned back in his chair, clasping his hands behind his head. "So you're a fan of mine?"

She looked away. Her clothes were baggy and formless, carefully chosen so as not to draw any attention to herself, a subterfuge that had the opposite of the intended effect on him; it was precisely the sort of detail he noticed.

"I'm sorry," he said quickly. "I didn't mean that in a pejorative sense. I'm flattered. I rarely get the opportunity to meet anyone who has read my books. Usually I only get letters."

"I wrote you a letter," she said.

"Did I write back?" he asked lightly.

"Yes." She lowered her eyes. "Thank you."

He rifled his briefcase again, finally locating her story in a folder that contained some of his own work. He did not remember reading it. After an afternoon of conferences, though, he thought he could fake a response without much trouble.

"I like your work," he began.

She looked shocked. She drew back slightly, as if he'd raised his hand to her. "Really?"

"Why are you so surprised? It's thoughtful, it's dramatic, and above all, it has feeling. Feeling happens to be something that's hard to come by these days."

He could have used a similar assessment to describe the work of nearly all his students, but in spite of his generic pronouncement, she appeared pleased.

"So how can I help you?" he asked.

She brought her hands out from under her thighs and laid them in her lap. "I'm so glad you liked the story."

"Why wouldn't I?" He sat on the edge of the desk and crossed his arms, affecting what he thought was a professorial posture. It was all part of giving her her money's worth.

"Some people think my work is too cruel, as if cruel things don't happen every day."

"Well, exactly," he said.

"People don't like to be shown things as they really are."

"An artist's job is to make reality palatable," he said.

"I know." Her eyes shone. He looked at her and smiled, remembering what it was like to feel the whole world turn around when suddenly you felt understood. It occurred to him that his boys were almost old enough to feel the loneliness that came with one's first grasp of abstract ideas. It always seemed that it would take forever before you could meet like-minded people; by then, chances were, you had become like-minded yourself. He promised himself he would do everything he could to prevent the boys from feeling as lonely as Rachel Morse did.

"What did you think of the ending?" she asked.

He started at the sound of her voice. "The ending?" he repeated stupidly. He'd almost forgotten she was there.

"Did you believe the choice she made?"

It would help if he knew what choice that was, he thought ruefully. But what would it hurt to say he believed it? Out of all the literate people in the world, no doubt somebody, somewhere, would.

"Oh, yes," he said.

She deflated with relief. "So many people who have read this story tell me that no one can actually make anyone else kill themselves if they don't want to. Obviously, I disagree. He kills her as surely as if he made her swallow the pills, one by one. I'm glad you see it my way, because if you had told me you thought it was unrealistic I probably would have abandoned this story. But what about the beginning? I always write a few unnecessary pages at the beginning . . ."

He sat quietly until she'd finished saying what she needed to say. She looked older at the end of her confession, as if she'd passed through a biological cycle that had transformed her. He was proud of himself for not having cut her off, even if he was humoring her at the expense of his own time. When it came down to it, that was what he had signed up to do when he accepted the responsibility for being a teacher, or a parent, for that matter. He had a theory of parenting that he applied to this situation as well; when they come to you for a hug, always let them be the ones to break away first.

He couldn't decide whether or not he should try to get out of going to Polly's. The case was strong for either course of action. He had, after all, taken the job in the hope of making friends, and Polly was offering him at least a trial friendship. He thought it would be good for him to talk about his work, as he hadn't written anything since he'd arrived at the college. Although he had his own set of tricks that he used to get himself going — Cézanne paintings, showers, arguing with the television — he thought it might be interesting to work through the process with another writer. *If* that was all they were going to do. He couldn't stop thinking about Polly's parting comment on his looks; it didn't strike him as the farewell of an uninterested professional.

Then again, she could have been making a straightforward observation. On principle, he should be the last one in the world to be suspicious. His specialty was creating strong female characters whose motives were often misinterpreted by a chauvinistic world, and the irony was not lost on him that he ran the risk of doing the same thing. His heroines always hated it when anyone tried to second-guess them, or to decide what might or might not hurt their feelings. At some level he felt that if Polly wasn't exactly one of his heroines, at least he could be his own hero. In the end, he decided to go.

"Ssh!" she whispered when she opened the door. He mimicked her by putting his finger to his lips. She turned around and swiftly crossed the room to a large desk that sat beneath a picture window. Her apartment was half the second floor of one of the quaint faculty houses that lay along a dirt road to the north of the campus. The house that Alex had been given for the summer was nearly a mile away.

"Am I early?" he asked.

She flashed him a pleading smile, reminding him that she'd asked not to be interrupted. A glance around the messy rooms showed him that no discernible preparations had been made on his behalf. He thought he might occupy himself by looking around at her things, to see what they revealed about her, but as soon as he began to do so, he found that he wasn't interested. He almost spoke to her again but checked himself before committing yet another interruption; he decided he would just have to give himself permission to wedge himself in between the piles of things on the sofa. He picked up a book. He had just become interested in the story he was reading when Polly came swooping at him, waving a sheet of paper in her right hand.

"It's finished!"

"Congratulations," he said automatically.

She held the paper with both hands at arm's length, as if she was about to have a dance with it. He wasn't surprised when she whirled around once, like a younger girl. When she'd finished, she pressed the paper to her upper chest so that it touched the skin in the opening of her shirt, as if she wished to absorb it into her body.

"I can't believe it," she said gleefully. "I've been blocked for months, but for the last two days everything has been flowing out. I feel like an erupting volcano. And the lava I produce will hopefully last forever."

Alex smiled, trusting his expression was bland enough to mask his embarrassment.

"Congratulations," he said again. His command of the language seemed to have evaporated in the face of her raw feeling.

She met his eyes, finally seeming to notice that she had company. She dropped her arms and cocked her head to one side. She was wearing shorts; her thighs had held up, he noticed.

"I'm sorry, Alex, I must sound like a fool."

She shoved a few things onto the floor and sat down next to him on the sofa. "I haven't given you much of a welcome, have I? But I don't have to explain to you. You of all people know what it's like when you're working well and nothing else counts." Her skin had the grayish look that comes from smoking too much, but in spite of it, she seemed to glow from within. "I have to tell you that I don't feel the least bit rude, because although it might not seem so, I have been thinking about you. In fact, it's to you that I owe this breakthrough."

"Me?"

"Don't act so surprised. You know what I'm talking about." She laid her hand on his knee.

"I do?"

"The car? The other day?"

They gazed at each other expectantly.

"When I drove you back," he said, to modulate the silence.

She snorted knowingly. "Yes. When you drove me back." She repeated his words in a tone of innuendo that made her interpretation of the events of the car ride clear.

Alex crossed his arms, then immediately unraveled them again when he realized the obviousness of his body language.

"You know as well as I do there was something going on," said Polly, who seemed not to share his predilection for subtlety.

"I do?" He stared at her legs and gave a helpless little laugh.

"Don't you?" She uncrossed her knees and planted both feet on the floor, her sudden uncertainty bringing on a more modest posture.

He frowned. "If I gave you the wrong impression, I think I was overly excited and had had a few beers."

She turned her head away, and her hair fell like a curtain over her face so he could not see her expression. He had spoken awkwardly, his thoughts backwards, and he had hurt her. She had no right to feel hurt by him, but he felt bad for her, anyway.

He tried to think of what to do next. He did not have any recent experience with unfamiliar women, and he could not remember how to mollify them without being affectionate. Desperately, he glanced around the apartment for something else to talk about. He saw a box of paints, but he instinctively knew she would find it a belittlement of her feelings for him to ask if she painted. Then he saw that she still held the poem in her hand.

"May I see it?" he asked.

"What?" She swiveled her head in his direction, still not revealing her face. He touched the paper.

"This. Your new poem."

"Do you really want to?"

"Isn't that why I'm here?"

Polly considered for a moment. She had a few gray hairs in the undergrowth around her ears that were visible only when she wore her hair pulled back. "All right," she said uncertainly. "If you're sure."

She stood up and took a practiced stance near the center of the room. Alex applauded himself for having come up with the right diversion.

"Are you ready?" she asked.

"I'm on tenterhooks," he said, inwardly cringing. He knew for a fact that he had never before used that expression in his life.

She paused, cleared her throat, and paused again. Then she began. Her voice was clear and strong when she read, much more appealing than it sounded when she talked; it took only a few seconds for him to be completely taken up by her words. She read for meaning rather than form, for which he was grateful. So many poets he'd heard read over the past few weeks were pretentious and ministerial in their diction. He really knew no more about poetry than did any former English major, but he was certain as he listened to Polly that he was in the presence of a person who had whatever it took to create transcendent work. When she came to the end and looked up shyly for his reaction, he returned her gaze and smiled broadly, feeling at that moment that he would do anything for her, for her tremendous talent.

"That was remarkable, Polly."

"Really? You liked it?"

"It was wonderful."

"I hoped you would. Look." She handed him the paper. Under the title, she had written "For Alex, who has restored my faith."

"Your faith in what?" he asked.

"You name it," she said tenderly.

"Thank you." His voice was hoarse with emotion, and he couldn't think of the appropriate words to express the great swelling of admiration he felt for her art. In lieu of naming anything, he held out his hand.

At six o'clock, when Alex left Polly's apartment, the sky was dark and it had begun to rain. A fresh, living scent rose from the ground as he walked down the hill, as if he were carving the world anew with each footstep. He thought, with a combination of serenity and shock, These woods will outlast me. On either side of my life, the woods have and will seem fresh and new to someone. Since he was two years old he'd known that he was going to die, but he still couldn't believe it. He forced himself to remember that Anne would also die, and the boys (but he had imagined their deaths at least once a day, every time a shriek pierced the quiet of the house; in the old graveyard near the college he couldn't even bear to look at the children's graves with the little stone lambs on top), that it was wrong and dangerous to attach significance to his own consciousness, to think, as he was thinking, that his large, full feeling when he was in the woods made the woods bigger. I'm not important, he reminded himself, none of us is, but even as he formed this thought, he realized that the impulse behind it was not truly philosophical or even modest: he had sat still and been honest for too long not to realize that what he was really trying to do was to convince himself that the fact that he had committed adultery for the first time in his life was not important either.

Committed adultery; the phrase hardly seemed adequate to describe what he'd done. It was too Biblical and clinical to apply to Polly, who had turned out to be soft, sensitive, and almost mystical in the level of attention she was able to pay to the moment. It *had* been important; no matter how small and insignificant his existence might be in the larger picture, this afternoon he and Polly had *mattered*. They had come together in the single connection capable of producing new life. As he went over and over the afternoon in his mind, he found that, in spite of all the minor embarrassments and awkward moments, he could not bring himself to feel bad about it. What had happened seemed natural, his remorse a false product of religious and social conditioning. Yet no matter what he told himself about the necessity of having a private life, or what he believed about the artificiality of monogamy, or what other reasonable arguments he could summon up to explain what he'd done, his thoughts always returned to one central reality: he would have to lie to Anne. If she found out, she wouldn't be philosophical about it, nor would she accept it. She would simply leave.

Twice, lights went on in the neighboring houses at precisely the moment he walked by, a coincidence that increased his sense of power. His conscience ordered him never to repeat this incident, but already he was unwilling to give Polly up; already he was beginning to think he could get away with having both her and Anne, at least for the summer. He knew that such an arrangement would be difficult, but the unpredictability of his own unseasoned responses to such a new situation had a hypnotic appeal. He had spent so many years immersing his imagination in the woman's side of not dissimilar affairs; now he convinced himself that he had the right to know what it was like to be the man. Naturally, it crossed his mind that a strict monitoring of his emotions under such a strain could facilitate a new depth in his work, but he was not interested in Polly only for pragmatic reasons. He also thought he owed it to himself as a man to affirm his aliveness in this instance, to live for once as a player rather than as a voyeur.

He stopped in the middle of the bridge that hung low over the body of water called Barton's Creek. The water swirled in circles that crashed apart on rocks, leaving clumps of leaves and twigs in their wake. It was too dark to see anything along the riverbank except for the bushes closest to him. Their leaves fluttered under the unstable burden of raindrops that collided and leaped to their dissolution on the ground. The grandeur of the natural world seemed an apt extension of his aching muscles, his quick thoughts, and he guarded himself with the aid of his throbbing senses against any intrusion by his suburban conscience, his guilt, his husbandliness.

"Alex?" said a small voice.

For a shining moment he thought he was about to be host to an apparition. He hadn't heard anyone walk up. He smiled as he realized that Polly must have come after him. Her pursuit of him into the damp woods would settle the question of the future once and for all. He was secretly grateful to her for taking the decision out of his hands. He envisioned leading her down onto the river-bank and repeating the slow steps toward the primal convergence that had bound them so closely only half an hour earlier. He turned around, his arms already outstretched.

"It's Rachel Morse." She materialized suddenly out of the dark and leaned with him on the rail of the bridge. "I was just taking a walk. I hope I didn't frighten you."

He jerked his hands back and took a deep, sonorous breath to reestablish his equilibrium.

"I *did* frighten you," she said gravely.

She seemed an odd, vulnerable lump in her shapeless army surplus jacket, her hair dripping.

"No," he said to the water, "I thought you were a friendly ghost."

She gave a little laugh that blended with the sound of the plashing creek. "If your ghosts are friendly, you must be very secure."

"Funny you should say that," he replied.

"Why?"

"I was just wondering where my limits end."

"Oh, I think you could get away with anything, at least in your writing. I've been rereading your books."

"You'll learn all the tricks, too," he said absently.

"I hope so." Her unpainted nails shone white as she gripped the wooden rail. "It's such a struggle. My scenes are either too short or too long, and even though I'm aware of it, I can't figure out how to fix them. Pacing is so difficult."

He barked a rueful laugh, then plunged his hands into his pockets. "It gets a bit easier, but not much." He looked at the water, which fluttered with silvery streaks. "I'm headed past the dorms. You?" he asked.

"Same."

"We could walk together."

They stepped off the bridge. The earth sucked at his shoes. He ran his fingertips over the wet leaves on the bushes along the path. "Let me ask you something," he said suddenly. "Do things still seem new to you? What I mean is, when you do something you have never done before, do you experience it just for what it is, or do you bring to it everything you know, so there are no real surprises?"

For a moment Rachel was quiet. The rain seemed to be letting up. "To be honest, everything surprises me," she said.

Alex laughed. Impulsively, he flung an arm around her and gave her a quick squeeze. "Keep it that way. The biggest sign of aging is the reluctance to take chances because one is already certain of the outcome."

They walked a bit farther. Rachel told him she had changed her story, but that the beginning was still wrong. Alex suggested that she skip the beginning until she had the end exactly as she wanted it. "There's no rule that says you have to write a story in any particular order."

"But I already have the ending," she said. "I know what happens. I just don't know where to begin."

"I suggest you begin as close to the end as possible while still having the story make sense."

She didn't reply, and though he couldn't see her face, he had the sense she was frowning.

"Forgive me," he said. "I don't think I'm being very helpful."

"I know you're trying to help." She was walking with her head bent nearly perpendicular to her back, the way his boys did. He wondered if she had any friends in the program.

"I have an idea," he said. "Why don't you come back to the house for dinner?"

"Tonight?"

"Yes, tonight. It will do you good to get your mind off your story, and if we really can't stop you from thinking about it, my wife is always full of good advice."

"Thank you. I'd like that, if you're sure it's okay."

He felt a flash of guilt for using Rachel Morse as a shield to hold between him and Anne's possible suspicions, but he told himself his baser motives were satisfactorily balanced out by the girl's obvious need for companionship.

He hadn't had sex with two women in the same day since college, when he had had that opportunity exactly once. After Rachel Morse left his house that night, however, Anne told him how much it had touched her to see him be nice to his student, and he knew she was really saying she wanted to be close to him.

"I missed you all afternoon," she said as she arranged her pillow.

"I know. It's just why I always avoided teaching before," he said. "Students want all your time." He paused. "But they're paying for it, after all. I'd feel the same way if I were in their position. I owe it to them."

It wasn't until he heard these words come out of his mouth that he knew he was going to see Polly again. He was paving the way for future excuses even as he reached for Anne, and found her reaching back.

The next day he found a present in his faculty mailbox. He wasn't even looking as he reached inside — there was never anything in there except student stories and the occasional flyer — so he automatically withdrew his hand when it alighted on something unexpected and strange. His shoulders quivered briefly as he thought of stories he'd heard about mailboxes planted with bombs or deadly snakes. When he had overcome the shock, and begun to analyze his reaction, he found that his response had been visceral rather than emotional; he would go so far as to characterize it as primal. He thought he must have a genetic memory of the horror connected with reaching a defenseless, bare human hand into an unexplored hole in the ground. His fantasies had suggested human malevolence — enemies, people out to get him — but his reaction had been deeper and less reasoned than that. Suddenly, in the intramural post office at a small New England college, he was a caveman. It was an odd aspect of himself to uncover, he who had lived such a cerebral life. Odd, but somehow exciting.

He looked in the box, this time reaching with his eyes as well as his hands. The object turned out to be a bird's nest with two cracked blue eggs still inside. Beside it lay a folded copy of Polly's poem, *The Last Man on Earth*.

Alex smiled and tucked the poem into his briefcase. As he walked toward the stairs that led up to the cafeteria, he dropped the nest and broken eggs in the trash.

"How are you managing this?" Polly asked.

"I'm supposed to be spending time with other writers," said Alex.

"Are you spending time with other writers?"

"When would I have a chance to do that?" Alex teased.

Polly smiled and folded her arms beneath her head, the force of which motion caused her breasts to pop out from beneath the sheet. He stared at them helplessly.

"It's an overrated pastime, anyway," she said.

"I wouldn't know." His hands crept toward her, as if of their own volition. He watched their progress tensely and cheered inwardly when they reached their goal.

"Take my word for it," she said. He didn't bother to respond, as the actions of his bold hands had already effectively ended the conversation.

Sometimes they talked more, but never enough so that the time got away from them before they had a chance to "get horizontal," as Alex jokingly put it. Polly had cleaned up the apartment after his first visit, a change he assumed was the result of a return to the everyday after the hypnosis of working on her poem, although he liked to believe she'd made things nice for him. She did make things nice, in other ways as well; in fact, it seemed almost too easy to be with her. It wasn't even awkward when he ran into her when he was with Anne, because he didn't feel anything inappropriate for Polly under those circumstances. In public she was Polly-the-Poet, as the boys called her. But when he went to her apartment she was quite another matter, and, to be honest, he wasn't himself, either, but more of a pared-down compendium of his more interesting aspects, slightly larger than life. Sometimes when he thought back over his performances on those afternoons, the wise things he'd said, his lack of inhibitions, he suspected he construed himself as a fictional character in order to be with Polly without feeling guilty about Anne.

Polly was smart about the whole thing, too. They never discussed when to meet; he went to see her when she left an offering in his mailbox. In spite of sending these little signals she always acted surprised to see him. The whole scenario of the mailbox had a nice romantic symbolism to it that he thought he might somehow work into his next book.

It was Rachel's turn to present her work to the class.

"I'm a little nervous," she said, "so please forgive me if I don't read very well."

She glanced at Alex, who tried to steady her with his eyes. She was right in her assessment of herself. In the beginning, she didn't read very well, but as her story went on her voice grew stronger and the restless movement in the room died away. She read what Alex recognized as the suicide story she'd been talking about for weeks, only now the heroine chose to live at the end, having come to the conclusion that living might indeed be the best revenge. She wrote it well, Alex thought. In spite of her age, or perhaps because of it, she expressed herself deeply, in elliptical sentences that led her audience through a wide range of emotion. When she'd finished, everyone clapped spontaneously, and Rachel winced with surprise, as if she'd caught them all reading over her shoulder.

"See? It wasn't so bad," Alex whispered as he joined her at the front of the room. "I think they loved you."

Her head jerked oddly and she said something very quietly that he couldn't quite hear — something like she loved them, too.

"I feel so guilty," Anne said.

Alex cringed at the mention of the word. "Why?"

"For leaving the boys with a stranger. Do you realize we hardly ever hire a baby sitter when we're at home?"

They headed up the hill toward the theater. Anne had a navy blue cashmere sweater draped over her shoulders, the sleeves dangling, a style Alex found womanly and refined.

"They'll be fine," he said as he took her hand. "They're both fast runners."

"Oh, that's reassuring!" She laughed.

They sat toward the top of the room, where they had a view not only of the stage but of the heads of all the other teachers and students. Naturally, he watched for Polly to come in, which she finally did in the company of one of the other poets, a man, but he'd been expecting that. Earlier that afternoon, when he had been just about to leave her apartment, she told him she had a date for the reading that night.

"Are you jealous?" Polly had asked. She was naked, lying on his chest. She liked to affect flirtatious poses.

He had been jealous when she told him, although he did not admit it — it seemed *too* adulterous to be jealous of Polly — but when he saw them together, he felt strangely glad for her, as if she were a sister of his who'd been unhappy for a long time. He hadn't really thought about what would happen when he and Polly went their separate ways at the end of the summer, but now he saw it would be all right. He would go home with Anne, his writer's block would lift, Polly would find someone else, and if they ran into each other again, they would compare notes on how they'd chosen to portray the summer in their work.

He watched as she and her date sat down. He knew she had located his position as soon as she entered the theater and that she was keeping track of him with the intuitive, poetic eyes in the back of her head. How long would it be before she turned around for a look? He bet two minutes. At a minute and a half, she dropped her silk scarf down her back and turned around to pick it up. When their eyes met, he smiled. He was still smiling, full of fellow feeling, when he turned back to Anne.

"I hope he reads the series about his children," Alex whispered to his wife as the lights went down.

"I don't care what he reads. I love it all," Anne said. "It's enough of a thrill to see him in person."

She didn't meet his eye as she spoke, but continued to gaze intently at the stage. Sometimes he thought he had learned to concentrate from her. Her eyes seemed to draw the famous poet from behind the curtains and pull him to the lectern, the same grave, gray eyes that had drawn him to her at a college party. He was a premed student who dreamed of writing; she made him write. She had read how Colette's husband locked Colette in a room until she finished a story, and she decided to try the same experiment with him one summer at a rented farmhouse in Maine. She was a gentler jailer than Willy had been, however; his confinement came with the added amenities of fresh blueberries and Anne's constant encouragement. By the end of the summer, he had completed the first draft of a novel that he was able to sell not much later. His career had been fairly straightforward after that, not in small part because Anne had always been there to remind him when to drop a note to someone, when to make a telephone call. She had been a perfect partner, always steering him in the direction of his best interests. If not for her, he had to admit, he would probably have become a mediocre doctor, pushing drug samples into the quavering hands of desperate patients whose cases didn't interest him.

An explosion of applause thundered through the theater like the reverse of rain, rain rising to the rafters. The famous poet accepted the accolades for a modest moment, then lifted his hand, and the clapping stopped.

For a moment the room was silent, and in that quiet moment, while the room held its breath in anticipation, he realized the enormity of what he'd been doing, what he was risking. In one of his books he'd written about a man who became sick with remorse after having an affair. Sick with remorse, he'd written, without having any idea what he meant; indeed, it had meant so little that, until now, he hadn't even connected it to his own life. The character in his book had become literally sick to his stomach, but for Alex the sickness was like being boiled in the ocean, rolled in wave after wave, picked up and smashed to the floor of the sea, the sea hot and without buoyancy.

"Let's go outside," he whispered. "I don't feel well."

Without glancing in his direction, Anne lay her hand expertly on his forehead. "You're cool."

"Maybe it's something that doesn't involve a fever."

She still didn't turn her eyes away from the poet. "I'll take care of you after it's over, okay?"

He sat through the reading as the waves washed over him. He didn't hear a word. He didn't think he would ever be able to read this poet's work again. During the final applause, Anne turned to him, flushed.

"I'm proud of you," she said.

"Me. Why?"

"For being a writer. I know your work does for other people what his work does for me. It's wonderful, Alex. There's nothing like it."

He stood up and pulled her arm through his and guided her toward an exit opposite the one toward which Polly was headed. "That's a rather backhanded compliment, isn't it?" he said as gaily as he could manage. "Are you saying that my writing doesn't do anything for you?"

"That's not what I meant." She nudged him playfully. "You seem to feel better."

"I suppose."

"Maybe it was just an attack of jealousy."

He started at her words, but saw from her warm expression that she'd merely been playing out the joke.

Outside the theater the audience was murmuring greetings and sharing critiques of the performance, their exhilarated voices whirling into the night. The air was chilly and clear, every star showed, and the thick belt of the Milky Way pulsed cold, indifferent light from its unthinkable distance above the tops of the pines. Anne spoke to several people while Alex stood to the side, watching her, assuming the role of the silent, supportive husband of the funny, vivacious wife. He had always supposed that he had left her open to doing what she wanted all these years, that she had had the social life she wanted. Now he saw how much she thrived on company and inconsequential social intercourse, and he realized that the restrictions he put on his own life had restricted her, too.

She reached an arm behind her back, groping for him. He took her hand.

"How are you feeling now?" she asked.

"Better."

"Better enough to go to the reception?"

"What about the sitter?"

Anne looked at her watch. "It's nine-thirty. If she hasn't killed them yet, she probably won't kill them between now and eleven," she said in a voice husky with fun. She was so intent on prolonging the evening that he checked himself from trying to talk her out of going to the reception, although he wanted her alone. On their way to the reception, she giggled in the darkness and even skipped a few steps, trading wry remarks with him as he wondered what grace had allowed him to be smart enough to have married her when they were barely more than children. He thought ruefully that he certainly wasn't as smart anymore — at least he hadn't been using whatever intelligence he had. The whole episode with Polly seemed to be the supreme folly of an ignorant, vain personality. It seemed beneath him. By the time they arrived at the house where the party was to be held, he had laid his feelings for Polly Larson irrevocably aside, as if they had material properties that rendered them fit to be thrown away and completely forgotten.

As he greeted several of his colleagues, Anne broke free and plunged into the living room, picking her way toward the famous poet, who was predictably seated in a wing chair in front of a large fireplace. Alex headed toward the bar in the dining room to get a drink.

"Dr. Quinn, I presume?"

He recognized Polly's voice. Another wave of remorse washed over him as he remembered what he had done with her that afternoon. Out of the corner of his eye he caught sight of the scarf she had dropped during the reading. Suddenly he recognized it as the same scarf that had been brought into play earlier in the day; he had a clear image of its being wound around a bedpost.

"Can't talk now," he managed to say. He pointed lamely to his drink. "I have to bring this to somebody."

Polly lowered her voice. "I'm having evil thoughts, aren't you?"

"Got to go." He jerked away as if he'd been spoken to by a devil, although there was no evil in her eyes, only desperation, and, as he brushed her off, confusion. The objective observer in him registered her expression even as he maneuvered to be free of her.

"Alex?" she called after him, but he kept going without looking back. He zoomed toward Anne, but the circle around her and the poet had grown thick as a fence and he despaired of working his way inside. He wasn't much in the mood to pay homage to the poet, anyway. The truth was, he didn't even like poetry — he thought that, as an art form, it was basically dead. For a moment he spotted Anne's head through a chink in the crowd. He willed her to intuit his presence, and when she turned around, he indicated with a hand signal that he was going to step outside. She acknowledged his plans with a small nod and quickly turned her attention back to the poet, as if she might have missed something.

On the porch, several of his students were sitting on the floor, smoking and drinking beer.

"Alex!" they called. "Come sit with us."

He waved casually, as if he hadn't heard their invitation, as if he were a celebrity keeping a friendly yet necessary distance from his fans. He walked around the side of the house and took a seat beneath a tree in the backyard, only to discover that there was no solace in the night. He might as well be inside talking to Polly for all the relief he felt. He had brought her with him. She was coiled coolly around his mind.

"I'm an idiot," he said aloud.

"You shouldn't talk about yourself that way."

He froze. "Who's there?" he called out, his voice hoarse. He heard footsteps on the leaves.

"It's Rachel. Rachel Morse."

He gave a wry, distant laugh. "Rachel Morse, Rachel Morse, I should have known it was you. You always seem to appear out of nowhere."

She walked into the light. Her hair was done in a thick, brown braid. "I'm sorry," she said quietly. "I came out here to get away from the party for a moment. I didn't mean to disturb you." She began to walk away.

"No, no, no," said Alex, "you're not disturbing me. I'm glad to see you. You're one of the few people I could stand to see right now."

Her head was turned away from him.

"Come on, sit down with me for a while."

He patted the damp ground at his side; she sat nearby. For a few moments they neither spoke nor moved as the shadows gathered around them in dark pools.

"Life sucks," he said finally.

"I know what you mean," Rachel agreed in a low voice.

Alex smiled. "Somehow I thought you would," he said, patting her on the foot. "You're one of my most sensitive students, Rachel."

"Too sensitive."

"Nope, no such thing. You need to be sensitive if you want to do really good work. Of course, it doesn't always make your private life easy."

"Don't I know it." Rachel sighed. "Either everyone thinks you're lazy because you lie on your bed and stare at the ceiling all the time, or else they think you're showing off. But it's worth it if you've got what it takes." She paused. "Do you think I have what it takes, Alex?"

"What?" He'd been thinking of Anne, how much fun she could be, how he'd wasted half the summer on Polly.

"You've read my work. Do you think I have what it takes to be a writer?"

"Why would you want to be a writer?" asked Alex. "It's not such a great life. You're young, you could still do anything you wanted."

"What do you mean?"

"I mean it's lonely and frustrating and thankless. It isn't as if the world is out there just waiting for you to write your book."

"But it's the only thing I care about." Rachel pushed her face into the light. The smooth plane of her forehead seemed to reflect his loneliness back at him. His life had been so busy that he hadn't even realized how lonely he was for someone with whom he could talk. He had stopped talking to Anne beyond the surface details and the necessary exchange of information about the boys since that first afternoon at Polly's apartment. He'd been afraid to talk for fear of blurting everything, including an apology he didn't exactly feel like making. Suddenly he thought that perhaps the difficulties he was having with his work were a result of having cut off his normal avenues of communication. Talking to Anne had always been a part of his creative process, although he'd never assigned their conversations a value before. Now he saw that he was a blank page without them.

"Will you excuse me? I have to go find my wife."

He stood up, and Rachel jumped to her feet too, with surprising agility.

"Wait," she said. "Do you really think I should give up being a writer?"

"If you can," he said kindly.

"I've put so much time into it. But if you don't think I'm any good . . ."

"That's not the point. It really doesn't matter what I think of your work, anyway." He looked over her head at the house and thought of Anne inside, glowing by the fire.

"But the whole reason I came here was to find out what you thought of my work. I used up all my savings for this."

He forced himself to look at her. "You're a fine young writer. But you could be fine at a lot of things that might make you happier. See what happens," he said.

"Yeah," she muttered. "Well, good night." She turned

abruptly and walked off, her footsteps so silent that she appeared
to be floating across the lawn, like a wraith.

"Good night, Rachel," he called out. "See you in class."

When she didn't answer, he headed back toward the party, his
conscience suddenly so clear that his mind began to fill with ideas
for a new novel.

He had no idea what he was going to say to Polly. He went over
and over possible speeches in his mind, but no matter how elo-
quent he tried to be, nothing could disguise his basic mission,
which was to tell her he couldn't see her anymore.

Finally he decided the best thing to do was to be straightforward. When he came to this conclusion, he thought it probably
wouldn't be too bad. Soon he was looking forward to putting the
whole affair gently to rest. Polly knew he was married. There'd
never been any discussion of altering that. He realized it was a
form of self-aggrandizement for him to imagine that a discon-
tinuation of their afternoon trysts would be a problem for her at
all. He was sure it had fulfilled a need for her as it had for him. He
began to conjure her as an old buddy with whom he would
always share important memories but not a real life.

Each morning he checked his mailbox for a signal beckoning
him to her apartment, but as the days went by, his box remained
empty. He saw her often, from a distance, across the green lawns
of the college commons or among the buzzing crowds in the
student dining room, but he never managed to catch her eye. It
seemed she'd gone her way at the same time that he realized he
had to go his, and that though the break had been relatively
painless, she didn't want to talk about it. Sometimes he saw her in
the company of the poet with whom she had had the date. That
was nice. He was happy for her. Soon the entire incident receded
into the background, less detailed and less deeply felt than it
would have been had he made the whole thing up.

As if paying a penance, Alex rededicated himself to his work
and his family, both of which appeared to thrive under his attention. The boys became miraculously more athletic, finally reaching the stage that men fantasize about when they have sons, the

catch-after-dinner, running-plays stage. Alex had never been much of an athlete himself, but the children didn't know that. They thought it was incredible that their father, who had what appeared to them to be a rather uninteresting job, was also capable of being compelling on their terms. He bought a map of the skies and together they explored the constellations as if they were foreign countries, occasions for which Alex granted them a dispensation to stay up late. When they finally were packed off to their twin beds, his life expanded even further, because it was then that he was alone with Anne.

"You're so beautiful," he told her.

"Uh-huh." She agreed, giggling.

"I can't believe I was smart enough to marry you when I was just a kid. Do you know what I mean?"

She turned on her side and propped herself up on her elbow. "I believe you're fishing for a compliment." Her mouth twitched with amusement. "I used to give you compliments all the time and you took them as a matter of course. Truly, you soaked them up like a sponge. I'm not so sure that was good for you." She glanced at him sideways. "I'm afraid I've made you a bit complacent. Perhaps it would be better if you worked for your compliments from now on."

"What do I have to do?"

"You're the creative one in the family. You think of something."

"Got you! That was a compliment right there."

"Think of something," she repeated.

"How about if I make you the heroine of my next novel?"

"Are you serious?"

"It's under consideration."

"Can you make her a pregnant heroine?"

His heart caught. "Anne . . ."

"I'm not pregnant yet," she said, playing with his fingers. "But I don't think it would be the worst idea in the world, do you?"

"It's the best idea I've heard all summer."

As the moon bloomed that month, they began the gentle process of trying for a new little Quinn, and with Anne's encouragement, he began work on a novel, finding that every time he tried to think of something, he could.

Had it been up to him, he would have let the students choose which one of them would give a reading on the last night of the program, but unfortunately, it was part of his job to decide. There was a stunned silence in the classroom for a moment after he announced that his choice was Rachel Morse, yet after the session he saw several of his more competitive students congratulating Rachel and remembered how it was at school when a mousy student won a prize; the triumph of the underdog imparted a feeling of solidarity to the group at large. He purposely hung back after the last student had left the room to afford Rachel an opportunity to thank him in private, but he saw her, through the window, walking away with her cohorts and supposed, in the first flush of her popularity, that he couldn't blame her.

After lunch he found a maple leaf in his mailbox. Polly's door was open when he arrived.

"Well, well, well," she said when he walked into the room. "This is a surprise."

Her apartment was empty, with everything stashed away for her imminent departure, he supposed, in the cardboard boxes that stood by the wall.

"You sent for me, so I came." He held his palms open toward her in a gesture meant to convey an acknowledgment of all the turbulent water that had flowed under their particular bridge.

"I sent for you?" she asked incredulously.

He hadn't expected bitterness. He'd imagined nostalgia, perhaps a mood of melancholy, but bitterness seemed ignoble, considering they might never see each other again.

"*I* sent for *you*?" she repeated.

He pulled the maple leaf from his pocket and held it out to her.

She parked her fists on her hips. "What's that supposed to mean?"

For the first time in weeks he felt himself pulled out to sea. "You didn't put this in my mailbox?"

"Why would I do that?"

She was flushed, as red as he felt, although his darker complexion was incapable of betraying shame.

"When you wanted to see me, you put things in my mailbox."

She shook her head. "You're the one who had to work me into your schedule. How was I supposed to know when you could get away? Your wish was my command. I just went along with what you wanted, like some stupid kid, and when you didn't want to see me anymore, you disappeared out of my life without a word said, although I'm sure you've written about it."

"Would it be so horrible if I wrote about it?"

She pressed her fingers to her temples. "I'm sure I can't stop you."

"Aren't you going to write about it, too?"

"Maybe in about twenty years. I don't tend to write out of pain."

"What about what's-his-name, Paul?"

"Oh, Paul," she said. "I don't see what he has to do with this."

"Aren't you and he . . . an item?" Alex asked awkwardly.

"You mean you thought — " She shook her head and rolled her eyes. "Paul's gay, which I would have told you if you'd bothered to ask."

"I didn't want to interfere."

"That's considerate of you," she said snidely.

"When you stopped leaving me things, I naturally assumed . . ."

"Alex, I have a lot to do. Is there a point to this?"

"I guess this is good-bye."

She had her arms wound so tightly around herself that she seemed in danger of breaking her own ribs. "It was good-bye a month ago."

"So." He backed awkwardly toward the door. "Are you flying home?"

"What do you care?" she wailed.

"I'm sorry." He held out his hand, but she made no move to shake it. "Good luck."

"Yeah, good luck," he heard her say as he sped down the stairs.

He stepped out into the sun and breathed deeply. He discovered he still held the maple leaf clutched in his hand, and he crushed it viciously, as if it was the symbol of all the lies attendant upon his relationship with Polly. Then, as he ran through this last ugly scene in his mind, he remembered that she had claimed she hadn't left the little offerings in his mailbox. He turned the mystery over and over as he walked down the hill until it came to him in a flash of illumination that it must have been Anne who had put the treasures there. She must have collected them during her daily nature walks with the boys. He pictured her sneaking into the faculty lounge and carefully filling his slot with birds' nests, wildflowers, curling pieces of bark. His unraveling of her secret missions suddenly rose up and converged with the lesson he had learned over the course of the summer; naturally, it had been Anne all along.

With her characteristic awkwardness, Rachel stepped up to the microphone, her aggressively plain glasses swinging from a string around her neck. For close to a minute she tried to position the microphone until eventually it became so agonizing to watch her that someone leaped from the front row to help. She poured herself a tumbler of water and, instead of taking a sip the way most readers did, she took another half minute to swallow the entire contents of the glass. Alex heard someone behind him joke that this was performance art, and Anne squeezed his hand sympathetically, as though Rachel's clumsiness reflected badly on him. When Rachel finally spoke, she was too close to the microphone, so her breath sounded heavy and obscene. Several people giggled. Shutting his eyes, Alex willed her to pull herself together, and as if having received strength from his wishes, she began again.

"I'd like to dedicate this story to my teacher, Alex Quinn, who told us on the first day of workshop to sit still and be honest, which I've been trying to do ever since."

There was a smattering of applause at the mention of his name, he presumed from his faithful students.

"Don't clap yet," she said quickly, mistaking the object of the applause. Alex cringed for her again. "I just finished this story, and it might still need some work."

"She's your student, then?" asked the woman next to him. Anne nodded proudly at her from his other side. The woman stared at him for a moment, her eyebrows raised in admiration.

There was another delay while Rachel organized a sheaf of papers that appeared to be covered with longhand. The audience shifted restlessly, but when she finally began to read, they settled as her voice grew strong and clear. Alex sat back and allowed his eyes to drift lazily around the room, absorbing the details as he went. Although he'd never bothered to study the auditorium before, or most of the people in it, everything looked warm and easily familiar to him, as if he'd been born here, as if it were his own hometown. He would miss this place. As he looked back over the summer and added up the events, the whole thing seemed like a noble experiment. Hypothesis: he needed other people. Conclusion: the people he needed, he already had.

He no longer regretted what he'd done. There was something to be said for the learning process itself, for smelling the scents, for having the conversations, for losing himself in a relationship with Polly, if only for a few weeks. Strangely enough, most of his lived moments were not as vivid as his imaginings when he wrote his books, but life was rounder, more subtle, more resonant of possibilities and of things going on beneath the surface. Going home meant being alone again, yet he suspected that though his life would essentially be the same, he would experience it more fully; he would appreciate his children, he would love his wife, he would honor his work.

As he pursued his thoughts, he was lulled by the warmth in the room and the swaying rhythms of Rachel's speech. The words he was saying to himself seemed to mix with hers, weaving back and forth, he the warp, she the woof, and he settled into a peaceful torpor as the sky darkened. He was thinking rather fondly about the first time he'd met Polly at the diner when Anne suddenly turned halfway around and stared at him, or rather, stared into him.

"What?" he whispered.

She kept her eyes on him for a moment longer, then turned back and stared icily ahead.

"Ramona was too shy at first," Rachel read, "to ask him all the questions she'd prepared for him over the years, but now that she was finally so close, she felt compelled to express her admiration for him and his great work in some small way of her own. For three nights she did not sleep as she tried to figure out what to do. On the fourth day, she put a bird's nest in his mailbox . . ."

Alex's scalp began to prickle.

"Have you read this story before?" Anne asked.

He shook his head.

"That afternoon she followed him to the house of a viola player. Through the windows, she watched them . . ."

His eyes were pointed toward the floor, so he saw the exact moment when Anne's hands, gripping the metal armrests, turned clawlike and hard. He saw by the look of her veins that he would be smart to die at that moment.

"Since she was only twelve he had been the person Ramona most admired," Rachel read, "but now she saw him for what he really was."

Rachel paused and looked up as Anne grimaced. Below them, Alex saw a foxy head dart back and forth, as Polly sought him out.

"He had taken her innocence, and she knew she would never again have a hero, not in the same way . . ." Rachel read.

"Well done," Anne whispered through clenched teeth. She stood up and steadied herself for a moment before pushing her way toward the aisle.

"Anne!" He rose.

She turned around and looked at him for a moment, her glare advising him not to follow her. He sank back into his seat as she disappeared. Several rows had craned around to see what the commotion was, but when they saw him sitting stonily alone, they returned their attention to the entertainment. It didn't matter, anyway, whether they stared at him or not, as he was no longer there. Anne would definitely leave him — he knew that —

and he was nothing. He was a corpse. He was a shell. He was a simple creature whose pain was merely a muscle spasm that would not reach the brain. He was dead, dead, nothing, nothing, a cipher who automatically mimicked the three-dimensional people when they broke into applause as the self-assured girl on stage finished her story. He watched dazedly as the vibrations from the clapping in the hall seemed to rock her body gently from side to side, like water lapping against a boat. Soon she left the stage and was swiftly replaced by an older woman who waited for the noise to die down so she could begin her own reading. Alex was suffocating, rolling on the ocean floor. He leaned over, thrusting his head between his knees.

"She's coming back out!" the woman next to him announced.

The ovation swelled with every dizzying breath he took.

"Aren't you proud?" The woman nudged him.

He couldn't bring himself to look up. He doubted if he would survive. The most he could do was wonder why no one noticed the drowning man among them as they sprang to their feet to applaud the artistry of his student, Rachel Morse.

Plans for Plants

SCOTT FORBES had already settled into his favorite chair and was flipping through a copy of *Adweek* when his wife, Emily, entered the room and began to massage the base of his neck. Emily smoked a cigarette as she rubbed. She calculated that there were six weeks left until she and Scott were due to renew their annual marriage contract, which they always did around the anniversary of their engagement in November. For the upcoming year, she was determined to cut out the daily massage clause. She supposed she'd been trying to be nice when she first volunteered to do it, but now she resented the time it took, especially since Scott hadn't offered her a comparable consideration. He seemed to think she could survive on compliments alone.

"Emily," Scott said, "one thing about you, your hands are great. I feel better, really much better."

Emily ran her thumbs up the sides of his spine. She knew the routine so well that she could perform it perfectly without having to focus on what she was doing, which left her free to think about her own projects. They'd recently moved from Manhattan to an old Victorian house in Dobbs Ferry that she'd vowed to finish decorating by the time their families came to visit at Christmas. She'd already built a greenhouse in the backyard, her first step toward starting her own nursery. That project had used up most of her creative energy, and she hadn't done much else. House-work alone took up more time than the job she'd had in New

York as a floral designer, and Scott was not much help. He seemed to think that the tribulations of commuting exempted him from any similar trials around the house. Sometimes she reminded him that they were supposed to share tasks pertaining to basic upkeep of their persons; most of the time, it was easier for her to go ahead and do what needed to be done. Not only that, she suspected he lied about what he ate when they went on a diet. He'd be thinner if he were telling the truth.

She glanced at the clock. Her massage routine took twenty minutes, and she was nearly finished. His body still felt tense, but less so than it had when she began. Considering the material with which she was working, less tense was an achievement.

"Mrs. Savich is probably taking credit for all my hard work," she said. "I don't see why you need both the Alexander technique and me. There's such a thing as relaxation overload, you know, or if there isn't, there will be. It's a problem that will no doubt come up on the talk shows quite soon. Don't you have a session with her tomorrow?"

"Uh-huh. Oh, that's good. Do that a little more, will you?"

Emily paused to take a drag off her cigarette. "In that case, maybe I can skip tomorrow night."

"No!" Scott wrenched around so violently that she was afraid he'd abrogated all her hard work.

"All right, all right, I'll do your massage," Emily said quickly. After seven years of marriage, she'd learned that you had to pick your battles. "You're awfully jumpy, if I may say so. Did anything happen at the office today?"

Scott closed the magazine. When Cayce, their cat, heard the pages snap, he vaulted off his perch on the sofa and sauntered over to Scott's chair. Scott tapped his hands on his lap as he coaxed the cat with little kissing noises. Cayce blinked, cocked his head, and after a respectable delay, crouched and leaped up, circled twice, and settled.

"That's a good boy," Scott said. He was quiet for a moment. "Actually, Em, it's something else. I have something to tell you. Maybe you'd better sit down."

"I'm fine." Automatically her knees locked, as they always did when she wanted to run away.

Scott inhaled deeply. "It's nothing bad," he said, making her suspect the worst. She had a fleeting image of him ducking into a Times Square hotel with his secretary. "It's just that I'm not doing the Alexander technique anymore. I quit a while ago because I didn't think it was doing much for me. I've been meaning to tell you, but the time was never right."

She slumped with relief, but Scott sighed in a manner that let her know she was not out of the woods yet. She glanced at the mirror on the far wall and saw herself standing above him as in a formal portrait, the two of them looking like siblings with their childlike haircuts and permanent, thoughtful expressions on their faces. Emily narrowed her eyes. Control, she thought, control. She took a deep, cleansing breath and tried to remain calm. "So what have you been doing when you have supposedly been with Mrs. Savich?"

"I'm still seeing her, but I've been working on something else instead." He paused. "I'm taking her astral projection class."

"What? Is this some sort of a joke?" She jerked her hands away from his shoulders as if they were on fire.

"I know it probably sounds strange to you, Em, but I want you to try to understand, because it's important to me. Mrs. Savich said she knew I had the potential to do it the first time she met me — you know I've always been slightly psychic — but she didn't press the matter until she was sure I was ready."

"Did she decide you were ready after you got your promotion and your *raise?*" Emily asked shrilly. She stared accusatorily into the mirror. Scott had recently become an account manager at the ad agency, which was how they could afford the mortgage for the house in Dobbs Ferry.

"It's not as unusual as you think," Scott said patiently. "A lot of people do it. Shirley MacLaine does it, and I know you like her."

"Only sometimes!" Emily wailed. "Only her acting, not the rest of it. Not even all her acting, either."

"Believe me, Em, it has nothing to do with you."

"Oh, thanks. That's supposed to make me feel better?"

"You know what I mean." His mirror image shot her a pleading glance. "Actually, I think I'm doing pretty well with it. I'm already in the advanced class. We go on simulated flights during every session. Even though we're not actually flying yet, it's exhausting. You have to go over every step of the way in your mind and visualize what you're doing as vividly as possible. This week we pretended to go as far as Chicago."

"Chicago?"

"We're supposed to go to California before the Christmas break."

"California?" Her voice ached with betrayal. "You're planning to go to California without me? Every time I've suggested we visit Carol, you've always found an excuse not to go." Carol was Emily's younger sister, a sophomore at Stanford.

"This would be completely different. I wouldn't go to the same places I'd go with you. I'd just have an aerial view."

Emily spread herself out in corpse position, just as her yoga teacher had taught her to do, on the floor in front of Scott's chair. The posture was supposed to be soothing, but she felt tight as a drum skin. "Scott, why are you doing this?"

"You have the greenhouse. I need something too."

"All right, I've heard enough. This is absurd."

"I know, I know. But just suppose it isn't? We use less than two percent of our brains, you know."

"At best," Emily said snidely.

"What's to say these things aren't possible? A lot of people think they are. You do yoga."

"Any real yogi would reject astral projection as being a false path. They have better things to do." She pressed her palms against her eyelids and saw colors whirling around. "It isn't fair of you to drag yoga into this."

Scott plunked Cayce onto the rug. He put his hands on the armrests of his chair and heaved himself up. "Look, Emily," he boomed down from above her, "look at me."

She wouldn't.

"It's not as if I'm having an affair," he said. "I think you could try to be a little more open minded. But even if you can't, I'm going to continue practicing, and I don't want to be disturbed, or teased, or whatever, about this. Understood?"

Emily grunted noncommittally. "It's your turn to make dinner!" she called after him as he left the room.

She heard Scott pound off toward the kitchen, mumbling under his breath, while she continued to stare at the backs of her eyelids in a doomed effort to make everything go away.

Some time later, Scott knelt down and handed her a plate of macaroni and cheese as she lay stubborn and disgruntled on the rug. They ate in silence, and when they'd finished, he curled around her and cuddled her until she temporarily forgot how angry she was. She was just thinking how nice it would be if he would give her a massage for once when, as if he'd read her mind, he straddled her and began to knead her shoulders. One thing led to the next, and it wasn't long before she slipped into her familiar habits and began to knead him, too.

"Is it safe?" he whispered, coming up for air after a long, heady kiss.

"I hope so." She tried to count backward to her last period, but she kept losing her place as numbers of the bulbs and plants she'd recently potted sprang to mind. "Maybe I should get something."

"Skip it. Let's wing it for once," Scott said as he matched the length of his arms to hers.

The next morning, while Scott was in the shower, Emily crept out to the greenhouse where she hid behind the last row of roses until she was sure he was well on his way to New York. When the coast was clear, she adjusted her apron around her hips and pulled on her gardening gloves, remembering as she did so how Cayce had nuzzled her at dawn when she'd woken up to find herself alone on the living room floor, freezing and stiff and irritated that she'd been tricked into forgetting how angry she was at her husband. She decided to proceed as if the last part of the evening had never happened. She simply wanted to be left alone to watch the river, do her yoga, and care for her plants.

A week later, the moon was full. On earth, the neighborhoods teemed with little ghosts and superheroes trick-or-treating from door to door while the heavens looked almost as sharp as they do in a planetarium. Scott settled himself among several of his classmates in a far corner of Mrs. Savich's living room and held a frothy mug up to the Milky Way.

"Here's to good friends" — he proposed a toast — "people who understand, people who don't demand an explanation for everything that happens."

"Hear, hear," said several of the regulars. They all raised their drinks and took long, satisfying swigs. Mrs. Savich was still in the library of her vast apartment, coaching a few of the slower learners, but as usual, she had prepared a postclass party for the hard-core group who'd developed a habit of staying late. Scott looked at the bottles and glasses lined up on the table and marveled at Mrs. Savich's generosity. He knew he'd paid to be in the class, but he still thought it was kind of her to provide refreshments. She could have asked everyone to leave as soon as she finished teaching, and no one would have minded. Instead, she welcomed them to stay as late as they wanted among her musty, esoteric books, the bowls of fresh flowers, the lavender-scented candles in the large silver sticks.

"I can't wait to get this technique down," said a man who ghostwrote a column for a famous astrologer. "Sure beats driving, doesn't it?"

"If I'd known about astral projection seven years ago, I probably wouldn't have gotten married," Scott said. "The only reason I did was because my parents promised me a car. Otherwise, Emily and I could have just kept living together."

The guys grunted and nodded. They were all married and they all had their reasons.

"Does your wife know you're doing this?" asked a professional ventriloquist.

"Yeah, oh sure, I told her, but she doesn't believe in it. When I met her, she was an independent, but she just reregistered as a Republican. Her true colors are coming out. Last Thanksgiving we went to her parents' house for turkey, you know? And her father told me with a straight face that people who live in hot climates never amount to anything." Scott leaned into the comfort of the velvet chair. "When Emily gets together with her old school friends, they still drag their hockey sticks out and crack the ball around the yard. That's what I'm dealing with."

There were sympathetic nods all around.

"Plus, she spends all her time breeding roses," he finished. "I can't talk to her."

"My wife used to want kids," said a man who was eighty percent accurate at picking out the black cards in a deck without looking. "Now she says she doesn't. Soon we'll be too old to start a family."

"Too bad we aren't older, though," sighed a short fellow who always wore cardigan sweaters. "Then we could legitimately have midlife crises and pursue college girls."

They heard a motor in the darkness, a plane. Soon they could see its silhouette against the moon.

"Doesn't that look like a witch on a broomstick?" someone said.

"Can't you come up with something more original than that?" Scott asked wearily.

His classmates turned to stare at him.

"I'm sorry. That's what I'm paid to ask all day long. I guess it's getting to me." Scott stood up. "Come on, who needs another beer?"

After passing around a few bottles, he settled himself near the window and raised his mug again, this time hoisting it toward the moon.

"To our wives," he said in a tone low enough not to be heard by the women across the room. His friends murmured their concurrence and thoughtfully drank up.

On the train ride home, Scott wished he hadn't talked so freely about his marriage. He felt he'd revealed too much, he felt disloyal. Poor little Emily, he thought. He noticed the way she stood in front of the mirror and pulled at the lines beneath her eyes to make them disappear for a moment. He tried to imagine her growing older, her mind becoming more rigid and her body cracking up, but all he could picture was how ceremoniously she would have opened the door to every tiny trick-or-treater, dropping her favorite candy bars into their paper bags.

Emily walked out of the hardware store without buying anything for the third time in less than a week. She couldn't bring herself to begin working on the wallpaper. She knew it was irrational, but she had a sense that she could escape from the house more easily if it was unfinished than she could if it were perfect. Lately she'd been having elaborate fantasies about how she'd dismantle the greenhouse, if it came to that. Her car could hold six rose bushes at a time without crowding, but she'd need to rent a small truck to move the larger plants. She could picture moving, but she couldn't focus on what would happen after that. The thought of dating gave her butterflies. Alcoholism was too sordid. The Peace Corps? That plan was old. She was old. She felt too old for a lot of things, but also depressingly dependent again, like a child. She thought maybe she had been too quick to give up her job. She couldn't wait to get her nursery business going, so she could regain her sense of independence.

She braked by the mailbox and jumped out to collect the mail. On the barrel-shaped box there was a painting of ducks flying out of a pond, headed straight for the sun. See Dick run, she thought bitterly, see Scott fly. There was no hunter in the picture, but the tableau gave the impression of one lurking just out of the range of vision. Everyone kept telling her how difficult it would be for her to start her own business, but she thought that if other people could do it, why shouldn't she? Then there were the skeptics who examined her small greenhouse and concluded that the diminutive operation she had managed to put into place betrayed a lack of resolution to follow through with her plan — as if winter was a good time to open a nursery! Most often, she was advised to get to know her neighbors, who would theoretically mushroom into a pool of regular customers when the time came. Every morning she awoke with decisions about the nursery weighing so heavily upon her that she'd developed a nervous stomach and rarely ate until noon.

The car stalled, then coughed furiously when she started it again and pulled up to the garage. Why does he get to drive the good car, she wondered, while I'm stuck in this piece of junk? It was nice when we received it as a wedding present, but now it's old. Everything is old, old, old. Scott is losing his hair in the back and he doesn't even know it. He can't see it. I see it, though, I see it every single day of my life.

Emily hoisted the garage door open, then stepped back into the car and slammed the door. She did it again, *slam*, and then again. As she was about to slam the door for the fourth time, she realized she was being watched.

"Good morning, Mrs. Simmons," Emily called out. Her neighbor's head was perched above the hedge like a jack-o'-lantern on a shelf. "Just a small problem with the door." She smiled confidently, as if she'd known exactly what she was doing all along.

Night after night, Scott practiced. He always pictured going west. He tried to expand upon his memories of coast-to-coast plane trips by thinking of how it would feel to fly through a cloud or over a mountaintop. His biggest problem was concentrating on exactly what he was doing. If he wasn't constantly vigilant, his imagination drifted to his destination, skipping the process of flying altogether. Sometimes he jumped from California to Hawaii and saw himself padding through a steaming jungle, the glut of green hues surrounding him almost sickeningly rich. Once or twice he envisioned himself pushing aside a moist branch only to see Emily standing in a cleared glen, wielding her pruning shears. He became indignant when she entered his fantasy life and swiftly worked to regain his equilibrium by counting backward from ten to one, then picturing a tranquil pond surrounded by tropical vegetation. He was supposed to be quieting his mind;

instead, in the pond's glassy surface, he saw his reflection. Hmm, not bad, he thought. Really, not bad at all.

The day before Thanksgiving, Emily called the local store and asked them to deliver a turkey to her house. When the delivery boy arrived, she peeked inside the bundle and began to cry. The poor turkey looked so naked and alone. She told the boy to keep the bird himself, and when Scott came home late in the afternoon, she announced that she'd become a vegetarian. The next evening they ate their Thanksgiving dinner in silence at a local restaurant. Scott had the turkey 'n' trimmings special; Emily ordered spaghetti. They were home and in bed early, but when her sister called at one o'clock, Emily was still awake. She grabbed the phone in the middle of the first ring, before the sound roused Scott.

"I hope it's not too late. I wanted to wish you a happy Thanksgiving," Carol said.

"No, no, it's fine." Emily searched through the items on her bedside table until she located her cigarettes and matches. "I couldn't sleep anyway. I've been sitting here making lists of all the things I can't bring myself to do and my mind is buzzed. What did you do today?"

"I ate with some friends. Otherwise, I studied."

"Wow. I was never that dedicated when I was in college."

"I'm trying to get all my papers done early so I can spend a few days in Los Angeles before I come to your house for Christmas."

"No comment," Emily said. "I've heard enough about the splendors of Los Angeles lately to last me the rest of my life."

"Sorry, I didn't mean to bring up any sore subjects. Are you alone? You sound like you're alone."

"Nope, Scott's right here. I've developed insomnia, but he's been sleeping better than ever since he added astral projection to his repertoire." Emily struck a match and took a long, death-defying drag off her cigarette. "At least I assume he's here. His body's here. That's as much as I can vouch for these days."

"He's still trying to fly to California without paying for a plane ticket?"

"As far as I know. The whole topic is a conversation stopper, so we don't talk about it much. I can't tell you how creepy it is when he practices. Remember in *Dracula* how Bela Lugosi crossed his arms over his chest when he got into the coffin? That's what Scott does, except rather than climbing into a box of dirt, he does it between my Laura Ashley sheets. I don't know how much longer I can take this."

"I never saw that movie. You shouldn't smoke in bed."

"Thanks for your concern, but there's not much chance of my falling asleep. What's all that noise in the background? Are you in a bar?"

"I'm on the street. There was a bomb scare in the dorm and we all had to clear out while Campus Security makes the usual flashy search for the usual nothing. It's such a pain. I have a test next week and I have to study."

"Doesn't anyone go home for Thanksgiving in the promised land?" Emily asked.

"Why should they?"

"Just asking."

She pictured her little sister standing on a lamplit street corner in Palo Alto. Emily had never been there, so she envisioned it to be like the California campus she always saw in movies, although she'd been told that was UCLA. Carol was a miniature version of herself in a lot of ways; smaller, younger, but practically a twin. She'd be leaning against the side of the phone booth with the sole of one sneaker pressed into the denim above the other knee. She was probably picking at her split ends. How great to be in college, Emily thought, such great problems. A bomb scare. A test next week.

"Carol, I'm thinking about getting a divorce," Emily whispered. She looked over at Scott, but he remained motionless.

"You can't do that," Carol said automatically. "A divorce would kill Mom. She's already furious because I'm taking Brit lit pass/fail. Can't you go to a marriage counselor?"

Emily lit another cigarette from the stub of the first. "And what would I tell this marriage counselor? That my husband is part bird? Anyone who believed me would be a person I wouldn't trust for advice. Besides, I'm beginning to think people are just vehicles on the road of life, no different than cars. If they break down, trade 'em in. I'm finally getting tough in my old age."

"You're sounding Californian, you'll be sorry to hear."

"Good Lord!" Emily hissed.

"I'm sorry. I was just joking."

"No, it's not that. Hold on a minute, Carol, don't hang up."

Emily pulled the receiver away from her mouth and held it like a weapon by her hip. Scott was moving. He appeared to be attempting to swim through the pile of quilts. He pursed his lips and kissed them, like a goldfish coming up for air, then shifted into what she'd describe, if pressed, as a weird back breaststroke, like someone carving angel wings in the snow. She forced the phone back to her face. "I'm glad you're not here to see this, little sister."

"What's going on?"

"I'm sure he's only dreaming, but my imagination tells me he's hovering over Cleveland right now."

Carol giggled.

Scott rolled onto his side and exhaled deeply. He seemed safe and familiar for a moment, the same old Scott who had a recurring nightmare that he'd lost his leader in a fog while ascending a slippery granite cliff. In a few minutes he'd wake up with a headache, and she'd stroke his brow until he fell asleep again.

"You're not really going to get a divorce, are you?" Carol asked.

"I don't know. I can't talk about it right now." She laid her hand on his forehead.

"At least wait until after Christmas. I already have my reservations, and I want to see the house."

"Forget I said anything. Just do your work, and watch some whales for me."

Just as she hung up, Scott hooked his arm around her waist and reeled her in.

She was lying on the bed thinking of all the Christmas presents she still had to buy when Scott came into the bedroom with a battered brown file folder under his arm. Emily recognized it immediately; it was the marriage contract. Scott tossed it on the chest of drawers and rolled up his sleeves, one of the gestures he'd affected recently that signified he was ready to get down to business.

"Emily," he said, "we have to do this."

"I'm not in the mood."

Emily lay on her stomach, her chin resting on her hands. She was reading a women's magazine, looking at pictures of girls who were young and hopeful and getting paid to kick their feet up into the air. She could still do high kicks herself, but she rarely felt like it. High kicking was a sacrament to high living, and her existence was the deepest bend under a limbo pole. Either way you had to be agile, but you developed very different muscles.

"Emily, the contract period has been up for several weeks. If we don't do this now, we might not get to it until after the new year and then our whole schedule will be down the tubes. I don't know about you, but I can't live like that."

"Try."

"You're resisting me."

Emily flipped the magazine shut and rolled her eyes at Scott. "That's what I love about you, you're so perceptive. I hardly have to say a word."

Scott crossed his arms over his chest and brought an index finger to rest on his upper lip. Emily knew he was planning his strategy. She watched his eyebrows squeeze together and remembered she used to love him when he looked like this. In the past, during similar moments, she had tried to figure out what he was going to say so she could say it first to prove how close they were. I was so young, she thought. I believed that if I could take the words out of his mouth, I could take his breath away.

Now she didn't try to figure him out; she merely watched him. The more details she noticed, the more he looked like a stranger. Suddenly she missed him. Here he was, standing right in front of her, and she mourned him, grieved for him as if he were dead.

"Let's try to keep this conversation civilized," Scott said. "Now, Em, correct me if I'm wrong, but if I remember the facts, the marriage contract was your idea in the first place. Is that true?"

"Yes," she whispered.

"What? I can't hear you."

"Yes, yes, it was my idea. I admit it. I confess. So sue me."

"Are you trying to get out of this marriage?"

"No," she said quickly and without conviction.

"Then don't be difficult."

"All right, all right." Emily dropped her chin back onto her folded hands and said slowly, deliberately, "I don't want to do massages anymore." She liked the way her words came out. Her head was heavy on her jaws, her teeth clenched, so she sounded serious and jokey at the same time. He can take it any way he wants, she decided.

"Okay!" He pounced on her suggestion. "No more massages, okay!" He paused. "How about if we give them to each other?"

"I don't have time."

Scott frowned.

"Can't you just hire somebody?" asked Emily. "Some nice, nonmystical, nonpsychic male masseur?"

"With what money? We're a one-income family now, remember."

Emily sighed. "You could give up Mrs. Savich. I don't think that would be the biggest loss in the world."

"We've been through this, Emily," Scott warned.

"We've been through this? Where was I when we were going through this? It seems to me that you made up your mind before you told me anything about it."

"Oh, Em, don't be like that. It's beneath you."

"Maybe. Or maybe it's beyond me."

She felt the force of tears behind her eyes, but they wouldn't come. She never cried anymore except when she was very tired or when she was watching television. Television killed her. Her eyes had been known to grow blurry during advertisements for the telephone company and the burger chains, a phenomenon that Scott thought was an indication of deep sensitivity and tenderness, an interpretation of her behavior that she in turn saw as the wishful thinking of an advertising man. She closed her eyes and tried to picture a particularly touching situation involving transatlantic telephone calls, but all she could envision was a stand of blooming cherry trees, the blossoms as delicate as a baby's skin. When she looked up, Scott was staring at her. He sat down beside her and took her hand.

"Remember how you used to bite your nails, Em? Not just the nail part, but all around the edges and the cuticles, too."

"You hated it."

"Did I? I don't remember that. I do know I used to feel sorry for those poor little hands. It was sweet the way you tried to hide them." As he spoke, Scott kissed her fingers one by one. "You didn't want anyone to see them."

"It's pointless to try to take care of them when I work in the greenhouse all day."

"I don't mind."

She shook her head. "Scott, does it really seem worth it to you to go on like this?"

He pulled back, dropping her hand as if it were something sharp and dangerous. "You do want out of this marriage, don't you?"

Emily chewed her lip. "It's not that, exactly. It's more that I want things to be the way they used to be. I don't feel those feelings anymore. You know how your mother describes what lithium is like? How she can remember her emotions but she just can't feel them anymore? That's how I am these days." She glanced at his hurt face. "I do remember that I liked you, though."

"*Liked* me?"

"Yes." Emily sat up. "I liked you. It wasn't only love, it was friendly, too. Now, it's all so dim. Maybe we need some time apart."

"Oh, Emily."

"Maybe it would all come back if we had some time apart."

Scott stood up and paced as he searched for a fresh approach. When he found one, he snapped to attention and gazed at her steadily. "What did you have for lunch?" he asked.

"What?"

He laid his hand on her neck and counted her pulse against his watch. "I think your blood sugar is low, you have that gravelly tone in your voice. How about some dinner? Do you want to go out?"

Emily lay back down and crooked her arm over her eyes. "You're not listening," she said. "You're making me feel like a discontented housewife."

"I think we should eat," Scott said abruptly.

Emily didn't move. She lay still, wondering how everything had spun so rapidly out of control. Even her body seemed odd and swollen. One of these days, she thought gloomily, I won't be able to stand it anymore. Scott will come home from work and find me in the laundry room, one arm clutching a bouquet of anemones, the other hand plugged into the light socket. The police will pronounce it a willful suicide, but Scott, never wanting to think her problems had anything to do with him, would demand an autopsy, to prove that a low blood sugar level had affected her better judgment.

"Who would like to describe their experience to the group?"

Mrs. Savich looked around the room. Scott averted his eyes, hoping he wouldn't be noticed. He was too tired to talk.

"Don't be shy," said Mrs. Savich in her booming foreign voice. She was dressed in a purple leotard and wore lots of glass bracelets on each arm that tinkled when she moved. "Remember, this is our last session before the Christmas recess, so I would like to accomplish as much as possible before we break for three weeks. Does anyone feel as though he or she is making progress?"

A man who'd predicted the World Series winner six years in a row raised his hand tentatively. "I think something happened to me," he said. "I felt a touch of vertigo, or at least a sensation of falling."

"Is that significant?" a man who saw auras asked petulantly. "I had a sensation of falling two weeks ago."

"Me too," said a woman who was a dream therapist. "When I

practice before I go to sleep, I can feel myself pulling away from my body."

Mrs. Savich raised an eyebrow. "How far away from your body do you go?"

"Not very far. I've never gone beyond the ceiling." The woman twirled a lock of hair around her index finger. "It's as if my soul is attached to my body by a rope, and before I stray too far, the rope jerks me back."

"Excellent." Mrs. Savich smiled broadly at the group. "She has just described the exact sensation you should all be experiencing soon."

The man next to Scott grunted disparagingly. He was an investment banker named Ted Warner who'd made a fortune off his prescience for likely takeover targets. "I don't believe her," he whispered.

Scott shrugged.

"I bet she lifted that from a book. I haven't felt anything, have you?" Ted asked.

Scott shook his head.

"I don't think I can input much more energy here unless something happens soon," Ted whispered. "I'm beginning to believe that having the ability that I do to project into the mind of Japanese investors is enough of a trick for this world."

"It must be nice," Scott said perfunctorily.

"I'm not complaining." Ted punched Scott familiarly on the arm, as if they'd reached an agreement.

"Have you something to contribute to the class, Mr. Warner?" Mrs. Savich squinted at them. Ted shook his head. "You, Mr. Forbes?" Scott said no. "In that case, I suggest you save your private conversation for the social hour."

Scott was relieved. He pulled away from Ted and concentrated on the testimonies of his classmates, but somehow they didn't seem as compelling as usual. He thought perhaps he was simply too tired to get anything out of it; then he wryly mused that it was his lack of participation in the discussion that rendered it dull for him. With a shock of self-recognition, he realized he had never really listened to the conversation before. He had always been too busy thinking of what he would say when it was his turn to talk. Now that he was paying attention, he was amazed by what everyone's descriptions of their astral efforts revealed about them. They all seemed anxious to fly away from whatever they had, to something they imagined would be better. As the class went on, the stories became both more fragmented and more transparent, and he grew increasingly ashamed of his own previous complicity in what now struck him as an example of mass delusion. He felt as though he had stumbled into a fringe therapy group. Yet he found his sense of empathy outweighed his embarrassment enough so that he was able to check his impulse to object to all the hocus-pocus, merely nodding encouragement instead. As the class drew to a close, he discovered he'd been sitting locked in one position for so long that his legs were numb. He stretched vigorously, bracing himself for an onslaught of creeping pins and needles.

"For the next few weeks, tell yourself you are light as a feather," instructed Mrs. Savich. "Say this to yourself all day every day, three or four hundred times. You will be amazed how quickly this works to change your whole perception of yourself."

"Should we picture any particular type of feather?" asked a woman who had recently lost her job.

"If you like," said Mrs. Savich. "Attention to detail will strengthen your visualization."

"This is where I draw the line," Ted Warner said to Scott.

Scott pretended not to hear, although he'd been thinking exactly the same thing. He made an excuse not to stay for the class party, and after wishing everyone a happy holiday, he hailed a taxi to Grand Central.

His car was the only one left in the parking lot when he got off the train. His windshield was crusted with a crystalline frost that felt like rock candy to the touch. Scott scratched away a small porthole through which he could watch the road on his way home. There were no other cars out, so he was tempted to ignore the five traffic lights en route, but when he made the first stop, the light struck the candied windshield at an angle that caused the glass to glow with a ruby luster. Soon the glass became emerald, then topaz, then ruby again. Without consciously deciding to do so, Scott sat at the light as it changed over and over. He looked in the rearview mirror and watched his face turn colors. He stared at his lurid features until he could no longer bear to witness the strange parody of himself that he had become. He closed his eyes and tried to envision the kind of man he wanted to be, but all he could see were the electric candles Emily had placed in each of the windows of their house, and the bright Christmas lights threaded with artless care among the bushes. When he opened his eyes again, he discovered it had begun to snow. The street stretched white and glowing before him like a trail of moonlight on the sea. He stepped on the gas pedal, suddenly in a hurry, not so much out of wariness of the shift in the weather, but because for the first time in a long time, he wanted nothing more than to be home.

Emily padded downstairs for the third time in an hour, her thick slippers muffling the creaking of the steps. She held her flannel nightdress above her knees, taking care not to step on the hem as she patrolled the rooms and inspected her decorations. The house finally looked like the cozy nest she had imagined a year earlier when she and Scott had made the decision to leave the city. She had decorated in a style spare yet rich in texture and hue, and now all her carefully planned open spaces that would make the house feel large and cool in the summer were filled with the flotsam of Christmas. She had just that afternoon found exactly the right tree. The house was filled with the scent of pine, which grew more powerful as the branches settled. She opened the boxes of ornaments that had sat unused in storage for so many years and laid them out on the table, so she and Scott could inspect them before hanging them up.

She watched the snow fall in large flakes past the window and peered anxiously down the road, praying that Scott had left the city before the storm hit. She tried to calculate how long it should take if he had left at ten, or ten-thirty, or as late as eleven o'clock. She wished she knew where he was. She leaned against the cold glass and had a mental picture of him in his car, only a few miles away. As she imagined him holding the wheel steady to keep the car from sliding off the road, she was suddenly filled with the odd feeling that she knew exactly what he was thinking at that moment. At first she was gratified to find that most of his thoughts were pointed toward home, but as she looked inside him more for more details, she found she barely recognized their home as conceived by Scott. It was a shock to see the same old furniture from a different point of view, but as she acclimated to the new perspective, she found herself taking note of ideas that would never have occurred to her, and she appreciated Scott's creativity. She felt a wave of shame pass through her as she acknowledged that she hadn't looked at things his way for quite some time. She tried to commit to memory exactly the vision she'd seen a moment earlier — she was particularly taken with a concept he had for the window seat in the bedroom — but there was a lot she already could not recall and she realized she would have to ask him about it.

Her eyes flew open as she heard his key turn in the lock. Cayce galloped to the door. Emily hung back shyly as Scott stepped inside, clouded with cold.

"I thought you'd be asleep," he said.

"Did you hear the news?"

He shook his head. She looks pretty, he thought.

"There was an earthquake in California," she said. "Mom called up afraid for Carol, but then Carol broke in on call waiting to tell us to stop worrying."

"I'm glad everything is all right." He hung his coat in the closet and laid his briefcase on a chair. "How long did it take to calm your mother down?"

Emily smiled. "About an hour. I had to let her give me her recipe for floating island." She paused. "How was class?"

Scott turned away. "It was okay."

Her cheeks burned. "I'm sorry, I didn't mean to pry."

"It's not that. The truth is, it wasn't so great. I don't think I'm going back."

"I don't mind if you do," she said quickly.

He shrugged. "I think I've gotten enough out of it already. Do I smell a Christmas tree?"

Emily led the way to the living room, where he saw the silhouette of the tree against the snowy sky. She switched on a lamp and curled up in a chair. Cayce explored the lower branches.

"It's terrific," he said.

"It's not perfect, but I thought it had a lot of personality."

"It does." He nodded.

Emily rested her chin on her knees. Scott wanted to go over and sit with her, but he wasn't sure he was welcome to do so. Instead, he watched her, and as he watched, he was filled with a sensation he hadn't experienced since he was young, when he was convinced he was psychic. He believed for a moment that he was inside of Emily. The entire workings of her body became suddenly accessible to him. He saw the blood course through her veins and arteries, gathering here, thinning out there, chugging up her leg to a point at the back of her calf where it hesitated, then finally pushed through. He saw her liver, her stomach, her supple intestines, then heard, like a great tornado, the breath rush in and out of her lungs. Farther up, liquid slipped down her throat as her mind wandered. He followed her thoughts as they slipped gracefully through the clean sponge of her brain: images of Carol, a fire in the fireplace, and something it took him a moment to recognize as an ornament they had once bought for the top of the tree. Reminders to go to the hardware store, and to buy more cat food. A plan to plant a row of silvery roses along the front walk. All these images had a familiarity about them that made him feel brave, capable of diving deep inside her where he spun in dizzy circles around her healthy heart. As he was about to pull away, he noticed a shadowy lump buried in her abdomen.

"Scott, I have something to tell you," she said.

At first he was afraid it was a tumor. It had the wild energy of a tumor, the frantic behavior of riotous cells. It grew as he watched.

"Let's go upstairs and talk."

He thought he could grab it and carry it away, sweep it off the spot where it clung to her body before it could do any harm, but as he leaned forward, it seemed to turn toward him, and he saw, as if in the slick mirror of a glassy sea, a tiny Scott with pretty eyes like Emily's, and a trembling hopeful soul all his own.

The Comfortable Apartment

FROM THE TIME she could crawl, my sister Josie was a wanderer. She was seven when I was born; by then she had run away twice. My first memory is of her lifting me out of my crib and carrying me over to the window to show me the sights. I stared at the reflections of trees in the glassy pool and the sleeping dog chained in the neighbor's yard while Josie talked about mountains and distant cities. She could envision these places from the confines of my room. I couldn't. I wanted to, I tried to, for her, but my vision stopped still at the horizon. For years, I thought my lack of imagination made me a realist. It was only recently that I realized how large reality is, and how the little part of it I could see was as much a distortion of the truth as anything Josie imagined.

She dropped in and out of my life like a recurring dream while I was growing up. She'd arrive home unannounced, dressed in some exotic costume, full of stories that my parents and I only partly believed. She lived in Paris, London, Rome. She hitchhiked the length of India "without getting raped," then spent a winter in the Amazon jungle, where she was raped by her jungle guide when they went out at night to shine their flashlights in crocodiles' eyes. While I was getting good grades at a local university, Josie was living in the Philippines with a famous psychic surgeon. On the day I married Kurt Nitze, she was on an expedition in Borneo, where she discovered a purple bird that was later named after her by the Audubon Society.

Just before she came back for good, Josie lived on a rose farm in South Africa and exported native crafts back to the States. It was in Cape Town that she met Willie du Preez. It was in the restaurant at the Boschendal vineyards that he convinced her they should move to New York. They arrived at the end of June, and signed a two-year lease for an apartment on the Upper West Side.

Kurt and I had recently bought a house outside Philadelphia, in a slightly less expensive suburb than the one where my parents live. It was particularly hot that summer. We hired a moving company, but we ended up doing all the packing ourselves, an economy that provided us with a lot to fight about when we couldn't find the things we needed in our new home. We blamed each other for every inconvenience. All that died down, though, after I fell over Kurt at the top of the stairs and broke my leg. To keep me comfortable, he bought an air conditioner, but he had it installed in the bedroom and I never went up there until I was ready for sleep.

All summer I got up at five-thirty to let the dog out so he could cruise around the block a few times before the humidity crawled under his fur and laid him low. I cracked an egg for Kurt and thought of Josie up in New York, starting a new life. I didn't see her for two months after she returned — my broken leg made it awkward for me to travel — but my parents reported back after they'd met her and Willie at the Algonquin for a drink. I pressed them for details, but they didn't come up with much beyond the fact that Josie was tan and Willie's clothes looked flimsy and expensive.

It wasn't what they said; it never is. What they didn't say, but what they made clear through polite omission, was that they didn't like Willie. That intrigued me. At the start of September, as soon as my cast was removed, I asked my husband if I could visit Josie at her apartment.

"When did you have in mind?" he asked. He glanced up from his paper, although I doubt whether someone who didn't know him as well as I do would have noticed this. He had the kind of eyes we used to describe as piercing blue; his necktie made them look bluer.

"Saturday, I thought. Just for one night."

"You know how she upsets you." He was looking directly at me now, pressing his advantage. One night I'd admitted my ambivalence about Josie to him, and I'd been paying for it ever since. Whenever I felt particularly unappreciated, whenever I tried my hardest to please and came up with nothing, Kurt dug the needle of Josie, effortlessly admired Josie, in deeper.

I assured him I knew, but that I was willing to risk it. He shrugged and offered to drive me to the train.

"Sit here, pet," he said, yanking me onto his lap. This was my cue to placate him with one of our private games, and I did.

I'd been standing alone in front of the information booth at Penn Station for fifteen minutes before Josie finally showed up. I was starting to panic when she tapped me on the shoulder.

"Hello, stranger!" she squealed. I barely had a chance to look at her before she threw an arm around me and led the way to the escalator. What I saw, though, was enough to reassure me that not everything had changed. Her hair was still the color of an Irish setter's. Her eyes were still green. She was still lovely.

"God, it's a beautiful day," she said as we hit the sidewalk. "How's Kurt?"

"Busy. Wrapped up in his experiments." I nearly started to tell her what had really been going on, but I'd learned to be more circumspect during the course of my marriage. Instead, I asked her why she hadn't been there to meet me on time. I was aware of how shrewish I sounded as I questioned her — it seemed an embarrassingly childish thing to do — but she was acting so damn jaunty that I felt she deserved it.

"Oh, I'm sorry, I hope you weren't worried." She was wearing perfume, a lot of it. I've never liked the scent of heavy perfume in the summer. "It was Willie. Our first fight, I guess you could call it. He ran out of the apartment and slammed the door, very dramatic. I began to cry, so I had to redo my makeup and then I waited around for a while to see if he would call. Luckily Tom didn't have any auditions today, so he cheered me up." She ran her fingers across the skin under her eyes, then pinched her cheeks. "There, how's my mascara? It isn't running, is it?"

I told her she looked fine. I asked her who Tom was. Tom was an actor friend from Los Angeles in town for an audition. The audition had been three weeks earlier but he had decided to stay on until he heard, as Josie put it, the verdict. In the meantime, he was being seen for commercials. He was sleeping on the living room floor.

"But don't worry," she said, "we have a bed for you."

We were on Broadway by then. At first it looked as though she meant for us to walk all the way home, but when I began to slow down, and to fuss when people bumped into me, Josie noticed my discomfort. She stepped out into the street and waved her arms.

"Now I want to talk to you about Willie," she said after she'd settled us into a cab. She lowered her voice and grew confidential. "He's a complicated man. Sometimes he isn't terribly friendly at first — and I'm not saying he's going to be like that with you — but if he is, don't let it put you off. He's really a remarkable person when you get to know him, and he's drop-dead pretty. God, he's made me happy!"

I didn't know what to say. I'm awful around people who claim they are happy. Josie's eyes glittered as she spoke, and I wondered if she was on speed. She was thin, too, thinner than I'd ever seen her, and she had frizzed her hair.

"Tom and Heather like him a lot," she continued. "You won't be able to help yourself."

"Heather?"

"She's a kid I met who needed a place to stay temporarily. Didn't Mom tell you anything? Anyway, I'm sure the argument wasn't important. It was bound to happen sometime, right? We'll get over it." She laced her fingers around one knee and stared out the window.

"You didn't fight because I was coming, did you?"

"Oh no, nothing like that. It's just that this isn't easy for him, even though it was his idea." She paused and brushed a few errant curls away from her cheeks. Her hairline was high, aristocratic, and the skin beside it smooth, unlike mine; I have a pair of forceps marks on my temples from where I was pulled out of our mother's body at birth. "I'm going to tell you something now, something secret. You can't tell the parents. Do you swear?"

I nodded.

"Before we moved here, Willie was living with a man."

She shifted around to watch my face, but I refused to give her the satisfaction of seeing anything in my expression except distance, sophistication, boredom. I kept my muscles still by staring at the cabbie's license, reading the letters on the placard over and over without linking them into a name. So that was it. Of course. There was no way our parents would accept a homosexual. Willie must be obvious, I thought. Once again Josie had moved center stage without even trying.

"I mean he had a male lover," she continued. "I hate the term 'lover' and here I am using it. I mean, he had a boyfriend, an older guy who immigrated to South Africa from Austria right after the war . . ."

She warmed to her subject and ripped the man to pieces while I ticked off the traffic lights on my fingers as we careened uptown. She had so much energy, I was exhausted just listening to her. She was still talking when we turned down her block. She didn't offer to help me pay the driver.

"So you see," she said as I fumbled in my pocket for a tip, "Willie had to get away. I like swimming pools as well as the next person, but Jesus, I knew I wouldn't survive if I stayed. Do you know what I mean?"

I nodded and passed another dollar through the opening in the glass shield.

"I mean, either you see the writing on the wall or you don't. We had to leave. A lot of people are still there and I feel sorry for them. They're going to get it someday."

I swung my bag onto the street, then hoisted myself out of the car. My knee buckled slightly.

"Janie, are you all right? You look like you're limping." My sister grabbed my elbow and looked directly at me for the first time since I'd arrived. "Oh my God, I forgot. How's your leg?"

The apartment was not at all what I imagined. I expected something glamorous, assuming that Josie would settle for nothing less than glamorous surroundings, but the place was so unpretentious and so artlessly decorated that it appeared, at first glance, almost sloppy. The kitchen was large and sunny, but I didn't get the impression that it was used very often. The shelves were empty except for a few cans of beans and sliced pineapple. A dark, moody portrait of Elvis Presley hung over the stove.

"Do you like it?" Josie kicked off her shoes and dropped her handbag on the dining room table.

"It's great. It's so big."

She laughed. "You've been reading all those horror stories about New York apartments. They're all true — I just got lucky with this one. It still needs some work, but I think it has a nice feel to it, don't you?"

I said yes, and I wasn't lying. The apartment was homey, cozy, and welcoming, personal in a way that made it universal; anyone would feel comfortable here. If I didn't know better, I would have thought the inhabitants had lived here for years, for ages, not two months. I wondered how it was possible to put down roots so quickly.

"Come in here," she said as she led the way through a small hallway, past the bathroom. "Talk to me while I straighten up."

Her bedroom could have belonged to a fifteen-year-old. Pictures of rock stars were taped to the walls and a pile of stuffed animals sat on a wicker chair in the corner. I noticed a photograph hanging on the back of the closet door so I pushed it shut to have a closer look. It was a picture of a woman and child, presumably her child. They were both hunched over, weighed down by heavy woolen coats, their faces covered with shawls. The mother stared straight ahead while the little girl clutched the material at her throat with a tiny, bare hand.

"Where did you get this?" I asked.

Josie glanced up from the other side of the room where she was busy sorting a heap of clothes into two piles. "Oh, that. I got that at Dachau," she said. "I had to go to a lot of trouble to get it. There was a huge enlargement of it in the museum there — that's where I saw it — and I loved it, so I paid them to find the negative and print a copy for me."

I hadn't heard this story before. "When were you at Dachau?" I asked.

"A few years ago. Wait a minute, let me get a cigarette."

While she was out of the room I studied the picture more closely. It looked different now that I knew the story behind it — a woman and her child on the way to the gas chamber. It was an excellent photograph, a work of art. The bleak forms, the placement of the figures in relation to each other, the angle of the camera: everything suggested utter futility. I tried to feel sad about it, but it wasn't sad. It was a lot worse than that.

"Do you like it?" Josie plucked it off its hook and pulled it into her lap as she sat down.

"It's very good."

"Mmmmm." She waved the smoke away from her eyes. "Do you remember me talking about Rebecca Gordon? I went to Dachau because of her. She always got mad at me when I told her about my concentration camp dreams because she claimed that no one who wasn't Jewish could ever really understand. I argued that no one who wasn't there could ever really understand, but I was sure I could empathize as well as she could. I went to the camp to find out who was right."

She paused. This was the way she told stories when she showed up unexpectedly with trays and trays of slides. She made her audience ask for more. Usually I tried to avoid being the one to fall into that trap, but now I was her guest.

"So, who was?" I obliged.

She ran her fingers across the top of the glass, tracing the figures over and over. "We both were, in a way. I understood the horror of it all right — anybody could — but what I didn't understand, what I don't think I'll ever understand, is why those people didn't get out when they had the chance. They didn't have to die. It was such a waste."

"Most of them didn't have a chance at all," I said. "Besides, it's not that easy to leave your home."

"It is easy. It's as easy as walking out the door and getting on a train."

She extinguished her cigarette by rotating the butt between her thumb and forefinger until all the unburned tobacco remnants lay clumped in the ashtray. She hung the photo back on the door. "Willie loves this picture. He found it in a box when we were unpacking and insisted on hanging it where he would see it every day."

I heard a clicking sound coming from the front of the apartment. I was jumpy from being in the city, so I immediately thought — burglars. I looked at Josie. She was as tense as I was, frozen where she was standing, listening.

"It could just be one of the roommates," she whispered.

Of course. Whoever it was had a key and couldn't be much of a threat. Josie was rigid. I felt stupid. I realized it must be Willie.

"Should I leave you alone?" I asked.

"No. Ssh. It *is* him."

Josie caught my eye. It wasn't a special look at all — she wasn't asking for anything — but I felt at that moment that I would follow her anywhere. Many times I had judged her harshly, often out of envy, without stopping to consider her point of view, her life, her vulnerability. Or the fact that she was, above all, my sister.

Willie came in grinning. I stood up to be introduced and he kissed my cheek.

"You must be Janie. Welcome," he said.

He winked at me as he pulled a bouquet of pink tea roses from behind his back and dropped them unceremoniously in Josie's lap. I smiled at her, but she wasn't paying attention to me anymore. Her gaze and her being had turned so completely to Willie du Preez that I doubt she even noticed when I left the room.

•   •   •

The next morning, I had tea with Josie before she left to do errands in the neighborhood. Tom and Heather were still asleep in the living room. I had met them briefly the night before; they were both very young. Young enough to be delighted with the fact that I was Josie's sister, and to accept me immediately because of that connection. They asked me questions I hadn't heard in years. Was I happy? Was I in love with my husband? Was I planning to have children? Did I think there would ever be another world war?

All this within twenty minutes of being introduced. It was easy to answer their questions, easy to tell the truth because I knew it didn't matter what I said. They were merely collecting data about adult life. I was a story they might or might not repeat. As I poured myself a second cup of tea I could hear them stirring on their makeshift beds. I thought of Kurt's pale body and how he liked to wind himself around me in his sleep. Often I awoke in his arms, not remembering how or when I got there. It was peaceful in Josie's apartment. I decided to extend my visit by a day or two.

I was just about to call home when I heard an odd noise coming from Josie's bedroom. I didn't know what to do; listening felt like trespassing, but there was no way to avoid hearing it without leaving the apartment, and I wasn't dressed yet. I tiptoed to the door and knocked. The sound continued, a mournful keening, a high, spooky wail. Finally I pushed the door open and stepped inside. Willie was doubled up under the blankets, hugging a pillow to his chest. I didn't hesitate before I crossed to the bed and touched him. I woke him as gently as I could.

"You were having a bad dream, I think."

He was facing the wall and didn't turn to look at me. He stretched his arms and I stared dumbly at the way his skin pulled across the walls of lean muscle that covered his back. He reached behind him and patted the bed. I wasn't sure he knew it was I who had woken him, but I sat down obediently, not too close.

"I've had a recurring nightmare," he said, "since I was a child. I'm out in a field near some railroad tracks, all by myself. A long train goes by, and for some reason I'm supposed to count all the cars. But it always goes too fast. I lose my place and become frozen with fear, knowing that someone will come along and yell at me for being so incompetent."

He rolled onto his back and faced me. Josie was right; he was the most remarkable-looking man. The hair on his chest was golden, yet his eyebrows were dark. When he blinked, his eyelashes cast spidery shadows on his cheeks.

"I know it doesn't sound so bad," he smiled, "but it has always terrified me. I'm sorry if I frightened you." He patted me absently on the hand, then pushed himself upright. "I guess it's time to get up. Do you want to shave me?"

I don't think "shocked" is the right word for how I felt, but I'm sure it is how I looked. He laughed at the expression on my face.

"Josie asked if she could shave me practically the first time we met. We tried it once, but we didn't get very far — she was a little heavy-handed with the shaving cream. I thought that since you're her sister, you might have the same inclinations."

I shook my head, no. I heard someone moving around in the next room, the closing of the bathroom door. I must have appeared to be about to bolt, because Willie gripped my hand tighter and rubbed my palm with the pad of his thumb.

"She's told you about me, hasn't she," he said.

It wasn't a question. I didn't answer.

"I know what you're wondering. Yes, we have a real relationship. I never thought I could change, but Josie is a very determined person. You should have seen her contracting for baskets in the Transkei; she knew who to bribe at a hundred paces. And she never tried to make the tribal people love her. She was honest, she paid them a fair price, and that was that . . ."

I nodded occasionally as he talked. I was willing to listen to it all, South Africa, Josie, everything, as long as I could be near Willie. It was all I could do not to reach out and stroke his stomach. When he finally did get up to shave, I followed him to the bathroom and watched. He thanked me, saying no one should ever have to be alone after a bad dream.

•   •   •

My husband, Kurt, is an epidemiologist. Lately he has been working on AIDS. Before that, it was toxic shock syndrome and before that, swine flu. He wears gloves and a mask to protect himself from the germs in the lab. He doesn't wear gloves around me, though. Instead, he washes his hands. He has a special bar of expensive black soap that I'm not allowed to touch. He washes after he eats, he washes after we make love, he washes after he hits me. Sometimes I call him Pontius Pilate in my mind.

I didn't tell Josie and Willie about him until the third or fourth time I visited them at the apartment. It's not the sort of thing you tell people right away. It's not the sort of thing anyone would suspect of a man I would marry, a man living in our neighborhood. Wife-beaters are supposed to live in a ghetto or in bland housing developments, not in the rich WASP suburbs of Philadelphia. Their lives are full of caseworkers and car payments, not country clubs and cassis. Kurt doesn't look the part and neither, I like to think, do I.

I finally told Josie about it because I thought she'd believe my story, and I was right. She didn't ask for any of the particulars; she just wanted me to leave him right away. I tried to explain to her that it was more complicated than that, that it wasn't just a question of leaving a single entity, Kurt. I would have to leave my home, my life, my marriage. The marriage was a country to which I'd pledged my allegiance and I couldn't surrender it without a fight. I had to believe that Kurt's rages were a stage he would pass through, and that we would still grow old together, rocking peacefully in matching wicker chairs.

Meanwhile, I began to visit the apartment with increasing frequency. Tom and Heather both moved out eventually, in bits and pieces. They'd disappear for a while and then drop by again for a week or a month at a time. They always left a few belongings behind as a sort of primitive gesture toward territoriality. I understood the impulse. It was for this reason that I insisted Kurt wear a wedding ring, and it was why I wore one of his T-shirts to bed when he was away at a medical convention. Josie teased me about my predilections for ownership, property stakes. At her dinner parties, she'd characterize me as the type who preferred stone walls to the fields beyond them.

When Tom and Heather weren't around, other people were. Josie decorated her rooms with interesting people. She had a talent for rooting them out, cultivating them for a while, then letting them go. She appeared to achieve in days a level of closeness with another person that it took me years to establish. At first I distrusted it. I thought that these friendships I saw forming before my eyes couldn't possibly be real. Gradually, however, I became friendly with some of the passers-through myself. After a while it didn't seem so painful when they left. It hurt me, but it didn't break me. There was always someone else.

I could have fallen in love with Willie if I'd let myself.

His body was perfectly proportioned and his hands were so soft they were a shock to touch. He took long walks early every morning, often to Times Square and back. Sometimes I went with him. In a sense, we became New Yorkers when we were together. We never noticed the dirt, the squalor, the sheer menace of the place. Instead, we made up fantasies and pointed out buildings where we would live when we were rich.

We laughed a lot. I could talk to him. He worshiped my sister.

Eight months after Josie and Willie moved to New York, Kurt put me in the hospital. I didn't feel any pain when he hit me — I never feel it when it's happening, the nerves go dead — but the next morning, I could not open my eyes. My nose was smashed over toward my left cheek and my lips were split. The doctor said it was lucky that a chip of bone hadn't traveled to my brain. I told him I'd been hit with a baseball.

"That does it," Josie said over the phone. "You're not going back to that man. When you get out of the hospital, you're going directly to the train station and then you're coming up here for good. I can't believe we have all sat by and allowed this to go on for so long. It's our fault as well as Kurt's. I'm sorry, Janie."

"That's okay." It hurt to talk.

"You promise you'll come?"

I promised. I tried to think about my situation, but I couldn't concentrate beyond the narrowest details. I had a sense that it was time to change, that I had to change, but all I could imagine was going through my closets and throwing a few things out.

"Well," she said, "I'll be down to visit you before then at any rate. But I wanted you to start thinking ahead. Are you all right?"

I nodded. She was my sister, so she understood without my having to speak aloud.

Kurt came to visit me every day. He always brought a present, flowers, a book; he was terribly contrite. His lab was in an institute directly across the street from the hospital, so he was able to come over both at lunch and after work. I was on a liquid diet, but he continued to eat well. He offered me bites of his delicacies and talked about politics and work as if we were on a picnic, while I reminded myself that each of these conversations was one of the last we would ever have. I wondered who would keep the dog, me or him. I thought about the language my parents would use to explain my absence, and I daydreamed about the apartment, about Josie and Willie drinking coffee, doing errands, sitting down to dinner. I kept track of the hours of their lives by the schedule of the television shows I watched, and when I knew it was time for them to go to bed, I slept.

I had an operation to straighten out my nose. Kurt told me I'd be beautiful when the bandages came off. He was tender toward my broken body in a way that appalled me. He reminded me of the sort of man people make excuses for, because they believe he must have a good side, because they have seen him be kind to animals. My will to leave was strong.

I was ready.

The night before my release from the hospital, Josie called.

"You have keys to the apartment, don't you?" she asked.

"Yes." They were in my purse and I had my purse with me.

"I think Tom will be there when you arrive, but I wanted to make sure just in case."

"Where are you going to be?" I asked.

There was a pause on the other end of the line. I heard a match strike.

"Willie is gone."

"No, he isn't," I said automatically.

"He went back to South Africa a few days ago. His mother broke her back and has to be in bed for several weeks, so he thought he should keep her company."

"Oh, is that all," I said.

"I hope to God that's all. I'm going down there tomorrow to find out. I'll call you as soon as I know what's happening. At any rate, I think I'm going to give up the apartment. The neighborhood is getting too druggie, even for me, and it's going to get worse before it gets better. How does Australia sound to you?"

"It sounds foreign. Josie, don't worry about Willie. He loves you."

"I really thought he could change, you know? I don't know why. People never change, not really. Damn it!" she moaned. I pulled the phone away from my ear and heard her voice then from a great distance, as if it were something I'd made up.

"Oh well," Josie said, "I'll survive."

The next morning I packed my bag and was dressed and ready to go by the time the doctor came in to examine me. He told me to keep my bandages dry; I signed the papers and left. The morning was balmy, and I was happy to be outside again. I liked hearing my flats slap against the sidewalk. It was the sound of dates and careers and futures, not like the dead-end shuffling of hospital slippers. I walked past Kurt's disease institute on my way to the train station. I pictured him with his eye to the microscope, watching worlds blow apart. He was supposed to pick me up at the hospital during his lunch break. I'd be in New York before he knew I was gone. When he figured it out, he'd cry. It was one of the endearing things about him that he could cry in front of strangers without being embarrassed.

I bought my ticket.

I hadn't planned on catching any train in particular, but at the information booth in Thirtieth Street Station, I learned I was in luck. An express I should have missed had been delayed and was due to arrive within the next few minutes. I took an escalator downstairs to the platform where a rather large group waited dispiritedly while departure times and tracks were announced. As I headed toward a spot where the platform seemed less crowded, I pictured Josie settling down in her airplane seat while Willie lazed at the shallow end of a swimming pool in Cape Town. A dark hand proffered Willie a sickly sweet drink. I blinked. People were staring at my bandages. I touched my fingers to the edge of the adhesive, and I wanted to rip it off the way I'd ripped my scabs when I was little. It always hurt, but something about it, perhaps the sight of fresh, bright blood, had made me feel alive.

The train pulled up to the platform. There was a moment of rushing, of people and baggage loading on and off, but for me, the train didn't seem to stop. I stood motionless as it roared through the station on its way to New York, a long train of cars, a long, long train of countless cars, hundreds of cars; cars, cars, cars, and then the caboose.

Buddy

OF ALL THE DOGS Charlie Whitman had known, the two that stood out in his mind as being ideal examples of the species had belonged to men who were strict with the animals, to the point of cruelty. The dogs, in turn, were so obedient as to seem clairvoyant. They sat before they were told to do so, and walked like supple shadows at their masters' sides. His family had owned a dog for a few years when he was little, but she was run over shortly after Charlie's father died, just when Charlie felt as though he'd been hit by a car himself. His mother refused to buy him a replacement, and in a short time he'd stopped thinking about his pet in the way that children who are forced to adapt to volatile circumstances learn to do, yet in the back of his mind he always assumed he'd own another dog someday, when he grew up and had his own life.

So far, the time had never seemed right; he worked long, irregular hours and traveled too often to accommodate a dog's schedule. He knew he wasn't set up for it, yet when his French girlfriend, Claudine, announced that she'd decided to get one he felt cheated, as though someone had stolen his best idea and made money out of it without cutting him in on the deal.

It was a humid New York evening in early June, and as usual they had outlasted their friends Todd and Sarah at a bar. Their table was wet with the leftover condensation of too many drinks.

"You can't do that," Charlie said automatically when she told him her plan. It was the wrong thing to say to Claudine, who was terminally literal and would take him at his word. Sure enough, her green eyes flashed as she gathered her considerable forces to mount a rebellion against him. It was too late to stop her, but if he didn't at least try to explain himself, she would accuse him of being hopelessly remote and not caring about their relationship, or her, or anything meaningful.

"Of course I don't mean you *can't* get a dog," he backtracked. "I just think that maybe you shouldn't."

"Why not?"

"It's a huge responsibility, that's why not. You'll have to go straight home after work." He heard himself sounding pompous and schoolmasterly as he spoke. He had met her when she was a student in his photography class, and he found it difficult not to continue lecturing her. "You won't be able to meet friends for drinks, or browse around the bookstores."

"So what? If I have something to go home to, I'll be glad to go home," she said pointedly.

"Is that what this is about?"

"No. Can't I get a dog without having you suspect my motives? Not everything has to do with you, you know."

"I do indeed know."

She regarded him suspiciously. He did his best to appear benign.

"Since you mention it, however" — she pronounced it how-ev*air* — "I told you two months ago that I thought we should live together, and you haven't said anything about it again."

Her triumphant expression as she finished this speech led Charlie to think she'd been working up to it for quite some time. He found it oddly exciting to realize that she'd hesitated to speak openly with him.

"I haven't had anything new to say on the subject."

"If I were you, I'd try to think of something."

When their eyes met, Charlie stubbornly made sure he was the last to look away, though he had an uneasy sense that he was making an empty gesture, that the advantage he'd unknowingly had only a moment earlier had disappeared. He closed his eyes briefly and wished that they were the kind of couple who could have a single drink before going back to his apartment, who went to bed early enough to have something more than brief, perfunctory sex. Instead, they were the kind of couple who spent their weekends hanging out in one uptown bar or another, ordering too many drinks while they each made their points. This particular bar had changed hands since the last time they'd been there — it now had a sculling theme — but the room was still filled with people like themselves who half believed they were missing something if they didn't wait until the last minute to disappear into their anonymous apartments and go to bed. To their right, a group of Young Turks from Wall Street were busy toasting each other in a boisterous manner that Charlie found dispiriting. Claudine glanced at them briefly. Those who noticed smiled at her. To Charlie's annoyance, she smiled back.

"I had a dog when I was little," he said grimly.

She turned to him with interest, leaning forward slightly to encourage his confidence. Unexpectedly, his voice had quavered when he spoke, and he blinked quickly to disperse the pressure swelling up behind his eyes. Lately he'd been beleaguered by sudden onslaughts of self-pity that he felt helpless to drive away before they'd run their course. It was difficult to pinpoint the reason for his bouts of unhappiness; on paper, his life looked all right enough. He was thirty-three years old and had just bought an apartment on the Upper West Side. He worked on his own terms as an architectural photographer, and had achieved a level of professional accomplishment whereby he had a recognizable style. Yet the apartment had saddled him with debt, and rather than his career affording him the life of independence he'd imagined when he chose it, he was constantly vulnerable to the whims of the editors at the big lifestyle magazines, most of whom were cynical and bitter because they made so much less money than the people they ran articles about.

And then there was Claudine.

He knew it would be a hard job to convince anyone to feel sorry for him because he had her. Yes, she was beautiful, and yes, she had all the characteristics that Frenchwomen were supposed to embody (including the one about the champagne glass), but she was only twenty-two. Her Sorbonne degree was so newly minted that she had not yet learned to temper her habit of questioning everything and having an opinion about everything else. Uncharacteristically, she listened to him without venturing more than an encouraging nod, and he found himself embroidering his story with incidents and vignettes he rarely thought about. He seldom spoke about his father, but now he told her that when his dog had chewed his father's shoe and he, Charlie, tried to lie about it, his father had beaten them both. When he finished, he saw by her tight mouth that he'd mistakenly provided her with details that evoked her anger rather than her sympathy. Suddenly the hours of sleep he'd missed recently crowded in on him, and he had an image of himself for a moment as a laughable older man pathetically trying to keep up with his young date.

"You must hate your father," she said, her cheeks taut with indignation.

"No."

"I would hate anyone who hit me with a belt."

Charlie shrugged. "Claudine, that was one small incident out of a long life. It's important to have some perspective about these things." He was sorry he'd brought his father into it at all. He should have stuck to the story of his dog's death. Drunkenness, he thought, the foolish confidentiality of drink. "Naturally, I did hate him for it at the time," he said, hoping to appease her and thereby put an end to the discussion.

"I hate him now."

"He's dead, Claudine. You can't hate a dead person."

"Oh no? What about Hitler?"

"We're not going to get into a discussion of Hitler, if you don't mind. And I'd prefer it if you didn't compare Hitler to my father."

"Your father sounds like a monster." She had a habit of reacting to anything he told her as if he'd told her something much worse. Her eyes widened and she began to clench her fists rhythmically, the way she always did when she was about to make a moral judgment. "I don't think there is any excuse for hitting a child or a dog. I would never." Nev*air*.

"You can't say that for sure. You don't have either, so how do you know what you'd do?"

Claudine planted her arms in the shape of a square on the scarred wood table, oblivious to the puddles that quickly soaked her sleeves. "For your information, I did have a dog before," she proclaimed loudly, causing Charlie to wonder if she was speaking less for his benefit than that of the money men behind him. "I nev*air* hurt him, and I wouldn't hurt a baby."

"We're not talking about hurting anyone. We're talking about discipline. It has its place, you know."

"Discipline yes, violence no." She glanced at her admirers at the next table, most of whom had loosened their power ties. They beamed back. It must be her accent, he thought, and her looks. Philosophically, he was sure they'd take his side.

"So what happened to your dog?" he asked.

"Like yours, he died. A stupid farmer shot him for scaring the chickens."

"How did he get off the leash?"

"I didn't use a leash. He wanted to run free."

"And how free was he after the farmer shot him?" Charlie asked meanly. "I'm sorry," he said immediately, hoping to prevent an episode of public tears and far-ranging recriminations. "I'm very tired."

"He was happy while he was alive," she said. "He wasn't chained down to someone's ego. A dog is not on the earth to obey you, you know. You train a dog so he will express his best nature, not so he will do what you want. You bring out his character. What do you think will come out if you hit him?"

"Maybe you're right," he said, trying in one stroke to mollify Claudine and end the conversation. "I don't know why I'm defending my father," he continued. "I suppose it's the old 'I can criticize my parents as much as I want, but no one else is allowed to say a word against them.'" He thought he sounded wholly unconvincing, yet Claudine appeared transfixed. He touched her hand. "Are you ready to leave? I think we should go home."

She picked up her heavy leather Coach bag and anchored the strap on her shoulder. She was wearing a tiny, tight, blue dress that looked as though it had been made for a doll. Like many European women, she seemed almost impossibly narrow. She made a brave show of pawing through her purse until Charlie told her to put her money away.

"I'm glad you're getting a dog." He laid his credit card on top of the check.

"You don't mean it."

"I do. I think it will be good for you."

The degenerates at the next table exploded into a round of applause, and Charlie jerked around quickly, afraid they were clapping to celebrate Claudine's victory, but they weren't paying attention to him at all. As he turned back, he caught Claudine watching him sharply.

"It *will* be good for me," she said evenly. "You always say I should take on some real responsibility."

"Yes, I guess I do."

"And I will prove to you what can be achieved by kindness," Claudine said. "I will make a good dog without ever hitting it. You will see, I am right."

"I hope so." He knew from experience that he could never score a clear victory once he started arguing with her, yet he felt he owed it to the forces of reason that guided his life to at least put opposing arguments on the table. However, he also believed there came a time to drink up quietly, to cut one's losses, to argue no more.

After much tedious research and many afternoons at the American Kennel Club library, Claudine decided to buy a sheltie. She made an appointment with a breeder on Long Island to see a litter of pups on what turned out to be the hottest day of the summer. Without knowing why he'd agreed to do so, Charlie found himself renting a car for the trip. Claudine met him outside her building wearing a green sleeveless dress, her hair tied back in a ponytail with a white chiffon scarf. She refused to allow Charlie to turn on the air conditioning, preferring instead to lean her elbow out the window and blow her pungent French cigarette smoke into the fetid air.

The houses seemed to grow larger and larger as they drove farther from the city. Finally, in the resort towns near the beach, the houses were so large that they appeared to bob like ships across the burned lawns in the hazy heat. At the address the breeder had given them, they found a ramshackle house at the end of a quiet road that seemed far from anywhere. As soon as Charlie saw it he began to think of improvements, imagining the porch rebuilt and the shutters painted black.

"Do you think we made a wrong turn?" Claudine asked uneasily.

"Not according to the directions you gave me."

"My English. Maybe I didn't understand."

A dirty child of eight or nine appeared in the driveway. Claudine walked over and bent at the knees, peering the child in the eye.

"Do you have dogs for sale here?"

The child hung his head. Claudine looked back at Charlie and shrugged. As he leaned forward to see if he could pick up any better clues, his soaked shirt peeled off the back of the seat like a Band-Aid. Annoyed, he swung out of the car and slammed the door. The child didn't look up, yet Charlie was sure his movements were somehow being carefully monitored. He walked over to the boy and sank into a deep knee bend, so they were on the same level.

"We've come all the way from the city to see the pups. I'll give you a nickel if you tell us where they are."

Claudine made a moue of disapproval at his suggestion of bribery. She touched the boy's arm.

"If I buy a dog," she said, "you can come visit it."

"Don't make promises you can't keep," Charlie said. He visored a hand over his eyes and surveyed the yard for signs of a person in charge.

"I mean it. You can come visit me," Claudine said.

The child looked at Charlie doubtfully.

"All right," Charlie said to Claudine as he straightened up, "I've had enough now. Let's go."

"The dogs are here, Charlie," Claudine said. "He's just pretending they aren't because he doesn't want to sell them." She turned to the boy. "You probably can't keep all the puppies, anyway, so wouldn't it be better to sell one to someone like me who will love the dog?"

"Let's go," said Charlie.

"Wait. He's thinking about it."

"How do you know? He could be thinking about doughnuts."

The child began to laugh. "Doughnuts!" he repeated.

"Oh, I didn't know you were here yet," spoke a disembodied voice. They looked up and saw a woman's head pressed against a dark mesh screen in a second-floor window. "Come inside, I'll be right down."

Reluctantly, the boy led them up the path, dragging the toes of his sneakers along the edges of what must once have been a front walk. They followed him through a dark hallway to a closed door at the rear of the house. Presently the woman appeared.

"Mrs. Adams?" Claudine extended her hand.

"That's me, for better or worse."

Claudine made their introductions with great aplomb; she always seemed more graceful and older when Charlie saw her in the company of other people. She chatted away charmingly about her reasons for wanting a dog and about all the research she'd done to pick just the right breed. Mrs. Adams listened with a shrewd expression on her weathered face. Charlie saw the price of the pups rising as Mrs. Adams studied their eagerness to get what they came for, and their expensive clothes.

"Each of the dogs has a different color collar around its neck," she said. "The red and the yellow are already spoken for, but you can have your pick of the rest."

As she opened the door, the boy slipped under her arm and rushed past her as she flicked on a light. In the center of the room was a pen made of old shutters placed end to end. Charlie automatically inspected the furniture that had been pushed to the walls and spotted a few surprisingly good pieces.

"Get back from there, Byron." Mrs. Adams grabbed the boy

just below the sleeve of his T-shirt. "Let these people look at the dogs."

Charlie gave a short, sharp laugh when he heard the boy's name; the absurdity of this scruffy child having a name like Byron was just the sort of thing that appealed to his sense of humor. Claudine smiled at him, clearly pleased yet puzzled by the sudden improvement in his mood. Byron, he mouthed silently.

"What?" she asked with her eyebrows.

He shrugged, and she shrugged back, then smiled. It was impossible to convey the joke across the room. Perhaps Claudine had never heard the name Byron. He gestured for her to go ahead and keep looking. She blew him a small kiss — *un bisou* — then turned to Mrs. Adams, who led her to the edge of the pen where she knelt down in a practiced manner that betrayed the influence of her Catholic upbringing. Her arms disappeared behind the wooden gating, and she began to croon to creatures that were still invisible to him.

"They're so adorable!" She sucked in her breath, creating an atmosphere of awe and wonder incongruous in the gloomy room. "So soft."

Byron crept forward and knelt beside her.

"Which is your favorite?" she asked him.

He pointed.

"Then I won't take that one."

The boy swayed with relief. She reached for the puppy he'd indicated and held it up for Charlie's admiration. The puppy seemed to fix its eyes on him.

"He likes you," Claudine said.

"Take him if you want," said Mrs. Adams. "They've all got to go."

"No!" the boy moaned.

"I'm sorry," Mrs. Adams said simply, in a resigned tone that made a lump unexpectedly rise in Charlie's throat. He had a sudden impression of the woman as being someone who'd started out in a place far better than where she'd ended up. Her features and coloring were not unlike his own. He was considering whether or not it would be rude to ask her if she was of Scotch-Irish descent when Claudine announced she'd made her choice.

"Is it a female?" she asked Mrs. Adams. The puppy wore a light blue collar around its neck.

"It's a bitch, and it's the only pup that's already weaned. You could take her right away."

"Why not this one?" Charlie asked, plucking Byron's favorite from the pen. "This is a good dog."

Claudine glared at him. He was annoyed with himself for becoming involved, but he thought the pup she liked was wild-eyed and showed all the signs of being incorrigible. For several minutes longer they debated the merits of the two pups under the respectively impatient and mournful eyes of Mrs. Adams and son, but Claudine had made up her mind and nothing he said made any difference.

"All right," he said finally. "That one."

Claudine cradled the pup and kissed its head.

"Three hundred dollars," said Mrs. Adams.

Claudine looked up. "On the telephone, you said two hundred fifty."

Mrs. Adams narrowed her eyes. "Bitches go for more. You could breed her."

The two women haggled for several minutes as Charlie made out a check for the full amount. He handed it to Mrs. Adams and steered Claudine toward the car. The last thing he saw as they left the house was the sight of Byron holding the good pup to his cheek as his mother pocketed the check in her dress.

"God, that was depressing. Good God, that was an awful, awful scene." Charlie laid his head back against the seat for a moment, both hands over his face.

"I felt sorry for the little boy." Claudine was busy settling the pup. She parted her legs slightly so that her green dress hung loosely between them, like a hammock. "I hope she lets him keep the other dog."

"She won't." Charlie started the car as Claudine laid the puppy in the bed she had made of her lap.

"Well, I hope she does. Anyway, I don't want to think about it anymore. I've picked a name for her. Do you want to hear it?"

Charlie grunted.

"I now christen her Buddy."

"Buddy's a boy's name," Charlie said automatically.

"Doesn't it mean friend?"

"It means a male friend, not a girl friend. For example, it would be right to say that Todd is my buddy."

"You are just being a chauvinist." She stroked the quivering puppy in her lap. "Her name is Buddy. It fits her."

"It suits her," Charlie corrected, but Claudine appeared to think he was conceding her point. He saw a deep contentment come into her eyes and he decided to let the matter go. When she gazed at Buddy, the wariness and acuity vanished from her expression, leaving behind a set of well-wrought features made slightly slack by tenderness. For her part, the puppy appeared to have found something equally soothing in Claudine; she stretched and promptly fell asleep. Charlie knew it was small of him to feel left out, but he did. He wasn't sure which of the two he envied more.

"I'm so happy," Claudine exclaimed. "Aren't you happy?"

Charlie let this go.

"This will change my life," she said matter-of-factly. It was difficult not to believe her. "For so long I have wanted another dog. I'll pay you back, of course."

"As you wish."

"She won't really be mine if I don't." She shot him an accusatory glance. "You paid too much."

"It wasn't worth the time it would take to bargain her down. Anyway, I'd be happy to consider it a present. Call it your Christmas present, why don't you?"

They both fell quiet at the mention of Christmas; it was a point too far in the future for them to imagine without bringing to mind the sticky question of what would have become of their relationship by then. For a while they drove in silence through the flat landscape. Charlie recognized the work — jutting out of the potato fields — of several architects he knew. For once he found the intrusion of man's odd fantasies on the natural world rather horrible, and he wondered what had compelled him to make a life's work of documenting them. Soon enough, though, these disturbing thoughts had passed, and he was able to spend the rest of the drive thinking of ideas for magazine articles, as usual.

Later, he remembered that, at the time, he'd actually been glad when Claudine said she wanted to become a more serious person. He'd always encouraged her to take herself more seriously. How could he have known that she would become immensely serious overnight, intense and fervid about all kinds of things? After two years of agonizing about the worth of her own photography, she began to take her pictures around to the galleries. She enrolled in a night-school class in English composition, and volunteered to work at an animal shelter on Saturday afternoons. Charlie had to admit that Claudine thrived under these conditions, but he resented being relegated to quality time, when he had, as it turned out, enjoyed quantity so much. He refrained from registering any complaints, however. He had tried to, once, but his objections had elicited nothing more than a few choice and dangerous words.

"Your problem, Charlie, is that you don't know how to make a commitment."

This was a topic he preferred not to debate. He did his best to ignore whatever she said when she was in this mood, and his self-control and equanimity won him the right to watch Claudine "train" Buddy. What Claudine called training was based on the theory that punishments work only in the moment, while rewards have everlasting effects. In practical terms, this meant that when Buddy did something right, Claudine praised her and fed her a piece of cheese or turkey, and when Buddy did something wrong, instead of disciplining her strictly the way Charlie often thought she should have, Claudine pretended nothing had happened and waited instead for the next good thing to come along. She refused even to say *no* to the dog and put Charlie under a stringent interdiction not to say *no*, either.

It drove him wild to have to stand by and watch Claudine coddle what he considered to be a particularly hard-headed, strong-willed pup. He had taken the opportunity when left alone with the beast for a few moments to make his displeasure with her as explicit as he could without doing anything physical, but every time he said *no*, or the even more satisfying *bad dog*, Buddy glared at him defiantly, as if to say *You're not my boss*.

But no matter how he felt privately, he forced himself to keep his mouth shut until one hot afternoon when Buddy chewed his loafers and he couldn't take it anymore.

"Damn it, Claudine, you've got to do something about that cur!"

"This is a symptom!" she yelled. "You are the one who cannot make a commitment, and yet you are going to blame Buddy."

"What? Who said anything about commitment?" Charlie asked. "I'm blaming the dog for chewing my shoe. That makes sense even in your world, doesn't it?"

"Buddy doesn't know what she's doing." She stood protectively in front of the hound.

"She damn well does! She did it on purpose!"

"She did not."

"Look at her." He pointed at Buddy, who was sulking on the rag rug. "Is that a clear case of *mens rea*, or isn't it?" Buddy glanced at Charlie, then quickly looked away, apparently deciding, quite rightly, that she'd do better to appeal to Claudine.

"You frightened her!" Claudine joined Buddy on the rug, and made a big show of kissing the dog on the lips.

"Claudine, please, that's repulsive." He flopped on the sofa, cradling the mangled shoe to his chest. He'd been working hard lately, and for the first time in a long time, a client had rejected a set of his pictures. The bigger surprise had been to find there was a strange satisfaction in being told he'd done unacceptable work. His failure was almost a reprieve that reminded him of the perverse pleasure he had always felt when a teacher had seen through him clearly enough to give him a bad grade on a paper he had banged out overnight. He respected the client for not allowing him to get away with his usual tricks. He had since rededicated himself to a pursuit of higher standards, but he still felt bruised and tender from the rejection, and he did not want to fight.

"There, there," he said to the shoe, "Daddy won't ever let that beast near you again."

He glanced at Claudine to see if he'd made her smile. For a moment he thought he'd succeeded, but when she saw him begin to grin, she collected herself and stubbornly continued to glare.

"It is typical of you to care more about your stupid" — *stupeet* — "dead shoe than you do about a live animal. Your priorities are all a mess. Many of your friends are married, and they're happy. And for your information, they all think something is wrong with you."

"Todd isn't married." He felt logically compelled to point that out.

"Todd is not afraid of marriage, though. You are."

"Claudine, the dog chewed a one-hundred-fifty-dollar pair of loafers. The dog is the issue here, not me, not Todd, not marriage. And anyway, weren't you the woman who said she wanted to be free, like Simone de Beauvoir?"

"Exactly!" Her voice rose and fell along the classic Parisian vocal scale. "Simone de Beauvoir was as good as married to Sartre, and he supported her while she wrote *Le Deuxième Sexe*."

"Are you saying you want to get married?"

She didn't reply.

"I've never deceived you about that, have I? Haven't I said all along that I don't want to get married?"

She wouldn't look at him.

"Haven't I been fair?"

"You have been straightforward, if you call that fair," she said. "I didn't want to get married either, but then something happened. I found out I love you."

Charlie sat up abruptly.

"Don't act so flattered," she said sarcastically. "I do think you should remember that most men would be happy to hear me say such a thing." She wrapped her arms ferociously around her narrow ribs; he had a vivid image of what she must have looked like in the lecture halls at the Sorbonne.

"I am flattered," he said.

"You could have fooled me."

Charlie dropped the mangled shoe to the ground and slid his foot into it, noting ruefully that it didn't fit him comfortably anymore, an observation he thought he could extrapolate to other areas of his life if he cared to do so. He ran his fingers through his hair. He tried to remain calm. "Claudine, this is not a conversation I care to be having, and I'd like to get out of it as soon as possible, so why don't you just tell me exactly what it is that you want from me, all right?"

She stood up, tugging at her tiny shorts. She seemed such a slight, dreamy little thing that it was sometimes hard to believe how much energy and stubbornness she could muster.

"I want to get married," she said.

He laughed sharply. "I guess I deserved that."

"I'm serious, Charlie. I'm tired of having you try to convince me that making a commitment is like tying a rope around your neck, when really it is just the opposite. Committing yourself to another person is what makes you free. What could be a greater freedom than having someone you can trust and talk to about anything? It is you who are not free, because you don't even understand the possibilities."

"I have a right to a private life. So do you."

"A private life is one thing. A paranoid, self-protective life is another. Independence is not a real philosophy with you. It's a fear." She clipped the leash on Buddy and walked to the door. "You'd better think about it."

For once, she opened the locks without fumbling.

"What about dinner?" He followed her to the elevator.

"Make it a rain check. If you're lucky."

When the door opened, Buddy bounded inside, pulling Claudine along in her wake. Out of habit, she turned around to wave at him, but dropped her hand midway.

Three nights later, Charlie was on his way to meet Todd at a restaurant when he saw Claudine enter a fruit stand on the other side of the street. They had not spoken since she walked out, although there had been a few empty messages on his answering machine, which he suspected of being failures of heart on her part. He did not call her. He wanted to — he missed her — but he couldn't think of anything to say that hadn't already been said. He couldn't change his position without changing everything about himself, so he held back, deciding it best to wait until he was sure of what he wanted. He never imagined he would run into her casually. He had already adjusted somewhat to moving through New York without her, so that when he saw her across the street, her head bent, her thin arm flexed under the weight of packages and her heavy leather bag, he felt as though he had come upon a mirage. It shocked him to see her alone, and he realized it was the first time he had observed her out of the range of his influence. Of course, he'd naturally assumed that she had a life of her own, that she crossed streets and ate food and paid her bills, but he'd never given that side of her much thought. Now he was shaken by the idea that her private life might have something more to it than prosaic detail, that there were depths to her he had yet to know.

He pressed himself against a granite wall, hoping he'd made himself invisible beneath the awning of a pizza shop. In a few minutes she reappeared, another bag in hand. She looked desperately sad and preoccupied. He watched her walk down the block until she disappeared around the corner, then he automatically moved off through the crowd of families and couples who thronged the sidewalk as he tried to figure out what had just happened. He did not believe in portents or signs, yet he had the uneasy sense that he'd been shown something he could not afford to ignore. For the first time in two years, he bought a pack of cigarettes. He chose a strong brand he hadn't smoked since college. He lit one on the street, hoping he wouldn't cough in front of strangers. He'd expected to feel slightly sick, but to his surprise, the habit returned easily and he immediately felt better for taking it up again. He had quit smoking before he met Claudine. The man who smoked was not the man who loved her, and it was easier not to be that man, not right now.

Damn it, though, he was committed to Claudine; that was what she didn't understand. He didn't believe in marriage unless children were involved, and he preferred to live alone, but aside from those considerations, he was committed. He hadn't slept with anyone else in nearly a year, which, in his view, was the biggest commitment he could make. He doubted she could say the same for herself, although he'd never directly asked her about it. He didn't really want to know. It was sobering enough that Claudine had once told him that she believed in free love, and that humans were not naturally monogamous. He told himself she said such things only to prevent him from feeling as though he was trapped, but he couldn't be sure. He made a point of letting her know that fidelity was important to him, if not to her. He knew himself well enough to know that he could not love her if she had sex with another man while she was with him. His attitude was less than modern, but he didn't care. The sheer visceral strength of his feelings on the subject struck him as being at least as valid as her social theories.

Todd understood his perspective. Since college, they'd kept abreast of each other's bachelorhood, which they pursued not so much by pursuing women, but by placing a high priority on distinctly unwomanly things. They hunted together once or twice a year. They bought each other expensive Christmas presents — silver flasks or beaver-skin hats or white silk scarves to wear with their dinner jackets. They knew all the pool halls and okay bars in Manhattan, and they stayed free by traveling among these sacred sites, doing so late at night when women were afraid to be out on the streets.

Until recently, Claudine had fit in well with the program. She never minded Todd's joining them for the evening, and it had been her idea that they all get naked for their ritual drinking sessions in the hot tub in Charlie's building. By making nudity a requirement, Claudine had effectively excluded most of their other women friends, who were no longer as confident of their bodies as Claudine could still afford to be. Ironically, however, she simultaneously rendered herself sexless for the duration of the sessions, as Charlie and Todd observed a strict taboo against ever becoming aroused around each other. But they had gotten drunk together, and laughed, and in those hours Claudine hadn't tried to be anything more than his friend.

He arrived at the restaurant, where Todd was already settled at a window table with a drink. Charlie lit a fourth cigarette.

"Don't say anything. I need this."

Todd shrugged. "Since when have I ever been the health police? Anyway, from what I understand, you have good cause to pursue a course of self-destruction."

"You talked to her?"

Todd nodded.

"Why would she talk to you?"

Todd drank bottoms up, then wiped his mouth with the back of his hand. "I've spent at least two evenings a week in her company since you met her. In her logical Gallic mind, that probably qualifies me as friendship material."

"What else did she say?"

"I didn't pay too much attention, if you want to know the truth. Basically, it was the same kind of commitment stuff that she's been talking about for months."

"What did you say to her?"

"Nothing. Why?" Todd asked.

"Oh."

"Oh. Asshole. You don't think I had anything to do with this, do you?"

"Somehow you've convinced her that you're not the wretched misogynist that I know you to be," Charlie said. "She used the example of your relationship with Sarah against me."

Instead of laughing, Todd slumped in his chair. "God, this is awful timing." He looked at Charlie. "There's something I have to tell you."

Charlie stared at him. "No. No. Not tonight."

"Come on, it's not the worst thing in the world."

"All right, all right. Just don't ask me to be your best man."

"I want you to be my best man."

Charlie signaled the waitress and ordered a bottle of champagne. When it arrived, he dismissed the waiter and popped the cork himself.

"To holy unions," he proposed.

"Let's not get crazy," said Todd, clinking his glass.

For the rest of the evening they tried to reassure each other that nothing would change after Todd was married, but the only thing Charlie felt he could trust was how quickly the champagne worked, and how convincing it was. His anger dissipated into thick sentimentality that allowed him to say many complimentary, even profound things about Sarah, which he talked himself into believing as he spoke. Todd laughed his cynical laugh all night, until Charlie realized it was the laugh that had had him fooled all along. Underneath, Todd was as susceptible as the rest of his married friends to alluring myths of domesticity.

"You think I should call Claudine, don't you?" he said, laying his credit card on the check.

"What's the worst thing that could happen if you did?"

"The worst thing that could happen is that I could end up in Greenwich with a train schedule in the inside pocket of all my jackets."

"I'll drink to that," Todd said.

Charlie looked at him blearily. "There's no way I can talk you out of this?"

"Sorry, pal. The harder they come, the harder they fall."

When Charlie arrived home, the doorman waved him over to the desk.

"Message for you."

My grandmother died. I have to go back to France for the funeral. Please take care of Buddy until I return. No one else can take her. I'll pay you back. Claudine.

"Is she gone?" Charlie asked. "Was she here?"

"Oh yeah, she was here." He beckoned Charlie to join him behind the desk, where Buddy stood up sleepily, wagging her tail.

For the tenth night in a row Charlie came home after having dinner out to find several turds in the middle of his living room floor. No, that was not precisely true. For the tenth night in a row he came home to find Buddy at the door, eager to greet him, eager to stand on her hind legs pawing at the air until he bent down to pat her. Although he was working hard on her training, he could not resist caving in to her enthusiasm when he first opened the door. Her teeth flashed and she flattened her ears against her head to show her excitement. As he flipped her over and ran his fingers across the soft fur on her belly, there were moments when he was glad to see her. "Hey, little girl," he would say tenderly, feeling himself at the center of an intimate, private world. "Did you miss me?"

It was always at about that point that he would find the turd. The evidence of her misbehavior utterly disheartened him; the close moments they had just spent seemed a sham in the face of her defiance. He did not understand how she could be so dull-witted. If her aim was to get him to stay home with her, she was going about it all the wrong way.

"Where the hell do you think this is going to get you?" he demanded.

She began to back away.

"Get back here!"

She turned her head slightly, displaying the whites of her eyes in a manner that made her look half-crazed.

"Come here," he said more evenly. "I just want to talk to you."

He held out his hand, palm up. Buddy glanced at his hand, then his face, then his hand again.

"Come here, Buddy," he coaxed.

She took a few steps toward him. When she came within reach, he swung his arm out to grab her, but she ducked and escaped sideways, like a crab. He called to her again; and again, after she'd come to him slowly, maddeningly slowly, she ran off just as it seemed he had a grip on her.

"This is not a game, Buddy. I'm too tired for this."

Buddy cocked her head from side to side and watched him with a quizzical, curious expression that he knew she thought was endearing. Claudine had spoiled her by applauding her manner-isms despite whatever perfidies they might conceal. He headed for her again, only to find his progress checked by a strangled sob coming from his own throat. He had to stop for a moment; he gripped the back of the sofa as if it were his heart that hurt, as if he needed to catch his breath.

"Good God," he whispered.

He wiped his brow with the back of his hand and found it wet, in spite of the air conditioning. For quite some time he had felt that something was wrong, but now he was sure of it; he was falling to pieces. The self he thought he knew was unraveling, and he honestly did not know what to do to make things better. He missed Claudine. He had never missed anyone before. He found it difficult to sleep without her, which made him realize that he'd fallen into the habit of doing so. Somehow the fact that they kept separate apartments had allowed him to ignore the realities of his life. The reality was that they had been virtually living together.

He poured himself a drink and called Todd.

"I was just about to go to bed," Todd said.

"Okay." Charlie paused. "This damn mutt is driving me crazy."

"Is that it?"

Charlie lit a cigarette. "No."

"I didn't think so. Go ahead."

"Actually, it's the French thing."

"Yeah, I was waiting for that."

"I think I need some advice."

Todd, who claimed to have been made brave by his own engagement, agreed to tell Charlie what he thought, on two conditions: (1) whatever was said would not interfere with their friendship, and (2) Charlie had to promise to seriously consider acting on Todd's recommendation.

"Done," said Charlie. "Tell me."

"Let me ask you a question instead," said Todd. "Look, I know you had a rough childhood and all that, but do you really want to allow all those childhood fears to run your life?"

"What do you mean I had a rough childhood?"

"Charlie, I was *there*, remember?"

"Have you and Sarah been analyzing me?" he asked angrily.

"I think you're afraid you're going to be as unhappy as your father was, but it doesn't have to be like that," Todd said, ignoring Charlie's outburst.

"Give me a break."

"You asked for my opinion. I'm just saying you should make your choices based on what you want now."

"So what do I want?"

"I think you want Claudine."

Charlie blew a cloud of smoke into the chilly air. "I think you might be right," he said finally.

"Just picture what it would be like not to have her. That's what I did with Sarah."

"We'll see. Anyway, thanks."

"I'll call you tomorrow," Todd said.

Charlie hung up. Buddy appeared at his feet and stretched her front paws up to his lap, apparently believing he was no longer angry at her. He picked her up and carried her over to the turd, swatted her halfheartedly, then went to the kitchen for a paper towel to clean up her mess.

The next day, he received a letter from Claudine saying she wouldn't be back for three more weeks. She didn't allude to anything personal, although he managed to leach some meaning out of the fact that she had signed off with the affectionate *je t'embrasse*. He was tempted to jump on a plane immediately, and he might have done so if she had provided him with an address. He tried to find her parents' number through information, but quickly discovered that their last name was as common as Jones, and there were hundreds of them in the Paris Minitel directory.

Having no way to reach her made him feel more out of control than he had during his adult life. It seemed unfair that just when he had decided he would at least give the kind of commitment she wanted a try, he was unable to put his decision into effect. The intensity with which he missed her was increased by his irrational anger at her for not letting him know where she was. He wondered if she was purposely manipulating him into acquiescing to her wishes by performing such a willful disappearing act, when it suddenly occurred to him that perhaps she did not want him to get in touch with her. It wasn't beyond her to take the practical course and cut her losses, leaving him behind. He realized he subconsciously had counted on her being shrewd enough to understand that patience might accomplish her goals in the end, but when he honestly reexamined the events of the last few months, he saw that he had given her no reason to believe that could ever be true. On the contrary, he had done everything he could to make sure she held out no romantic hopes for a turnaround on his part. He had backed himself into a corner with his own insistence on having his freedom, and ended up in the sickening position of being chained to the vague hope that she would take him back.

Although he couldn't reach her to plead his case, he needed to do something constructive that would at least provide him with the illusion of a happy outcome to the frustration of the waiting period. He thought of painting the apartment, or going daily to the gym, but he knew Claudine wouldn't be swayed by gestures that could be construed to be more for his benefit than for her own. He was casting about for a better idea when he heard a noise in the kitchen, and in exploring the cause of it — Buddy had paddled the water out of her bowl — he realized that fate had already handed him a trump card.

All right, so she was never going to be the perfect dog he would have chosen for himself, but he could make her into a perfect dog for Claudine. The thought of handing her a champion upon her return rather than the mongrel she left behind filled him with the sense of purpose he needed to make the time go by quickly. It was additionally inspiring that everyone thought she was such a beautiful dog. He couldn't walk two steps without someone stopping him to ask about her breed or to admire her looks. He found himself saying that Buddy was his dog; it was easier than explaining the entire situation, and anyway he found he had developed a masterly attachment to her. She was doing quite well when he took her out on walks. In the beginning she had pulled a lot, but he bought a good choke collar and gave her a solid jerk whenever she pulled forward, and in a short time she was heeling at his side, trotting along to keep up with his long strides. He taught her how to sit by jerking up on the collar while simultaneously pushing down on her rump, and he taught her not to jump on the furniture by laying mousetraps along the edges of the sofa and chairs. Once he had made it clear that he knew all her tricks and that she wasn't going to be able to put anything past him, her behavior improved enormously. After two more weeks had passed, he had no major complaints except that whenever he left her alone in the apartment, she expressed her anger at him by presenting him with a turd upon his return.

"Buddy, damn it, I've really had it with this. I had a hard day at work. I don't want to come home and have to clean up a mess."

He placed his hands on his hips and widened his stance ferociously. Buddy slunk along the perimeter of the sofa and tried to squeeze behind it, but he swooped down and caught her by the leg. He lifted her up and forced her to look into his eyes. Just as he was on the point of beginning his lecture, she bit him.

She was as surprised as he was; immediately, she tried to pretend the bite had never happened by licking the site of his wound.

"It's too late for that," he snorted. "Damn you, Buddy, damn!"

He was about to carry her back to the turd for her punishment when he spotted something equally suspicious. There were a few tufts of a cottony substance near the corner of the sofa. He peered behind it and found the needlepoint pillow that had been left to him by his grandmother. It had been chewed to shreds. He stared at the ruins in disbelief.

"How could you do this to me?"

He held her at arm's length. She struggled to get free.

"So you're beginning to realize this isn't a game?"

He shook her.

"Look at this!"

He bent down and shoved her face in the remains of the pillow. She made a halfhearted effort to mouth the filling.

"Drop!"

She looked up at him quizzically.

"Drop!"

She opened her mouth, allowing the tufts of stuffing to fall to the floor. He carried her over to the turd.

"Bad dog!" He shoved her face in it. She opened her mouth as if to take a bite.

"Are you crazy?" he growled. "Doesn't anything get through to you?"

She swung around frantically, wiping a nose full of dung across his shirt.

"That does it."

He hurled her on the sofa and pulled the belt off his pants. Holding her head tight, he began to beat her. At first she struggled, but soon her body went limp. He didn't know how many times he hit her before he was able to stop himself. When he had finally had enough, he let her go, and he saw her slink off to the kitchen as he headed for the bathroom to wash his face and hands.

He stood on the second level of the international arrivals terminal until Claudine's plane landed, then headed downstairs to wait with all the other anxious relatives and lovers and limousine drivers behind the metal barricades. Finally she appeared, pushing her suitcases on a cart in front of her.

"Claudine!" He held his arm straight up in the air and did not move it until he saw her find him in the crowd. When she spotted him, she looked as though she'd seen an accident, or as though a flash bulb had gone off in her face.

She still loves me, he thought. It was going to be all right.

"How did you find me?" she asked as he steered her toward the exit.

"I met all the planes from Paris that were coming in this afternoon."

She glanced at him quickly, searching his face for clues to the truth. Whatever she saw made her laugh a little.

"I suppose there was only one plane from Paris this afternoon?" she teased.

"Two." He carried her bags outside.

"I'm sorry about your grandmother," he said after he'd settled her into a cab.

"I was too. I can't stop missing her."

"It takes time."

Charlie saw the cab driver staring at him in the rearview mirror and realized he hadn't told him where to go. He gave his address.

"What about my bags?" Claudine asked. "Shouldn't we drop them off at my apartment on the way?"

"I was thinking we could make room for them in my apartment." He looked at her. "I was thinking you should move in with me." He paused. "I was even thinking that maybe we should get married."

There was a long quiet moment before she threw herself on him in a great oceanic wave of tenderness, and in that long moment, he knew he had made the right decision. Even if she rejected him, at least he had run the ball all the way down the field, and he could look back with no regrets. His sense of inner peace made the moment even more poignant as she accepted his proposal. He had imagined this moment so often that it was already like a memory, and he had to remind himself to pay attention while it was actually happening. As she nuzzled his neck, her rich perfume settled over him and he felt lucky and grateful that he'd woken up before he'd allowed her to get away. His chest ached with the weight of his past, his emotions, his decisions. There was too much there to call it happiness yet; the ache was happiness's messenger, happiness coming.

"What made you change your mind?" she asked when they broke apart.

"I didn't really change it at all," he said. "I just shifted it a little, and then everything looked different. Clearer."

She squeezed his hand, her eyes bright.

"I realized you were right about a lot of things," he said.

"Of course I was." She crossed her legs, her stockings making a swishing sound that filled him with nostalgia for the colder seasons, all the icy winters he had known.

"You won't be sorry," she said.

"I know."

She leaned her head contentedly against his shoulder for a moment, then suddenly twisted to face him. "How's Buddy?"

"Wait until you see her. She's doing great."

It was true. He could not think of the night when he'd beaten her without shame, but when he got up the next morning, it was as if a miracle had occurred. Buddy stayed on her rug in the kitchen until he called her, and she sat still as he clipped her on the leash. When he took her outside, she did her business right away, then heeled step for step when he went to buy his paper. She didn't try to pull him over to the other dogs, nor did she strain against him even the tiniest bit when he turned to go back inside. And that night, when he came home from a dinner with Todd and Sarah, he found Buddy lying peacefully in front of the sofa, not a mess in sight. It had been like that, and even better than that, ever since. "She's the perfect dog."

"I told you," said Claudine.

"And you were right. It was just a question of bringing out her potential."

When they arrived at his building, the doorman fetched her bags from the trunk of the cab while Claudine raced ahead to the elevator. By the time they reached his apartment door, she was squealing.

"Buddy," she called. "Here I am, Buddy!" She turned to Charlie. "Hurry up, open the door!"

He turned the key in the lock.

"Hurry, hurry!"

She placed her hand over his as if the process would go more quickly if she helped him turn the knob. He watched with amusement as she flung open the door and rushed into the dark hall.

He flicked the light switch. "How does everything look?"

She took a step forward, at the same time reaching her hand behind her, groping for him. "It looks beautiful. Where's Buddy?" she asked.

"She's probably asleep on her rug in the kitchen."

"She doesn't come to the door anymore?"

"Not unless I call her. She obeys all my commands now."

Claudine looked at him uncertainly. "She does?"

"I've worked with her a lot." Charlie dropped her hand to pull her suitcases into the front hall. "Go to the kitchen. She'll be there."

Claudine slipped her high heels off and padded in her stocking feet along the runner, then across the parquet floor. As she stopped still in the kitchen doorway, he watched the back of her head, noticing with an odd new sense of intimacy the blond, wispy hairs that escaped from her ponytail. For a long moment she did not move. He was about to put his hand on the back of her neck when something about her steely posture, her fixity, made him wish he had his camera in hand. He hadn't even considered photographing a human subject in at least ten years, but he wanted to capture Claudine. He closed his eyes to help him remember exactly what he saw so he could reproduce it in the studio. When he looked up again, she was gazing at him, her face twisted in an odd half smile.

"Is this some sort of a joke?" she asked.

"What are you talking about?" He was still thinking about the image of her he wanted to make.

"Did you go back to Mrs. Adams and get that other dog?"

"Don't be silly." He pushed past her into the kitchen. "This is Buddy, right here." He nudged the dog with his foot. "Go say hello to your mistress."

With apparent great effort, the dog rose to her feet and lumbered toward Claudine.

"No," she moaned hoarsely, pressing her hands to her cheeks. "Oh, no." She leaned against the wall. "That's not my dog."

Charlie picked up the puppy and kissed her on top of her head. "Why don't you hold her, darling?" he said gently.

"What did you do to her?" Claudine whispered.

He placed the puppy back on the floor and commanded her to *sit*, then wrapped his arm protectively around Claudine's shoulders. "You're still upset."

"I want to go home, Charlie," she said in a low voice.

"Claudine, this is your home." He squeezed her tighter. For a moment she went limp, and he felt a great painful ache for her, a desire to protect her, to pull her out of the path of daily dangers, to make sure she had everything she needed. His hands on her back seemed to pick up every tiny sensation in her body, all the little sighs. He didn't think he had ever felt quite as capable of making a difference in the world, and he had to wonder where he'd gotten the idea that loving a woman was a small thing.

"I'm sorry, Charlie," Claudine said softly. "Please let me go."

He heard her words, but she didn't really pull away. She merely leaned backward on his arms as she pushed lightly against his chest.

"Please. I want to go back to my apartment with Buddy."

"Ssh." He stroked her hair. "You've had a really hard time these last few weeks, not to mention a long trip. Why don't you go to the bedroom and . . ."

Then, before Charlie had time to finish his sentence, as if anticipating the exact words he was planning to say next, Buddy lay down.

Naked to the Waist

"WHAT's the worst thing you've ever done?" Lucy asked.

Nick thought for a moment. "I'd have to say it's more what I haven't done that counts against me. Everything that ended up bringing me here, in other words."

"Oh, thanks a lot!" Lucy elbowed him without opening her eyes.

"Not *here* here, silly. Hugh's house."

"I knew what you meant."

She hadn't expected such a serious answer, but she supposed that, given the circumstances, it wasn't surprising that Nick was prepared to talk. They'd driven to a nearly deserted island an hour north of Key West, and then, to ensure their privacy, they'd walked at least a mile along the empty shore from where they'd parked the car. To the east, the ocean stretched to Africa, while behind them the island was flat, sandy, and overgrown with scrubby vegetation. Lucy rolled onto her stomach on her beach blanket, burrowing herself into the sand. Before laying her head to rest on her folded hands, she pulled her dark hair to one side of her neck so her shoulders would tan evenly. When she was settled, she examined her conscience to discover whether or not there was any good excuse for looking at Nick at precisely that moment. She considered it an indulgence that bordered on idolatry to look at him without having a reason, and lately she was trying to be spiritually strict with herself. In view of the fact that thinking about his life with Hugh usually undermined Nick's good humor, however, she decided it was allowable to check on him, for his own sake.

"You're staring at me, aren't you?" he asked.

"Sort of."

"Don't." He clapped his hands to his cheeks. "I'm ugly."

She knew that sometimes he really believed this. "Do you think I would spend so much time with you if you were ugly?"

"Yes."

"Do you think Hugh would?"

Nick laughed sharply. "You've got a point there."

Lucy crossed her eyes for a moment, turning Nick into a ruddy blur. This was one of the deterrents she used when she found herself staring at him for her own enjoyment. She shifted her focus to the top of his head, making his sunbleached hair disappear into the sandy terrain as she purposefully tried to deconstruct his physical presence to get at the essence underneath, which was theoretically not as hypnotic or unsettling as his looks.

So far it hadn't worked very well.

"I guess the worst thing I've done lately," Nick said, "is that I agreed to go on this cruise with Hugh without putting up a fight. I don't want to go, not at all."

Lucy didn't want him to go either, but she saw no point in spelling it out. When it came to the subject of Hugh and Nick, her opinion went without saying.

"Hugh will embarrass me on the ship, I just know it. He'll go out of his way to make sure we sit at the captain's table, and then he'll go out of his way to make sure the nature of our relationship is perfectly clear to everyone. Then I'll have to act as a walker for all the rich old ladies who think they can use me the way Hugh does. And there will be tons of food at every meal, but I'll be too sick of myself to eat."

"It will be fun," Lucy said.

Nick sat up abruptly. His thin back was as expressive as most people's faces; there was scorn in the muscles around his spine.

"That's easy for you to say, but I know what you're really thinking. You think that I should tell him I'm not going, but I'd have to leave him to do that. I couldn't just stay in the house while he's away." He sighed. "If I left Hugh, I'd have nowhere to go, except to someone else like Hugh."

"You could come home with me," Lucy said carefully. "You could live with me and take courses in New York, maybe even finish your degree, if you wanted."

The silence that followed had a dangerous feel to it.

"Maybe he'll fall overboard and leave you all his money," she joked. She glanced at him and saw by his pinched lips that, if anything, she had made things worse. A vein in his neck throbbed, and Lucy realized she had crossed the line into his fantasy life. "It's only ten days," she said quickly. "I'll be here when you get back."

"But not for long."

"Not necessarily. I'm not in a hurry to get back. I could stay."

Her current visit to Nick had been designed to coincide with the last wearying gasps of a five-year relationship that went the way of oblivion rather than marriage. The trip to Key West was for purposes of rest and recovery, and her offer to house-sit for Nick and Hugh while they cruised was to afford her quiet time to decide what to do next. "I could even move down here. I can do anything I want."

There was a pause. She watched as he erased all traces of concern from his features, and presumably from his mind. When he'd composed himself, he turned toward her, offering up one of his bright, expansive smiles.

"Don't do that," Lucy said impatiently.

"What?"

"Don't try to snow me as if I were Hugh. You can't just smile at me and expect me to forget what we're talking about. You can't avoid your feelings forever."

Nick regarded her quietly for a moment, a curious, impersonal expression on his face, like a deer's. "Wanna bet?" he said finally. He stood up. "Anyway, I'm going swimming."

Lucy groaned. She hated it when Nick cloaked himself in this particular mood. He had the capacity to sink to his lowest ebb in a matter of minutes; then it could take several hours to buck him up again. By the time he was back to normal, it was usually time to deliver him back to Hugh. Suddenly she didn't feel like repairing Nick for Hugh's benefit.

"I feel like a swim myself," she said. She jumped up and walked to the ocean without looking back. Nick walked past her and dove gracefully beneath the flat surface of the sea. As she stood ankle-deep in the soupy water, she saw in her mind's eye a picture of how her current situation might move forward if only she could have what she wanted. She could live with Nick and save up the interest from her trust fund instead of spending it to travel around. They could both get jobs and schedule simultaneous vacation time like other, regular couples. To punish him for having such a grip on her, she rolled her bathing suit down around her hips, the way European women did. When Nick resurfaced she was standing naked to the waist in the clear water.

"Lu, what are you doing?" He blushed and giggled, pushing his index fingers into his eyes like a shy boy. "What if someone sees?"

"What if they do?"

Nick visored his eyes with his hands and made a great show of searching the shoreline for signs of life. He had brought her there because he wanted to be alone, which he assured her he could manage in her presence, but now she had reminded him how different they really were, and she saw by his vexed expression that he wished that someone, anyone else was around.

"We're alone here," she said, dropping into the water up to her chest. Unfettered, her breasts bobbed to the surface. She couldn't recall being topless in the water since early girlhood, in the lake at camp or at the pool, places where she had enjoyed her animal vitality without connecting it to anything or anyone, before sex. She spread her arms beneath the sea and waved them back and forth, her muscles churning with the effort of pulling the water's full weight. Burrowed in the sand, her knees looked substantial, trustworthy. Above them, her stomach gleamed white as the inside of a shell.

She caught Nick looking.

"Well, you're allowed to go around with your shirt off." She slapped a handful of water at him.

"I don't think I can handle it."

"Don't you like them?" She looked down at her body, then coolly back at him.

"I do like them. They're pretty. That's the problem."

Nick took his hands from his eyes and smiled sheepishly. Once again Lucy felt guilty for pushing him. She slid deeper under the water, no longer inclined to expose herself. When she was hidden up to her neck, Nick stood up, taking a position between her and the sun, shading her face. She appreciated his protective gesture, but the day was still so bright that she couldn't look at anything without squinting. Yet no matter how impaired her vision became, she could still discern the tiniest shifts in Nick's expression. She watched him go from embarrassed to ashamed to somewhat composed, and frighteningly serious.

"Nickie, it doesn't matter."

He held up his hand to silence her.

"Doesn't it?" He stared at her intently, as if to excise that last lie of hers forever from her heart and mind. "It matters to me. You asked about the worst thing I've ever done? Let me tell you about the worst thing I'll ever do." He touched the surface of the water lightly, with his fingertips. "You always say I have everything? I don't, you know. I do not have the capacity to touch you, and I never will. Do you understand?"

She looked away from him, toward the beach. "I don't believe that," she said finally. "I think you're afraid, and that once you overcome your fear, you could do anything you want."

"Oh, so all I need to do is overcome my fear?" His tone was hateful. Whom he hated most at that moment, she wasn't sure. "Well, I can't argue with that."

Down the beach, three people had appeared and were pointing excitedly at a school of dolphins swimming close to shore. Lucy dove and lay for a moment on the ocean floor, keeping still by holding on to the sea grass. Slowly she pulled herself over to Nick's feet and cupped her hands around the backs of his ankles.

He jumped skittishly, so she quickly let go, as though her intent had been to surprise him, not to hold on. She pulled her suit up and heaved herself skyward. When she resurfaced, he began to giggle again.

"I'm such a child," he said.

"You're a porpoise," she replied. With her index finger she touched him in the middle of his chest and he fell backward, as if she'd shoved him. Wet, his blond hair darkened.

"This could be perfect," Lucy said.

"I know. If it weren't for me."

Hugh laid a hibiscus flower in a bowl of water and sat it on a table by the pool. Just inside the open sliding doors, Nick was setting up the bar while Lucy mashed several packs of onion soup mix into several pints of sour cream. The party was a combination bon voyage for their trip and a celebration of Hugh's election to the board of the Theater by the Sea. Earlier, while Nick was at the store, Hugh had confided in Lucy that he'd donated money to the troupe in the hope that Nick would take an interest in the theater, that it would give him something to do. As always when Hugh tried to manipulate her into taking an objective interest in Nick, she pretended she didn't quite know what he was getting at. She wanted no part of helping Hugh manage Nick.

"Are you going to change your clothes?" she asked.

"I don't know. Should we?" Nick was wearing jams and a T-shirt.

"It's our party. We can change if we want to," Hugh called from the deck.

Lucy and Nick exchanged glances. When they said "we," they did not mean Hugh. They cast him as a bothersome parent who interfered with their important, private games. Lucy shrugged. "I'm sure I'll get cold later, so I may as well put on some pants now."

She went upstairs to the guest room and changed quickly, in the dark. She could hardly bear to be away from Nick during any moment that she could possibly be with him. Frightened by her longing to be downstairs, she forced herself to hang up her clothes and neaten her things. Then, sitting cross-legged in the middle of the bed, she took twenty deep breaths under the ceiling fan. By the time she returned to the kitchen, the first guests had arrived.

Lucy spotted Nick across the living room, showing off the cow-shaped Christmas tree lights they had draped over the plants. He was laughing happily, his mouth wide. He pulled a section of the string of lights away from the plant and handed them to a thin girl in a green silk dress. She gushed over the plastic cows in a manner familiar to Lucy; it was a disguise for gushing over Nick. She scanned the crowd for Hugh and found him talking seriously to the director of the company, who also owned theaters on the mainland. Out of the corner of his eye Hugh was keeping track of Nick, but he didn't appear to be concerned about the girl in the green silk dress. Although she knew she didn't need to be either, Lucy was. Nick was one of the few people who'd ever made her look at other women as anything rather than friends and sisters, and Nick didn't even want other women.

She went to the bar. Hugh appeared behind her and wrapped his arm around her shoulders. He made a point of behaving as though she was his friend, too.

"The icemaker is broken," he said. "I have to go to the corner and buy some bags of ice. Would you take care of the drinks until I get back?"

"Sure, but my skills are limited."

"I'll go, Hugh," said a man standing nearby who'd overheard their conversation.

Hugh accepted the offer and reached for his wallet, but the man held up a hand in protest. "I've got it covered. You can pay me later."

"Thanks, Dennis."

When Dennis walked away, Hugh turned back to Lucy. "I guess you're off the hook."

She smiled. "I'll handle it. You go be the host."

Hugh squeezed her briefly, then disappeared into the crowd. Although she felt vaguely uneasy at having taken on the responsibility for everyone's thirst, she was glad to have something to do. People struck up conversations with her as they waited for their drinks. When they heard she'd be house-sitting while Nick and Hugh were away, they promised to invite her to dinner to break up her vigil, and she found herself wishing they meant it, as some of them seemed nice. Nickie bopped in occasionally to giggle with her between trips to the pool deck or into Hugh's red and gold library to entertain the artists and their patrons. Lucy drank rum as she poured.

"Boston," said a man's voice close to her ear.

"What?" she asked automatically. She'd heard what had been said, but she wasn't sure what it meant.

"How about Maine, then. Or Baltimore?"

Lucy looked up. The person speaking to her was the man who'd gone for the ice — Dennis, if she remembered correctly. He appeared to be about forty, although it was hard to be sure about people who had spent a lot of time in the sun; he was tall, and good-looking enough, she thought, that under other circumstances she might find him handsome, if she hadn't been so spoiled by Nick.

"If you're asking where I live," she said, "the answer is New York."

"I didn't ask anything. I was guessing where you're from." He popped a slice of lime into his mouth and extracted the fruit from the rind.

"Oh. Why?"

"Only a certain kind of person cracks ice the way you do."

"Really?" She handed a drink to a woman on her left.

"Most people put the cubes into the glass without cracking them."

"Really."

"Stop making drinks for a while. Watch what people do."

He pinched the material on the sleeve of her sweat shirt and pulled her away from her work. He stationed Lucy and himself against the counter, where they had a perfect view of the drinks table. Every time someone dropped a cube of ice into his or her glass, Dennis made a mark in the air, keeping an invisible score.

"All right, you win," Lucy said finally. "How did you know?" She glanced at him sideways, her eyes following her lashes up to his face.

"I was a bartender for a while after I got out of the Army, first up in the Hamptons, then down here."

"So what kind of person cracks the ice the way I do? You said it was a type."

"It is a type. It's the type who take their drinks seriously."

"Surely you can do better than that," Lucy said. "You can't go around telling someone she's a type without telling her what it is."

"Okay." He turned toward her. "I'd say you're the sweetheart type, or maybe you're simply an angel." He pushed a hank of her hair behind her shoulder and trained his wet blue eyes on her as if he could hypnotize her with his gaze. She was embarrassed by the intimacy of his tone, and felt as though she had wandered into a party for older people, that she had mistakenly given a grown-up man the wrong signals. She realized how accustomed she'd become to Nickie's blushes and giggles. Dennis seemed out of her league.

"I'm not really such a sweetheart, not unless you get to know me very well." She lowered her eyes and hoped she would not say another stupid thing.

"That doesn't sound like a bad idea," Dennis said.

She looked across the room at Hugh, who was gazing at Nick, who was staring back at her. Holding his attention, even if it was only from across the room, made her perversely happy.

"Maybe I could stop by sometime while they're away," Dennis said.

"Sure."

"Maybe tomorrow?"

"I don't see why not," she said lightly, as if she flirted with strangers all the time.

The next afternoon, Lucy and Dennis stood in the pool up to their waists, trying to get to know each other over the din of activity nearby. On one side of the house was a small hotel, on the other, another private house. Nick and Hugh had built a fence around their property and lined it with palms, but the second floor of the hotel hung above the barrier and it was usually possible to hear people fighting or drying their hair or making love. She and Nick had a notebook in which they wrote down phrases they overheard spoken by the hotel patrons, among their other secrets. As Lucy tried to talk to Dennis, someone at the hotel called out "Martha, Martha," frantically. Meanwhile next door, a man was trimming the hedge with a power tool that made the water vibrate as it buzzed.

Dennis was oblivious to all the noise, or so it appeared. If Nick had been there, they would have huddled together in the deep end, their fingertips hooked over the edge of the pool as they whispered about what might be happening to the person who had called out for Martha. Lucy would have guessed that the man and Martha were probably having sex, a conjecture Nick would find disgusting. He did not believe sex was an appropriate activity for the afternoon, or for people who liked each other well enough to rent a hotel room together. He had sex only in the middle of the night, with the lights out and the shades pulled, so he could not see his partner. Later, he always tried to convince himself that nothing had happened, that it had all been a peculiar dream. For a long time he'd had Lucy convinced that he and Hugh never had sex together. It was only from Hugh that Lucy learned differently.

Nick pretended to have no idea of how much of what went on had to do with sex. He had gotten her in the habit of not allowing herself to think about it, either. With him gone, those restrictions automatically lifted, and she found herself looking at the hair on Dennis's chest and the veins in his arms.

"Are you married?" she asked boldly. She wrapped her arms around her waist.

"No. I was, but not anymore."

"I'm sorry."

"Don't be. She joined the Navy, so Uncle Sam is supporting her and I'm off the hook."

Lucy laughed nervously. She wasn't sure if he was joking or not.

"Them's the breaks." Dennis shrugged.

"Well, I'm never getting married," Lucy said firmly.

"Bully for you." He looked away.

She ran her big toe across the bottom of the pool, feeling the heavy weight of the water against her leg. "I like to be free, you see." She tried to sound nice; she didn't want to hurt him. It wasn't his fault that Nickie had left that morning to go on a cruise. "I like to travel when I want to, and visit my friends."

"That's not hard to understand." The buzz saw stopped for a moment, and the hotel was quiet. Dennis lowered his voice. "I think I'd like to do some traveling, too."

That night Lucy walked through the half-dark, fragrant streets to the Little Theater, where Dennis was selling refreshments. He made a living by supplying and operating the concession stand at local theaters, a profession she thought enterprising. He got her in free to see the show, but she couldn't concentrate on the drama. She thought the lead actress looked sad, and that the old velvet curtains that hung at the edges of the stage smelled musty. At intermission she left through the back and smoked a cigarette behind someone's refurbished antique car; from there she spied on Dennis. He was wearing a flannel shirt with the sleeves rolled up, a look that reminded her of boys she'd known in college, who had all copied Neil Young. She quickly instructed herself not to pretend that Dennis was Neil Young; in her experience, that kind of association led to big trouble.

A bell rang and the crowd went back inside. She'd been curious to see what he would do when he was alone, yet with everyone else gone, she suddenly felt that she was the one alone. Dennis seemed to be surrounded by decent companions in the form of boxes of homemade brownies and jars of lemonade. She stepped into the driveway, grinding her cigarette under her toe.

"Come here, Lucy," he said without looking up.

She walked up to the stand. "I was spying on you," she confessed.

"Likewise." He snapped a large plastic lid on top of a tub of brownies.

"I'm not going to watch the rest of the play."

There was a pause.

"Should we go get a drink, or something?" she asked.

Dennis leaned across the refreshments table and laid his hands gently on her shoulders.

"Lucy, I have someone," he said. "I'm not really free."

Although technically nothing had happened, hearing him explain why nothing would made her feel as though something had, and she was automatically embarrassed for both of them.

"I wasn't suggesting anything but a drink." She forced herself to smile. "There's nothing wrong with a drink, is there? Between friends?"

It rained for several days, a warm, sweet rain that made the house smell like soil. The deck and the front walk were covered with flattened flowers and mushroom-colored slugs. On the first morning of the rain, Lucy woke up shivering. She pulled the blanket up to her chin and lay still on her back, watching the water fall like silver necklaces past her window. She imagined Nick lying in his bed on the ship, doing exactly the same thing. When she finally got up, she discovered that the roof had sprung leaks in several places. The floor was slick and icy-looking, the edges of the rugs heavy and dark. She went through the cabinets in the kitchen and placed as many pots as she could find strategically beneath the drips. Immediately the rooms grew loud with the pinging of rain on metal. It was as though the house had been turned inside out. She was nearly at the top of the stairs, on her way to take a shower, when the doorbell rang.

"You look like you have your hands full," Dennis said, eyeing the pots.

"That's all right, I'm glad to see someone from the outside world." She led him in. "I've been mopping and doing damage control since I got up." She smiled broadly, as though the morning had been funny, as though she was adaptable and carefree.

He placed his hands on his hips and thoughtfully examined the leaks in the ceiling. "The whole roof needs to be replaced." He spoke with a confidence that made her wonder how she'd managed alone. She wasn't up to roofs that needed replacing. She felt guilty, as though the leaking roof was her fault.

"What should we do?" She blushed. "I mean me. What should I do?"

"What you've done is just fine. Hugh will have to deal with it when he gets back. Do you have a backgammon board?" Dennis asked.

"What will that do?"

"It will kill some time."

"Oh." She shook her head, fanning her hair over her hot cheeks. "For some reason I thought you meant it could help with the rain."

He looked at her steadily. "It could."

She almost asked how, when she understood what he was really talking about. He likes me, she thought, and I . . . like him. Suddenly their attraction to each other seemed obvious, and she felt foolish for having allowed it to creep up on her by surprise. It was typical of Lucy to ignore the largest aspect of any situation, concentrating instead on the little details that, when she described them to other people, always sounded insignificant. In theory, she believed that the particular mirrored the general, but privately she thought the general was too much for her, that by its scope it was too apt to touch on her fears. In the big picture, she had to make decisions, whereas if she kept things small enough, there was a chance they would go away.

"Hugh keeps his games in the library. I'll go look," she said.

"Actually, I have a backgammon board in my car. You know how to play, don't you?"

"I always win."

"So do I."

They walked to the car, ignoring the rain. There were two dogs in the back seat, a shepherd mix and a Norfolk terrier.

"Oh, bring them inside!" Lucy said.

Dennis opened the door and the dogs leaped at her, scratching madly, clawing white marks into her tan. She patted them tentatively. It occurred to her that the dogs might belong to Dennis's girlfriend.

She tapped her leg, coaxing the dogs to follow. If they did belong to his girlfriend, she didn't really want to know. As she glanced back to make sure the dogs were following her up the steps, she saw Dennis take a bottle of wine from the car.

"You had all this planned, didn't you?" she said later.

"I didn't dare plan anything. Don't you remember, I left all my props outside."

His face hung so closely above hers that she couldn't look at him without feeling her eyes begin to cross. He smelled of wine and aftershave, and of the kind of perfumed soap she never used except in hotels. Already the mixture of these scents was familiar, even comforting.

"That was the cleverest part of the plan. To make it seem as though you were just stopping by to be nice, when all along you wanted to ravish me."

"I did?"

"Didn't you?"

He kissed her again. They were lying on the sofa in the living room, fully dressed, and he'd been kissing her for hours without doing anything else, which put her in the position of being the one to want more. She disguised her own growing warmth by laughing every so often. The dogs, however, circled excitedly, tongues out, noses in the air, and she knew she wasn't fooling anyone.

"You're not stupid," she said.

"And you're an angel."

It was nice to lie on the sofa and kiss. It was like being the teenager she never was, a girl who necked with boys cautiously, ready at any moment to break apart if her parents entered the room. She had never been like that. When she was a teenager, she believed that if she kissed a boy, she was obligated to go all the way; anything else was dishonest. As soon as boys realized she was as willing and reckless as they were, they didn't bother to take their time seducing her. She kept expecting Dennis to figure out that she was easy, and to respond by speeding up, but he seemed content just to kiss her as the rain plinked into the cooking pots.

No matter what he says, he must be getting bored, she thought. Anyway, she was ready for a cigarette. She sat up.

"Well." He stretched. "I guess I should go."

"Fine." The wine was gone, the daylight going. Her voice sounded sharp.

"I have work tonight," he said quickly.

"I thought this was a dark night at the theaters."

He colored slightly. "I didn't think you were paying such close attention."

"It doesn't take much attention to figure that out," she said. "If you have to go, you have to go, but don't lie."

"I do have to go."

"I understand. But remember, you owe me a rematch."

"No way. I know how to quit when I'm ahead." He smiled. "Walk me out?"

"You can't be a legitimate world champion unless you're willing to accept the challenge of a rematch."

He looked at her uncertainly. "Now?"

She nodded.

He looked at his watch. It was a good watch, she noticed.

"I need to make a phone call," he said.

She pointed at the wall phone in the kitchen and immediately ran upstairs. She sat down on the edge of her bed. The tree branches seemed ponderous and drained of color in the fading light. She heard his voice, little bursts of talk in a register slightly above the low steady drone of the rain. She couldn't hear what he was saying, but she felt sure he was making excuses to his girlfriend. She thought she should have let him leave when the moment had arisen; instead, she'd made an inference that amounted to her word, and she couldn't go back on it now. After all, she had already kissed him.

He slipped into the room. "I can stay, at least for a while."

"I'm glad," she said, lying back, her dark curls billowing out.

On all the rainy mornings, before Dennis came by, Lucy sat on a high stool in the kitchen and called her friends in New York.

"He's incredible," she said. "He knows exactly what to do without me having to tell him anything. All I have to do is go along for the ride, but somehow it's my ride. He's not very sophisticated, or educated, or any of that, but he has a real erotic intelligence and that is rare."

Her friends were happy for her. Since her five-year relationship had begun to fall apart two years earlier, she hadn't been interested in anyone except Nick, and none of her friends counted Nick.

She was afraid that when the rain ended it would all end; instead, when the sun emerged and she was able to lay the damp, animal-smelling rugs on the deck to dry, Dennis appeared on a motorcycle and began to take her out. He liked a different set of bars and restaurants than the places she went with Nick, which were either stylish or sleazy. Dennis didn't notice as much. He rarely looked around. He trained his eyes on her and kept them there until the bill was paid.

"What shall it be today, piña coladas or sea breezes?" she asked. "Whatever it is, I think we should order a pitcher."

Dennis frowned slightly.

"My treat," Lucy said.

"That's not right." He stared at the menu without reading it. They'd been to this restaurant three times in as many days and knew the menu by heart. When they arrived, the hostess had automatically led them to their favorite table on the balcony.

"What's not right? For me to treat you? I don't mind paying."

He pressed her foot with his. "But I like to take care of you, baby. It's just that I'm a little short this week."

"Don't worry about it. I'm not."

"Okay, I appreciate it."

"I think everything evens out in the end, don't you?"

He nodded.

"Dennis," she said quickly, before she lost her nerve, "how are you managing this?"

He stopped smiling. "She's visiting her grandparents."

"For how long?"

"Another week." He wrapped his hand over hers, squeezing hers against the glass. "She isn't here," Dennis said.

She isn't here, Lucy repeated to herself, and soon, with the help of the pitcher of planter's punch and Dennis's insistent presence, she forgot about his girlfriend. The afternoon slid into evening into another afternoon, a haze of rum and sun and breezes under ceiling fans. Once they took a tourist tour of the island and once they drove up the Keys, but usually they sat in one bar or another until they could no longer reasonably stay apart and had to head back to Hugh's. The first time they went out they made complicated arrangements not to be seen together, but once they were in each other's presence other concerns always evaporated, and it wasn't hard to convince themselves that the island, if not the whole world, was on their side.

On the day Nick and Hugh were due to return, Lucy and Dennis lay in bed, dozing lightly, the ceiling fan cooling their sticky bodies. They had not yet talked about what would happen when they no longer had the house to themselves, but it was clear that they wouldn't be able to meet as they had, and Lucy was beginning to feel bereft. Somehow she had lost control of the relationship. Their sexual connection had undermined her ability to be alone. Whenever he left, she grew fearful and couldn't wait to have him back.

"You look like a little boy." She touched the clean-shaven hollow under his lower lip. "Were you cute as a little boy?"

"My mother thought so."

"Were you thin, like you are now?" She pinched the skin on his leg.

"I was skinny. My sisters used to make me drink huge glasses of chocolate milk."

"I don't blame them." She burrowed closer, draping her leg over his abdomen. "It would be fun to have a little boy who looked like you."

He squeezed her. "Do you really think so?"

"Sure." She was looking at the ceiling, but she could feel him staring at her.

"I'd like to have a child with you," he said at last. He propped himself up on his elbow. "I can't believe I'm saying this, but it feels totally right." His features bespoke both tenderness and excitement. "We could have a baby."

Lucy had played this game before, with other boyfriends, too often to take it seriously.

"What would we name it?" she asked lightly.

He gripped her wrist. "I mean it, Lucy. We could have a baby, or two babies, or three. We could be together all the time. I'd love to be able to wake up every morning with an angel like you. Do you know how much that would change my life?"

"Are you asking me to marry you?" To her own ears, her voice sounded far away.

"I guess I am, if that's what you want."

She faced him. "Do you love me?"

He furrowed his brow. "Can't you tell?" He ran his fingers down her arm. "Haven't I shown you?"

"You've shown me you want me, but what I want to know is, do you love me? I mean really."

He was quiet for a moment. "Well, I want to know everything about you," he said. "I want to have a house with you, and kids, and old age. I want you to be happy." He looked at her questioningly, to see if he'd said enough.

"What about your girlfriend?"

"That's my problem, not yours."

She lit a cigarette and got out of bed. He sat up, pulling the sheet modestly over his lap.

"Should I really think about it?" she asked as she pulled on her shorts. "Are you sure it's what you want?"

"I promise I'll make you happy. Yes, I'm sure."

"Just tell me what you would do about her. I hate to think of myself as a home wrecker."

"If I loved her, don't you think I would have married her by now? There's no home to wreck with her. If I have a home at all, Lucy, you're it."

"I'm serious, Dennis."

"So am I."

Nick was paler than when he'd left. When Lucy asked him if he'd enjoyed himself, he said it had rained often on the trip, and when it was sunny, he hadn't liked lying by the pool. He brought her a straw hat, a straw bag, and a metal sculpture to hang on the wall. After giving his presents to her, he went upstairs and shut himself in the bathroom, leaving her to listen to Hugh's long-winded descriptions of the meals on the boat, the people at their table, and the major attractions of each port. She nodded and tried to ask polite questions as she emptied the dishwasher, thinking with some irritation how typical it was of Hugh to go on and on with his dry recitation without ever wondering if she was interested, without thinking to ask what had happened to her. He didn't offer to help her put the dishes away, and she realized with a flash of anger that, because she had taken care of his house, he now saw her as a species of servant, someone whose interest in the details of his life could be taken for granted.

"I'm driving up to Miami on Monday," Hugh said. "I could give you a ride to the airport then."

He'd finally come to the point of their little conversation, she thought. She sometimes suspected that he put up with her only to use her as a distraction for Nick, a way to sublimate energy that might otherwise have been drawn to more threatening pursuits. Hugh had a habit of telling Lucy intimate details about his life with Nick that were designed to demonstrate how hopeless her own case was; instead, Hugh's stories made her feel sorry for Nick, and determined to rescue him. Nevertheless, no matter how many skirmishes she outlasted or battles she survived, she had to admit that Hugh was winning the war. On an earlier visit, he'd been so anxious for her to leave that he'd paid for her ticket.

"Thanks," she said, "I'll let you know." She snapped the dishwasher shut. "By the way, when it rained, your roof leaked. I think it may have to be replaced."

Hugh immediately looked up.

"It was worst in the living room. I tried to keep everything dry, but there are some water stains on the ceiling."

He beckoned her to follow him, and she pointed out the areas where, in her own assessment, the problem was most serious. Hugh was immediately absorbed by the problem, so much so that he didn't hear the folding bedroom doors open upstairs. Soon Nick appeared in his bathing suit. He glanced at the two of them, his expression sullen.

"I'm going to the beach," he announced.

"I'll go with you," Lucy said.

Without giving any indication of whether he'd heard her or not, Nick strode through the house and allowed the front door to slam behind him.

"Excuse me, please," she said to Hugh.

She ran to the porch and quickly spun the lock on her bicycle. The combination sprang to mind automatically, although she hadn't thought of it for over a week.

She always kept her goggles and her flippers in the basket of her bicycle, so except for a bathing suit, she arrived at the beach prepared for a long, purifying swim. Nick had sped ahead of her and was already in the water by the time she reached his spot on the pier. She jumped into the water in her clothes.

"You're such a hippie," Nick giggled. Away from the house, his mood had improved.

They swam from their pier to a hotel pier a third of a mile away, where they climbed up the water-smoothed wooden ladder and lay on the hot boards. She pulled off her T-shirt and unhooked her bra.

"Not this again!" Nick cried. "All I saw on that boat were boobs."

"Any nice ones?"

"I guess. If you like that sort of thing."

She rehooked her bra and turned onto her stomach.

"You're such a baby," she said.

"I told you I'm emotionally arrested at eight. Eight-year-olds don't like boobs."

"Eventually they do."

"When they grow up."

"Exactly."

"Well, Lucy, do you think I show any signs of growing up?"

There was a pause.

"Could a cruise be that bad?" she asked at last.

"It wasn't the cruise, although that was queer enough. It was the company."

"So do something about it," she said coolly.

Nick flipped over and rested his head on his folded hands. He faced away from her.

"I'm sorry," she said.

"Don't be. You're perfectly right. I have no right to complain if I'm not willing to lift a finger on my own behalf."

She made a pillow of her soaked shirt and tucked it under her head. "No, it's all right. You should be able to complain to me whenever you want. I'm your best friend."

"You won't be, if I don't do something. You'll get sick of me."

"Why don't you at least get a job, so you can have your own money?"

"Because whenever I get a job Hugh buys tickets to somewhere and I have to quit to go with him. And don't say I don't have to quit. Objectively, I probably don't, but the reality is, I always do. For one thing, Hugh is my primary employer, and for another, when he dangles Egypt or Italy in front of me, it's hard to resist, although I usually wish I had by the time we're ready to leave."

"Listen," she said, "I've gotten myself into a situation, too."

"Really?" He brightened.

"Don't be such a voyeur. This is my life."

"Your life is my movie."

"Oh, great." She sighed. She'd had a respite from cleverness with Dennis, a break from Nick's rapacious need to be entertained and astounded, and, she saw in retrospect, it had been a relief not to have to bury her real desires in light amusements. She opened her eyes and stared at the sun for a few seconds, then shut her eyelids and watched the black and pink patterns that formed in space a few inches away from her head. The truth was, he wouldn't even acknowledge her needs or what she wanted, yet, because he was the one in the position to say no, he had forced her to accept him. The injustice of it maddened her. Yet how could she be truly mad at an eight-year-old?

"I have a new boyfriend, Nickie," she said in the tone with which she would address a child.

He propped himself up on his elbows. "Are you kidding? Do I know him?"

"Sort of." When she told him it was Dennis, he didn't move a muscle. "He wants to marry me."

"Don't we all." Nick rolled his eyes and nudged her with his elbow. "Get to the good part. What else?"

She laughed. "You have a way of putting things in perspective, don't you?"

"If perspective is what you call it."

"I think perspective is what I need at the moment."

She gave him the blow-by-blow, making fun of herself and her excesses, making it sound as though it had been just a fling, something for her to do while he was away.

Dennis left an envelope on the doorstep of Hugh's house with a note inside saying he was waiting for her answer to his proposal; he wrote that he could barely sleep. She hadn't spoken to him in the three days since Nick had come home, although he had called once and spoken to Hugh. She considered calling him back, but she had never called him before and was reluctant to change the pattern of how they knew each other; anyway, she figured his girlfriend must have returned. She had learned from Nick, who had been filled in by Hugh, that the house where Dennis lived belonged to his girlfriend, Babe Watkins. Lucy felt dizzy at the thought of calling and having her answer the phone.

"Are you seeing Dennis tonight?" Hugh asked.

"No, I think he's working," Lucy said. She had stayed close to the house, close to Nick. She didn't want to run the risk of running into Dennis before she knew what she wanted to say.

"So come to the Arts Council fund-raiser with us. It will be your last chance to see everyone before you leave."

She hadn't said anything definite about leaving, but in case she lost track of leaving as being her goal, she could always rely on Hugh to bring it up.

"I don't know anyone," she said.

"Does anyone really know anyone? You know who they are," Hugh said.

"We'll have fun. Please come, Lulu. What are you going to do here, watch television?" Nick asked.

"Since when did you have anything against television?"

"Please," said Nick pointedly, conveying the promise that if she came he would hang out with her, that he didn't want to be alone with Hugh.

"Yes, please," Hugh repeated politely.

"All right," she said to him, as if he had persuaded her, when the truth was that it still wasn't in her to forgo a minute when she could be with Nick. She thought there was not much chance that Dennis would be at the fund-raiser; the party would be for the patrons, and Dennis was the help.

An hour before they were due to leave the house, while she and Nick were in her bedroom trying on clothes, Hugh knocked on the door. They exchanged the resigned glance of children who know they are about to get into trouble.

"Come in," Lucy said.

Hugh had a box under his arm. "What are you guys wearing?" He always tried too hard.

"That's what we're figuring out," said Nick, an edge in his voice.

"Well, here, this may help." Hugh opened the box; it was full of jewelry.

Both Nick and Lucy sat down on the bed and began to pick through the treasure. There were several diamond necklaces, a stretchy diamond bracelet, nearly a dozen pairs of earrings, and various unidentifiable items, the uses for which had passed out of fashion.

"Where did you get this stuff?" Nick asked. "I've never seen it before."

"It was my mother's. I haven't had any reason to bring it out. None of it is real," Hugh said to Lucy. "It's all just paste, but you're welcome to any of it you'd like."

A bribe, Lucy thought.

"You mean to keep?" Nick asked, speaking for her.

"Oh, I couldn't," Lucy was then free to reply.

"Why not?" Hugh asked. "I have no one else to give it to. I doubt I'm going to get married."

Nick gave a sharp laugh.

"Try it on, at least," Hugh said.

Lucy picked out a heavy gold, sapphire, and diamond bracelet and tried to fasten it around her wrist.

"Allow me." Hugh hooked the catch.

"I love it," she said, turning her arm back and forth. She held it up for inspection.

"It has a couple of stones missing." Nick gripped her under the forearm with his right hand; with his left, he pressed the pads of her fingers back, as if he were a fortuneteller exploring her palm. His hands were moist and clung to her skin.

"Oh, that doesn't matter. It's so heavy! I love the weight of it." She stood up cautiously, being careful not to take her hand away from Nick, but he let go anyway. She kissed Hugh on the cheek. "Thank you."

"I'm not going to do anything with them," he repeated. His eyes darted around the room. Suddenly Lucy was struck with the realization that Hugh had given her the jewelry to gain entrance to their latest game, to try to be part of the group. For the first time in a long time she saw things from his point of view, a perspective that left her feeling sorry for him and ashamed of herself. No wonder nothing ever happened between her and Nick. She couldn't wrest Nick away from Hugh in his own house. As she looked back and forth between the two of them, she realized that no one but she had ever thought it might be possible.

"Why don't you show us what you're going to wear?" she said to Hugh, trying to make all her perfidies up to him at one stroke.

"Okay." Yet he didn't move. She guessed he was afraid to leave the room for fear that his welcome might be revoked in his absence.

"Would you like me to look in your closet with you?"

Nick glared at her.

She followed Hugh to his bedroom and made a great game of playing with his clothes, just as she did with Nick. Hugh warmed under the blaze of her attention and soon she was actually beginning to enjoy herself, even apart from the obvious pleasure she derived from effecting a transformation in Hugh. When they had nearly arrived at a decision — white pants and a light blue shirt, conservative yet complementary — she heard Nick enter the room and flop down on the bed. He began to sing in a soft, melancholy voice designed to pull them back into his orbit. What a baby, Lucy thought as she rolled up Hugh's sleeves.

For a while, as she watched Nick moving easily through the throngs at the party, complimenting a dress here, delivering a drink there, nonchalantly ignoring her, she thought that she had created a monster, but that, of course, was flattering herself; the monster had been created long before she came along. It astonished her that someone so childish could be so effective, yet once again she acknowledged that, in spite of all her insights and her current mood of detachment and disdain, he was controlling her even now by making her keep track of him. She couldn't even get Nick to take her seriously or feel jealous when she flirted with anyone else, which she supposed was her fault as she had made it clear over several years that she found no one else as compelling as Nick. He hadn't been at all convinced of the importance of Dennis. Without trying, Nick had forced her to worship him from afar, and the contortions she went through to maintain her equilibrium as she controlled her passion were efforts she cast as a path to strengthening her character. It came to her now that people had tried to tell her all along that she was deluding herself; she had thought they didn't understand.

Nick disappeared into another room with several acquaintances from the theater boards, affording her an opportunity to escape. She felt more in control the moment he was out of her sight, when her memory and sense of self weren't so obliterated by his perfect features. She retraced the route to the front door and left the building. As she walked out the driveway, she looked up at the hundreds of stars that hung low in the dark sky. The street was quiet except for the occasional crunch of a leather shoe on asphalt, or a burst of laughter ricocheting among the old brick walls of the refurbished commercial buildings along the harbor. As the party went on behind her, the sound of individual voices leaped out, as if sent as emissaries from an invisible spirit of the night to draw her back into the fray. Once or twice she was sure she heard Hugh's nasal drone and Nick's attractive laugh rising above the din, their voices brushing by her like bats. She had once believed that everything had a material existence, ideas as well as things, which explained why words had so much power to hurt. Now she thought it might be more comforting to believe, as Nick did, that nothing was real. Again she imagined she distinguished Nick's laugh from among all the laughs that floated like ghosts across the lawn. Quickly, and with great purpose, she walked away from it.

She'd been walking for some time in a deep state of self-absorption when she saw that she'd arrived in front of the Little Theater where she'd assumed Dennis would be working that night. The building was decorated with strings of white lights along its edges, making it look Christmassy and quaint. It actually wasn't a theater at all, but a converted barn in back of an old house on the main street. In the old house someone was practicing piano, someone who played well. Lucy crept up the driveway, wincing at the din created by her own careful footsteps. When she came to the end of the drive, she saw that Dennis's refreshment stand was empty. She walked around it, touching the wood and the padlocks as if there had been some mistake. For the past two days she had been carrying him and his proposal around in the back of her mind, calling up images of him whenever she wanted, assuming that she knew where he was and what he was doing at all times, as if he would remain in a state of suspended animation until she was ready to conjure him up again. It shook her to realize she had no idea where he was. Suddenly she longed to see him, and wondered how she could have stayed apart from him for so long.

It was too far for her to walk back to the house in her sandals; she steeled herself to return to the party, where she could get a ride from somebody, if not from Hugh. As she headed back toward the wharf, she tried to keep her attention in the moment by spying on still-life tableaux through lighted windows and trying to distinguish the scents of flowers one from the other, providing them with names if she wasn't sure of them. She remembered that she'd been artistic until she met Nick; now she was merely creative, expressing herself by naming scents or setting a beautiful table. She realized that, though she'd never looked better in her life, she'd actually let herself go. It was Nick's fault. She was turning herself inside out to be attractive to him, and what for? She wasn't even sure how she'd drifted into this predicament.

When she'd met him at a dinner party in New York a few years earlier, she'd thought of him as a little brother, a friend. She'd even been amused when he seemed to have a crush on her. He'd been the one who called the next day; he started the friendship. He was the one who kept in touch with her when he returned to Key West. He wrote. He called. He adored her, and it was easy to adore him back. It had been easy right up to the moment when it became impossible.

Back at the bar, she asked for a rum and Coke. Hugh was in a conversation with some people she recognized from previous parties. He shot her a mute plea for rescue, but she pretended not to see it. She spotted Nick standing in the doorway that led to a large room set aside for dancing. When Nick saw her, he shook his head slightly, a gesture she later realized was a warning to turn back before it was too late, but she had armed herself against him so thoroughly by then that she saw him only as a reflection of her own defenses.

"Excuse me." She pushed past him as if he were a stranger.

She felt him grope for her hand, but she wrapped her arms around her rib cage and he couldn't catch her. She was still holding her drink; the condensation on the outside of the glass dampened her cotton dress. A band was set up in the far corner of the room, but the seat behind the drum kit was empty, the other instruments on nearby tables or on the ground. A man she recognized from afternoons at the pier stood protectively by the electric piano. The rest of the room was filled with people she didn't know or knew only slightly. She was working up her courage to go speak to the man by the electric piano when she spotted, tipped back in a chair by the far wall, her lover, Dennis. He looked more deeply tanned than she remembered. He wore a pair of new jeans that she didn't think she'd ever seen, and an Oxford shirt with too many buttons undone. At his side, in another chair, sat an older woman whom Lucy intuitively recognized as Dennis's girlfriend. She had her hand in Dennis's and she sparkled as she talked to him, making an effort to please. Dennis smiled perfunctorily as Babe spoke to him. He drained his beer. When he stood up and headed for the bar, she went with him, her bare arm wrapped around his waist. Lucy watched them work their way across the room. They seemed to know everyone. They behaved as a couple, but not as an old married couple who were content to split up and work the room separately; they behaved more like newlyweds, or people who'd met on vacation and were now intent on sharing their hazy bliss with the real world.

"Do you want to leave?" Nick tugged at the back of her dress, his eyes blazing with concern.

"I'm all right," she snapped.

"She's not very pretty."

"She has a womanly look, though. Men like that."

"She *is* friendly."

"You've met her?" Lucy asked in surprise.

"Once or twice."

"Why didn't you tell me?"

"I don't really know her, and frankly, I didn't want to talk about it."

"That's not like you. You usually love to talk about people." Lucy studied his profile. In spite of her new resolve, she was still moved by his face. "You disapprove of me." As she spoke, she knew she was right.

"I have no right to."

"That doesn't mean you don't."

"Don't look now, but we've been spotted."

Heat crawled up her neck; she turned her back to the bar. "What are they doing?"

"He's coming over."

She reached for Nick's sleeve. "Stay with me."

"Lucy?"

She heard Dennis's voice behind her. She turned around.

"Hello, Dennis," she said formally. "You know Nick."

Nick said hello.

"Lucy, may I talk to you alone?" Dennis asked.

"You're not exactly alone," she said bitterly.

"Should I be?"

"I'll see you later," Nick said.

"What do you mean, should you be?" She saw Nick join Hugh in the doorway. "You asked me to marry you."

"And you didn't give me an answer yet."

"So what are you doing, hedging your bets?"

"I want you, Lucy. I want to be with you. You're the one who hasn't made up your mind yet."

"So if I say no, you'll stay with her?"

"Probably."

"That's a little cold, isn't it?"

He shrugged. "I'm in love with you, but I don't like to live alone, either."

Over his shoulder, she saw Babe coming toward them. "I don't want to fight," she said. "Your friend is coming this way."

Babe slipped her arm through Dennis's and proffered Lucy a small, freckled hand. "Hi, I'm Babe Watkins."

Automatically Lucy held out her hand.

Babe turned to Dennis. "I'm getting tired. Would you mind going home early?"

"Would you excuse us?" Dennis said awkwardly.

He took a step backward, and Lucy felt everything slipping away from her as he moved to leave. She could not put the pieces of everything that was happening together fast enough to see clearly where she belonged among these people; all she knew was that she could not bear to have Nick go off with Hugh and Dennis go off with Babe; she could not bear to be the one left alone.

"Yes, you're excused," said Lucy. She looked straight at Dennis, willing him to understand that she would marry him. "My answer is a definite yes."

🐦

When she reached Miami on her way back to the island from a two-week stay at her parents' house in Philadelphia, Lucy found that all flights south were canceled owing to a sudden storm. Impulsively, she followed the signs for the VIP lounge. When no one stopped her, she took a seat and ordered a drink. Soon she was joined by a trio of businessmen, and she laughed with them freely as the rain battered the picture windows in rhythmic waves. Her engagement to Dennis had rendered her invulnerable to the kind of attention that used to be confusing and, most often, unwanted. Saying that she was getting married was a passport to a world she hadn't known existed. It was a pleasant world, full of inside tips and helpful hints, but there was something creepy about it, too. As she talked to her married friends and her mother's married friends, she almost felt as though her engagement had caught her in a net that was tightening by the minute.

She supposed she was having pre-wedding jitters. Everyone she knew had had them to some extent. She reminded herself that, in this instance, a case of nerves was particularly justified. Her whole life had changed so quickly. If Dennis hadn't come back to Hugh's house that night after he'd taken Babe home from the fund-raiser, Lucy might have lost her nerve. He had appeared in her bedroom and made her know that the hardest decision was over, promising he would make things easy from then on out. The next morning, he surprised her by asking Nick to be their best man, and she trusted him to go on figuring out what to do next.

When the rain let up, she headed over to the runway. The plane was a small eight-seater. She'd been told it was safer than a jumbo jet, but it didn't feel safer. Whenever she'd flown down to meet Nick, she'd imagined the plane crashing into a mangrove swamp, Nick crumbling onto the tarmac when he heard the news. Now that she was flying to meet Dennis, she wanted desperately to stay alive. She wasn't sure how he would react if she were killed in a crash, but he was too stalwart for his response to make her death worthwhile. If she died in a crash on her way to meet Nick, the incident would fester in him forever, and he would tell it as a secret to anyone who became important in his life. Dennis would grieve, but eventually he would get over it.

She willed the plane to stay afloat.

"Vacation?" the man across from her asked. She could barely hear him over the roar of the engine.

"More like relocation," she yelled. "I'm getting married and moving down here."

He gave her a thumbs-up sign. It was another example of how her life was continually being validated since she had become engaged. She pulled a sweater over her head and squirmed in her seat, trying to find a comfortable position. When she admitted to herself that there was no chance for a nap, she pulled the packet of letters Dennis had sent her from her bag. He'd written her every day during her stay at her parents' house as she planned the wedding. His letters were barely grammatical, a discovery that had made her uneasy at first, until she reminded herself that literacy was not the most important thing in a marriage. She had plenty of friends to talk to if she wanted to discuss books. When she'd finished reading the letters and drawn what strength she could from Dennis's sweet, misspelled, romantic remarks, she closed her eyes and leaned back against the seat, her body vibrating to the rhythm of the engine.

She remembered talking to Dennis on the phone in the library of her parents' house, her mother looking on, nodding encouragement, which was so unlike her; the role of mother-of-the-bride had brought out unseen aspects of her personality. It was important to her mother that "things be done right," no matter how modest the wedding plans. She refused to waste money on a florist and planned to do the flowers herself, with the help of her friends, but she insisted on buying decent champagne. She thought it was silly to spend money for engraved invitations when thermography produced perfectly acceptable results, but she was willing to pay for first-rate musicians, on the condition that there would be no flutes, and absolutely no harps. They planned the wedding for the beginning of June, to be held at her parents' house. Rows of chairs would be set up for a ceremony in the yard, followed by a reception indoors and out: the rugs rolled back but not removed, the flagstone terrace decorated with azaleas, butter-crème icing on the layer cake.

Dennis had called her father, who made Dennis promise to buy a life insurance policy before the wedding day. Dennis made a separate phone call to her mother to say how privileged he was to be marrying Lucy, how great his luck. He called Lucy every night after work from a pay phone outside the Theater by the Sea and made her laugh as he described the people walking by; through his descriptions, she pictured island life vividly. He mailed her a blank check for the wedding rings, and a brochure of the Caribbean hotel where he wanted to take her for their honeymoon. She existed in an impregnable bubble of excitement until she could see him again.

Unlike Nick, who always stood on the tarmac waving his arms as the plane banked in, Dennis waited until she entered the terminal building before he sprang at her, a glass of planter's punch in one hand, a Polaroid camera in the other. He kissed her deeply, as if they were alone, but not before she saw him notice that she'd gained several pounds.

"I have the car outside," he said when they broke apart. As if to demonstrate the truth of this, he jangled his keys.

She laughed.

"What's so funny?" His face clouded with bewilderment. He had dressed for the occasion in shiny brown loafers and a new shirt.

"I don't know. I mean, I assumed you had the car outside. How else would you have gotten here?"

"I could have gotten a lift from somebody," he said dejectedly.

She slipped her arm through his with a deep sense that it was up to her to rescue the event.

"Here's the ring." She held her hand up to him. Her mother had given her a family ring.

"It's awfully plain," he said. "Are you sure it's what you want?"

"Yes. I love it."

"As soon as I have enough money, I'll buy you something better. Did you get the wedding rings?"

"They're being engraved." She looked at her ring again and was about to explain to him what was so special about it when he gripped her arm tightly, as if to steady himself, and she saw he was exhausted. His skin was gray with strain. He held on to her for a moment, then seemed to pull himself back together. A little color returned to his face.

"Are you all right?"

"I stayed up late, cleaning."

They collected her bags and walked to the car as he told her about the house. He had arranged for them to stay in a place that was being renovated by a friend for future sale.

"I can't wait to see it," she said breezily as they crossed the parking lot. He perked up and began to tell her all he'd done on their behalf, but his voice was the voice of a stranger and his descriptions of what she could expect from her new life seemed all to do with another girl. She realized she'd backed herself into a corner by saying she wanted to see the house. Being at the house would mean being in bed, and she hadn't had time yet to get used to Dennis again enough for that; she needed time. In the car, he leaned his forehead against the steering wheel and sighed deeply.

"What's wrong?" she asked, frightened by his intensity.

He wiped his mouth with his hands, then ran his fingers

through his hair. "I'm so glad to have you back. Come here, kiss a boy."

She went into his arms, but the first moment he came up for air, she asked him if they couldn't go somewhere and get themselves a drink, before they went home.

"Nick? We're here," she said in a singsong, imitating a line from a movie they'd seen together.

There was a pause on the other end of the line. "Welcome back," he said finally.

"I just got in this afternoon. Dennis had to go to work and I'm supposed to be unpacking." She looked around at the piles of sheet rock leaning against the walls, the layer of sawdust on the floor and windowsills. "Do you want to come keep me company?"

"Can't tonight. I promised some people I'd go out with them."

"Oh."

"Sorry."

She looked up at the ceiling and blinked, her eyes stinging.

"Are you still there?" Nick asked in a friendlier tone.

"Uh-huh."

There was another, longer pause.

"How about meeting for a swim tomorrow?" she said when she had regained control of herself. "Usual time, usual place?"

"Sounds good, but I won't be able to say for sure until tomorrow."

"Did you get a job?" If she remembered correctly, she'd talked to him ten days earlier, and he hadn't been so busy then.

"Fiske Larson asked me to be his assistant on the new play, so I have to go to rehearsals every night."

"Congratulations!" she said brightly. "What are you doing?"

"*Bye Bye Birdie,* in drag."

"That was my idea."

"That's right, it was. I forgot about that."

She was hurt. More than anything, she hated not to get credit for her ideas, meager as they had been lately. She asked more questions about the play. She even tried to coax Nick back into their old private world by making a joke about Hugh, but Nick remained distant.

"Is anything wrong?" she asked when she sensed he was about to hang up.

Coolly, he replied that everything was fine; it was the way he talked to Hugh.

"Well, I'm glad you're all right. Tomorrow, then?"

"I'll call you."

"Great," she said, feeling homesick for the first time in years.

The next day, she went shopping with Dennis for flour and sugar and spent the morning helping him mix up big vats of brownie batter. When Dennis wanted to take her out to lunch she made an excuse to stay at the house so she could be close to the phone. Whenever Dennis left the room she lifted the receiver to make sure the equipment was working. She was almost relieved when Dennis said he had to make several calls; she could tell herself that Nick was trying to call her but couldn't get through. When he hadn't called by three o'clock she rode her bike over to his house, where she found Nick and several other men lying on beige plastic chaises around the pool. One of the men held a finger to his lips and pointed to Nick.

"Ssh. He's asleep."

She smiled and stood there awkwardly for a few minutes, watching Nick sleep, not knowing quite what to do next. Normally she would have headed to the refrigerator for a glass of iced tea or a slice of the Key lime pie that Nick made on a regular basis, but that option no longer seemed open to her; she did not live in the house anymore. She almost wished Hugh would appear. He would, at least, be polite to her.

She walked toward the umbrella-topped table and chairs on the other side of the pool and was about to sit down when Fiske Larson materialized out of the shadows of the house and sped toward her. He wore an open shirt that emphasized his emaciation, and a bright green bikini.

"Welcome back," he said.

She shook his hand. It was light and formless. "I hear you're doing *Bye Bye Birdie*," she said. "That was my idea."

"Really? Yes, I suppose Nick mentioned that." He looked across the deck at Nick's placid face. He loves Nick, too, Lucy thought. He turned back to her. "And you're getting married?"

"That's the plan."

"Congratulations."

They smiled awkwardly.

"Well, as you see, Nick's asleep. He had a late night," said Fiske, "and he's in store for another one, so I don't think we should wake him up now." He flicked his index finger like a windshield wiper across his mustache as he peered at her intently; she had a sense that whatever gesture she made next would be something he would someday use in his work. She chose not to move at all.

"Do you want to wait for him to wake up?" he asked.

"No, that's all right. Just ask him to call me." She looked at Nick again. His chest rose and fell gently. "He's supposed to go swimming with me later."

Fiske considered this information. "He made plans with me for the whole afternoon."

"Well. Tell him to call."

Dennis was out when she arrived at the house. There was a note for her on the bed saying he'd gone to the pier in hopes of finding her there; if not, he planned to swim anyway. Automatically she got back on her bike and had ridden two blocks in the direction of the beach before she realized she was too tired to go anywhere. She returned to the house and ate a spoonful of brownie batter before lying down for a nap.

"Why don't we take a drive, sweetie?" Dennis said a few nights later, on an evening when he didn't have to work. "Put on something nice, we'll find some place to eat."

Lucy shut herself in the bathroom before removing her clothes to shower, because if she undressed in front of Dennis he would want to make love and, once they started, they might never leave the house all night. She wanted to go some place clean. The floor of the bathtub was gritty with the sawdust that had penetrated everywhere. She was certain her lungs must be full of it. She didn't want to ruin Dennis's high opinion of her by being anything other than the kind of girl who never complained about superficial things, but privately she'd begun to resent the mess. After drying off, she put on a purple sundress and asked Dennis to zip it up for her. He gripped the material at her waist and tightened his lips as he concentrated on his chore, but the zipper stopped midway up her back and would go no further.

"Is it stuck?" she asked, holding her hair off her neck.

"I don't think so." He grunted with effort. "I think it's just too tight. You'd better wear something else."

She quickly put on a bra, which she hadn't needed under the sundress, and changed into a skirt and blouse.

"How's this?"

Dennis was shaving. He glanced at her out of the corner of his eye as he pulled at the skin on his neck. "You look fine. Your hair looks pretty."

"I wish we had a full-length mirror. Maybe I'm gaining weight because I can't see how I look. Also, I'm not smoking as much," she added defensively.

Dennis laid his razor down and faced her. "This place isn't working out, is it?"

"It's okay," she answered automatically.

"No it isn't. It's a mess and you've been incredibly sweet and patient to put up with it, but I think we should start looking for our own place."

She laughed lightly. "Well, I have to admit, the thought had crossed my mind."

"Why didn't you say anything?"

"I don't know. I guess I didn't want you to get mad at me."

"Come here. Come on, come over here." She obeyed and was rewarded with a hug. "I can't think of anything you could do that would make me mad at you. I'm going to be your husband. You have to tell me when you're unhappy, otherwise the marriage won't work."

"You're right," she said, although she didn't completely believe that he wanted to hear about her unhappiness. It had always undone her even though it was her own and she understood it. Why should he handle it any better?

"We'll start looking tomorrow."

During the drive up the islands they discussed how they wanted things to be when they returned from the honeymoon, and though Lucy had the sense that everything they said had been said before by other couples, the conversation still seemed fresh and thrilling, as though they were affording a striking and original interpretation to the lines of a great play. They decided they needed a new car, as his was Babe's old one and he would be obliged to return it soon; they discussed what a waste it was to pay rent, how it would really be more economical to buy a place — they could always rent part of it or even start a bed and breakfast; they decided that she should try for a job on the paper, or better yet, at the radio station. She was starting over; it was an opportunity to try for exactly what she wanted.

"You won't have any trouble finding something," Dennis said. "I'm sure you can do whatever you want."

"You too."

All during dinner she gazed at Dennis gratefully. She knew that marriage was a big step, but somehow it hadn't registered until now that what it really meant was that she no longer had to be alone. She felt wave after wave of gratitude toward him for picking her, for always shaving so he wouldn't scratch her, for insisting the hostess move them away from their window table when she could no longer bear to watch the porpoises swim circles in the cement tank outside, for not criticizing aloud when she drank and smoked, for providing her with a constant supply of brownie batter and lemonade.

On the dark ride home, they stretched their arms out the window to feel the push of the hot wind. Dennis sang along with a Sam Cooke tape; Lucy counted seven shooting stars. On their way past an empty stretch of beach, Lucy suggested they get out and take a walk. Dennis pulled to a stop.

"It's so beautiful," she said. She reached for his hand.

Dennis looked at her. "Wait here a second."

He hopped out of the car, leaving the door open. She heard his leather shoes scrape the grit on the road, then the sound of him rummaging around in the trunk. The trunk slammed shut and he appeared beside her on her side of the car. He handed her a canvas bag.

"Go ahead," he said. "Look."

Curiously, she reached her hand into the bag and pulled out a variety of strange objects that she didn't recognize for what they were until she looked up and saw the twist in Dennis's grin. She dropped everything back into the bag and thrust it at him. "No," she said, unable to manage anything more.

"What?" He took the bag, but still held it toward her.

"That stuff is not for me. I'm not interested."

"There's nothing wrong with it," he said. "It can be fun to experiment a little."

"I'm not into it," she said. "Maybe I'm a prude, but I've never wanted to try anything like that."

He slid into the car beside her, wrapping her in his arms. "Ssh, it's all right. Ssh." He soothed her as though she had been crying.

"Let's just forget it, okay?"

He smoothed her hair. "Ssh."

She closed her eyes and leaned against him. He whispered to her and stroked her until her mind went blank. He laid her on the seat and undressed her slowly, urging her to be with him with nothing but his own hands.

After looking for several days, they rented an apartment on Flagler Avenue in what had been advertised as a contemporary building, which turned out to mean it was constructed of cinder block. It was owned by a middle-aged couple who had come to the island as hippies in the sixties and grown rich by buying property in the right places at the right time. Dennis and Lucy rented the first floor of the building. They had a living room/ dining room/kitchen, a bedroom and bath, and a fenced patio where they could lock their bikes. Their rent was six hundred dollars a month, more than Lucy paid for her rent-stabilized apartment in New York, but there was no security deposit and no length-of-stay requirement, which was why they decided to rent this place rather than one of the more charming apartments they looked at in the older part of town. They figured that they'd be buying a house soon enough, so there was no point entering into any arrangement from which it might be difficult to free themselves when they wanted. As soon as they'd paid the first month's rent, however, Lucy knew they'd made a mistake. There were no rugs on the poured cement floors and the rooms received only a sliver of sun in the late afternoon, and only in the back. Her feeble efforts to rearrange the furniture and decorate the walls with her scarves and necklaces made the apartment look worse.

"Let's go to my storage locker," said Dennis. "We can get some things out of there to make it nice."

The storage company was on an island near the Naval Air Station. When they arrived the ground was shaking with the vibrations of jets revved up and ready to take off, and they had to wait for the military activity to die down before Dennis could hold his hand steady enough to fit the key in the lock.

"There's nothing to most of these islands," he said. "Either you've got mangrove or coral, neither of which is anything to bank on in my book."

He didn't seem to be talking to her. She looked down the rows of storage lockers and wondered if owning a storage facility was a good business, as her mind was on money these days. Somehow it seemed to be a very American business; she couldn't remember seeing private storage facilities in any other country.

"Who uses these anyway?"

Dennis squinted at the sky. "You'd be surprised. The guy who manages the place told me that it's mostly people from the trailer parks. Then, of course, there are the Key Westers who leave their houses empty all summer. They usually want to put a few things away." He grinned. "I could tell he was fishing around to figure out which group I was in."

"Did you tell him?"

"I said I was getting a divorce."

"Did you tell him your wife had left you to join the Navy?" she teased.

"It wasn't funny at the time."

Lucy's heart bumped. "You mean it really happened? I thought you were joking."

He turned the key and lifted the door. "It really happened all right."

A blast of heat blew out of the locker. Lucy followed Dennis inside, hooking her index finger through a belt loop on his shorts as though he were guiding her by touch. Although they were only a few feet from the sunlight, the locker was musty and dark. Dennis pulled a chain, lighting the naked bulb overhead. The locker was the size of the maid's room in Lucy's apartment, which was similarly packed to the ceiling with all kinds of boxes and upturned furniture. Dennis squinted at the labels and began to pull things down.

"Don't just stand there." He nudged her. "Look around; let me know what you think would be good."

She reached out a hand toward nothing in particular; she touched a piece of frayed rope. Everything had been packed carefully, as though it were all precious cargo being shipped to a pretty house rather than the detritus of what even she, his fiancée, would characterize as an unspectacular life. As she studied the careful descriptions of contents that Dennis had written in black Magic Marker on the sides of the boxes ("*National Geographic* Dec 1974–Aug 1978," "Letters from Family," "Narrow Ties") she had some sense of what he had gone through on her behalf while she was talking to caterers and studying typefaces in Philadelphia.

She wondered if Babe had left the house while he packed, or if she had stayed to make sure none of her own things disappeared into his boxes. She wondered what they had said to each other when he left for the last time. Had he given her back the house keys? Did he say good-bye to the dogs? Did he feel regret at the last moment, or was he sure he was doing the right thing? For that matter, what had he and his first wife said to each other when she left him for the Navy?

"This has been hard for you, hasn't it?" Lucy said.

He wiped his forehead with the heel of his palm. "These are interesting times."

"There are so many things we haven't talked about. I don't really know about your relationships, for example."

"We'll have plenty of time to talk."

"I don't even know what your first wife was called, or if you still keep in touch."

"Christmases." He piled several throw pillows in a corner and hoisted a carton back to its former spot. "We send cards. She's stationed in Germany. Her name was Marybeth."

"Did she take your last name?"

"Yes. She still uses it."

Lucy wondered what he expected her to do about her name; she had always planned to keep it as it was. She decided to let it go for the moment. "Why did she join the Navy?"

He pulled another box down. "She was working at a time-share resort, trying to sell slots, and all of a sudden she got the idea that her job was a dead end. She wanted a real career. Every day she drove past the naval base and that big Recruitment Center sign. She put two and two together and joined up."

"It sounds like something out of a movie."

"I guess I didn't help," Dennis said. "I told her a lot of stupid things about the Army, to impress her, you know, and I guess she just wanted to see it all for herself." He grunted ruefully. "The Army should hire her to do their advertising."

She leaned against the wall of boxes. "You were in the Army?"

"I never told you that?"

"I think I would have remembered that." She shook her head.

"Well, after what happened with Marybeth, I don't really play it up, either."

She couldn't do anything but stare at him. She didn't know anyone younger than her father's general age who had joined the Army.

"Wait a minute." He held up a finger, signaling her not to move. She stood obediently still as he rummaged among the boxes, finally locating the one he wanted on the floor against the back wall of the locker. Rather than moving everything above it, he worked his hands along the side of the box and crouched in front of it. For a moment he was completely still; then, in one swift motion, he pulled the box toward him with the assurance and dexterity of a magician pulling a tablecloth out from under a set of plates. The other boxes fell easily into place, making only a small thump as they landed. He looked up at her and grinned.

"Old Army trick." He cut the twine securing the box with a pocket knife. "See, here's my dog tags." She bent down to look, and he slipped them over her head. "Here's all my stuff."

She curled her fingers tentatively over the rim of the box and peered inside. There were clothes and metal dishes, a canteen in an olive drab canvas case, some yellowed magazines.

"Here's the real pièce de résistance of even more interesting times than these." He handed her a helmet. Rather than the French pronunciation, he had used, on purpose she thought, the English "peace" and "resistance." The helmet was covered with a worn netting. Several folded sheets of paper and what looked like an animal tooth were lodged beneath the chin strap.

"It's ARVN."

"Really? How did you get it?"

"Take it if you want," he said. "Take it back to the apartment, but don't ask me any stories about it because I ain't got no more to tell," he said, lapsing into a diction she'd never heard him use before. In the past, she would have assumed the accent was a joke; now she wasn't sure.

"You were in Vietnam?" she asked quietly.

He pointed to the helmet. "Here it is, thirty-two, my unfucking lucky draft number. Yes I was in V-yet-nam."

"What was it — "

He held up his hand. "Don't bother asking, honey, 'cause as it happens these days I can't remember anything about it."

He stood up and began reading the labels on the highest boxes. He stretched his arms up, untucking his shirt, baring his torso so she could see his slight hipbones, his fragile spine.

"I'll take this, if you don't mind."

"Huh?"

She pointed to the helmet.

He shrugged. "Sure, I said you could. It's all yours."

The radio station didn't have any openings, but the manager told her to make a demo tape and they'd keep it on file. The editor of the newspaper, although he seemed to believe her when she said she knew she could write if given the chance, would not hire her without clippings or at least a few writing samples.

"Just get out there and put a few articles together," Dennis said. "There are a million stories on the naked island — if you count the fish."

"Very funny. Anyway, I doubt they'll like what I have to say. My perspective is too dark."

"So? Don't write from your perspective. Write the kind of article you think they'll want to read, the kind that will get you the job. Work your way up to dark."

"You don't think it's unethical for me not to say what I think?"

"Honey, frankly no one cares what you think. Just write about something they want to, or better yet, need to know."

She considered writing witty, upbeat articles about the restaurants she'd gone to with Dennis, or the sights they'd seen in the first flush of their romance, but she didn't want to expose her own secrets, and anyway, she wasn't convinced that her tastes were universal. She thought about writing movie reviews, but the people on the island were strong-minded and had opinions of their own. What did the people want? If they were anything like her, she thought, they might want to know what was going on every night at the Theater by the Sea. She decided to interview Nick.

She'd barely seen him at all since she'd been back. Once she'd run into him at the supermarket and once she'd followed him on her bike until he noticed her and stopped to say hello, but each time he'd been in a hurry to get back to the theater. At least, if she interviewed him, she'd have a chance to spend some time with him.

She decided to include Fiske Larson in the deal, both to preclude any awkwardness with Nick and to validate her purpose of producing a salable article for the newspaper; she made it clear that the topic was to be *"Bye Bye Birdie:* Why Everyone Should Come Out to See It," which, as a working title, provided her subjects with a structure they would think of no reason to fear. She arranged a lunch meeting with them at the Flamingo Patio, calling ahead to reserve an out-of-the-way table where they wouldn't be disturbed, a touch that seemed professional if unnecessary in those particular environs. Ten minutes before the scheduled rendezvous, she checked her tape recorder for the hundredth time and ordered a drink.

Nick arrived first. She watched him swing his bike in a wide U-turn in the street, his shirttails flapping in the wind. He locked his bike to the peeling picket fence in front of the building and pulled himself together by using his fingertips to comb his white-blond hair. Suddenly he stopped and looked at the restaurant. She began to raise her hand to wave at him, but even as she tilted her fingers to the left she knew it was a superfluous, girlish gesture, all right for Dennis, utterly beside the point with Nickie. After all, he was already staring at her. If nothing else, she thought, she still had the capacity to will him to look at her across a crowded room, which effectively answered the most pressing question she had for him.

He spotted her and joined her at the table. "Are we recording?" he asked.

"Not yet. Should we start?"

"Fiske would probably want us to wait for him."

She placed her hands in her lap and tried to wait with some composure through the awkward lull in the conversation.

"You look pretty," Nick said finally.

"I'm too fat."

"You're hiding it well. Would I be scared to see you in a bathing suit?"

"No more than usual."

Nick laughed. They ordered drinks. He grabbed her wrist and looked at her watch.

"Fiske is definitely coming. He's really nervous about the show," Nick said, as if nerves were a known cause of tardiness.

"How's it going?" she asked.

"Good, good. I can't believe how talented the people here are. The girl who's doing the sets is incredible."

Lucy thought that she could have done the sets if anyone had asked her. She hoped Nick hadn't forgotten that she was incredible, too.

"Is Hugh letting you do your job, or has he scheduled a trip to Europe for opening night?"

Nick flinched. "He's been great. He's into it."

Lucy saw he wasn't going to talk to her, not really. She actually was relieved when Fiske showed up, so she could turn on her tape recorder and ask the questions she'd prepared.

Later, after she'd transcribed the interview and sat down to write the piece, Lucy found herself incapable of coming up with an acceptable first sentence. Each time she tried a new approach she inserted a fresh sheet of paper into Dennis's old typewriter. Each time she failed she pulled the paper carefully out of the platen and laid it in a pile beside her, thinking she could use it for future drafts. At the end of the evening, just before Dennis was due home, she counted the discarded sheets and found that she had written thirty-nine lead sentences. The fact that she had spent an evening writing the same number of failed sentences as the number of years her future husband had been alive was a detail that did not escape her attention, but she refused to make something of it and wrote one last sentence to break the spell.

> Nick Stephanhoff has said before that he considers it to be his tragic flaw that he cannot be with Lucy Langworthy in the way that men can be with women. Shrewd observers will perhaps see some connection between his perceived personal failure and the professional success he is currently enjoying in his role as director's assistant to Fiske Larson for the current production of "Bye Bye Birdie" at the Theater by the Sea, which was Lucy Langworthy's idea in the first place.

She took the stack of sheets that she had planned to use for other writing and carefully cut them into two-inch horizontal strips. She placed the blank strips along with her new blue pencil on the counter in the kitchen, figuring that Dennis could use them for shopping lists, figuring that she was no longer even creative but merely crafty, and capable only of coming up with small ideas that might make life easier. In this spirit, she soaked a cotton ball in witch hazel and used it to clean the typewriter keys. She sealed the sheaf of sentences in an envelope and walked to the corner of her block, where she threw them away in a municipal scrap basket.

It isn't Dennis's fault, she told herself, it isn't Nick's. A man can't write your sentences for you, or keep your weight down. A man couldn't even give you the courage to leave the house if you were too afraid to leave the house; unless, of course, he was willing to leave with you. As she admitted this, she realized that in the part of herself that was most reflective of her own interior life, her own perception of what excuse she had for liberty, her own relentless if not obscure pursuit of happiness (she had never thought of herself as the sort of person who valued happiness, but now she saw that it was what she had been after all along), in the part of herself that made her get up in the morning and make her bed and wash her hair and return phone calls and go to the doctor when she found a mole on her ankle or a lump under her arm, in the part of herself that kept her going, she believed that if she were with the right man, she would be able to manage it all.

After giving up on writing, Lucy began to go to work with Dennis.

At the Little Theater, she sat beneath a street lamp in a low beach chair and read first novels that she checked out of the library three or four at a time. At the Theater by the Sea, she sat on a folding chair in the room behind the refreshment stand and read hagiographies, also from the library, the more obscure the saint, the more extreme his or her behavior, the better. She particularly liked the stories of girl saints who would not eat. She was considering the idea of writing a book about these girls who starved themselves in the name of God when just such a book appeared in the library. The fact that "her" idea had already been done made her feel more tired than had the prospect of doing the research for the book, and she stopped reading about the saints, and history, and anything she liked that someone else might have gotten to first. Anyway, how could she legitimately write about anorexia when she had no memory of what it was like to be hungry?

Not eating was not her problem. She was not allowed to eat brownies from any of the large pans that Dennis prepared for sale, so she had to acquire the batter before it ever went into a pan, when it was not yet officially a part of their livelihood. Usually, during the preparation of a fresh batch, Dennis left the room often enough for her to be able to fill an old margarine tub with the amount she needed for her own supply. Sometimes she baked it on a cookie sheet; sometimes she preferred to eat it raw.

"Have you weighed yourself lately?" Dennis asked one night when she said she wasn't in the mood to be on top.

"Where would I have a chance to weigh myself?" she snapped. "Anyway, I can't help it if I'm gaining weight. There's nothing for me to do around here but eat."

Immediately sorry for sounding so childish, she laid her head on his shoulder and stroked his chest. "I'm sorry," she said. "I suppose its pre-wedding jitters or whatever they call it, but I can't seem to concentrate on anything. I feel superfluous here. Everyone has something to do but me."

There was a pause. She heard Dennis catch his breath, as if he was about to say something, but he seemed to reconsider, and she was silently grateful to him for not reminding her of her plans to storm the bastions of media on the island.

"Why don't you work with me?" he said finally. He lay naked in the dark, invisible except for the pale strip of untanned skin around his hips.

"I have been going to work with you, in case you haven't noticed."

"Yes, but you haven't been working. Maybe if you worked."

Lucy's first impulse was to mount a defense against what she perceived as a criticism; she felt stung, as if he had called her lazy and fat. She was glad the lights were out. She got off the bed and went to sit in a chair across the room. As she moved away from him, she got a grip on herself that allowed her to consider the possibility that her defensiveness was a response to her own guilt rather than to anything Dennis had said. She smoked a cigarette as she sat in the chair, then brushed her teeth and returned to bed. Dennis had fallen asleep by then, so she had to wait until morning to tell him she'd decided he was right.

"Congratulations," she said to Nick when he appeared at the concession stand during intermission. It was the opening night of *Bye Bye Birdie* at the Theater by the Sea. During the first act, while she and Dennis had set up the stand, there was hardly a moment when the building hadn't been filled with echoing laughter or a burst of clapping that sounded like rain.

Nick grinned. "Isn't this wild? Look at my back." He turned around and dropped his sport coat off his shoulders, as if it were a stole. "I'm soaked, aren't I? You should see Fiske."

Lucy handed someone a brownie for a dollar.

"The mikes are blanking out again, but no one seems to care," said Nick.

"I gave you a five. You owe me four," a woman in a long dress said to Lucy.

Dennis materialized at her side. "Is there a problem?"

"I gave her a five."

Dennis handed the woman four dollars.

"I don't think she did give me a five," Lucy said when the woman was gone.

"She didn't." Dennis flipped open the tackle box where she kept her money. "There isn't a five in here, see? You've got to pay attention."

"I'm sorry. I was congratulating Nick."

Dennis reached across the counter and slapped Nick on the back in a gesture that seemed to Lucy unnecessarily manly.

"All set to be our best man?" Dennis asked.

"I'm going up to Miami to look for a suit."

"That's not a bad idea. I'm going to have to do that myself one of these days."

Lucy was relieved when Dennis returned to his post at the other end of the counter.

"That was pleasant," Nick said, his eyes alight with humor and the triumph of the night. "Anyway, I'd better get back. I don't think Fiske can live without me at this point."

"I can relate."

Nick blushed.

"Here," Lucy said quickly. "One for you" — she pushed paper cups full of lemonade across the counter — "and one for Fiske."

"Are you sure you can afford this after being so reckless with the company profits?"

She rolled her eyes. "He's a slave driver."

"Well" — he toasted her with his cup — "thanks again." He began to walk away, then spun around. "Listen, there's going to be a cast party at my house. Why don't you come?"

"Because I'm not in the cast?"

"You're in the cast," he said.

They looked at each other for a moment, then started to laugh, just as they had always used to do.

"Whatever that was supposed to mean, I still think you should come to the party. I wouldn't feel right having a party at the house without you being there."

"Maybe I will."

He turned and the thirsty crowd surged to take his place at the counter. Even after she'd lost sight of him, she could not stop smiling. She chided herself for thinking Nick had been avoiding her, when the truth was he had been busy working on the play. She was ashamed to realize how often she invented connections between events that had nothing to do with her or her own frail emotions. For the first time in weeks she felt as though she was seeing things clearly. She wanted to go to the party.

Alone, so she wouldn't have to worry about whether or not anyone else was having fun.

In other words, without Dennis.

She didn't return to the cinder block apartment until seven in the morning.

At which point she was still wide awake, after having done some coke for the first time in years. Her hair was wet. She carried her sandals in her hand.

"Come here, baby," Dennis said. He swiped his arm toward her, his face still buried in the pillows.

"I'm going back out. Go back to sleep."

She changed into shorts and a T-shirt.

She discovered she had no money, so she took fifty dollars from the tackle box, leaving in its place an IOU scribbled in blue pencil on one of the horizontal pieces of paper she had cut.

She left Dennis asleep under the ceiling fan and rode her bike past the corner where she and Nick had parted ways half an hour earlier after staying up all night, after lying on the pier counting shooting stars, after skinny-dipping just before the sun rose, disturbing the last traces of phosphorescence. As they were walking toward their bikes, about to leave the pier, Nick had kissed her. It was a strange, fierce kiss — their teeth scraped, his tongue studied the roof of her mouth — that left her wondering if this was what he thought kissing was. It reminded her of the way dogs bite each other on the back of the neck in preparation for sex. She tried to kiss him back more gently, but he pulled away. She saw him touch his finger to his lips. She wondered if he had dared himself to do it.

But he kissed her again when they parted ways, a perfunctory kiss on the lips that she liked much better.

It was more like a boyfriend.

"I thought you couldn't touch me," she said.

"I thought you said I could overcome my fears."

"Do you admit I was right?"

"I admit I'm on drugs," he said.

She rode her bike past the pier again, past the large house where she often saw a beautiful Hispanic girl leaning against the porch rail staring out to sea, past the house of the famous dead author, past the house of the famous dead naturalist, past the pink and turquoise houses in Black Town, past a cruise ship docked in the harbor, past the stores and the seafood shacks, through all the sleepy, sweet-smelling streets to Nick's house.

He was on the upstairs balcony.

He had a towel wrapped around his waist.

"I can't go out to breakfast after all," he said.

Someone in the hotel next door stuck his head out the window.

"Hugh needs me to help him clean up. The place is a mess."

"I could help too."

"I think we've got it covered." He leaned on the balcony rail and lifted his feet off the ground for a moment, like a small boy testing his strength.

"How about later?"

"Maybe later."

"Lunch?"

"I'll call you."

The man at the hotel window pulled his head back inside. When she looked back at the balcony, Nick was gone.

"I think we should start looking for a house," Dennis said. "I think it would be good if we bought something now so when we come back from the honeymoon, we can move right in and get started."

"Get started on what?" Lucy asked.

"Our lives. The future. The baby boy who's going to look like me."

She had forgotten about the baby boy.

"It can't hurt to look."

They drove to a real estate agency where they introduced themselves to a man who was ready to go right out with them. Lucy recognized him as a friend of Hugh's. She decided to pretend she had no idea who he was unless at some point she needed the connection.

If Hugh still counted as a connection.

She loved the third house they saw. It was painted yellow and surrounded by a five-foot wall. There were four small buildings in the compound. She could have her own art studio where she could draw or write or do whatever she wanted. They could rent out two of the buildings, thereby bringing in enough income to cover the mortgage. They could take out a mortgage large enough to put in a pool immediately.

For the first time in several weeks she pictured herself doing something. She pictured herself swimming in her own pool.

"We'll get back to you," she told the agent.

That night Dennis sat on their patio, scribbling numbers in a notebook. She hung up the phone.

"They can't lend us the money right now. After all, they're paying for the wedding." She sat down on the bench next to Dennis. "We'll just have to wait."

"I can't believe they don't have the money."

"I hope you're joking."

"I'm not joking. I don't think they're being straight with you."

"What are you talking about? You've never met them."

"I just don't like them jerking you around."

"They're hardly jerking me around. It's not exactly jerking someone around to tell them you can't just give them thirty thousand dollars. And even if they did have it, they're under no obligation to give it to us. It's their money."

He stared at the label on his beer and frowned.

"Did you expect my parents to buy us a house?"

He shrugged.

"I don't need a house," she said carefully. "It's not the most important thing."

"How much would you lose if you took your money out of CDs now?"

She looked at the wood grain in the picnic table. Beside her, he finished the bottle of beer. She pushed her arms through the sleeves of her sweater and hugged herself.

"I asked you a question," he said.

"I would lose a lot. Is that what you want?"

There was a pause.

"What I want," he said slowly, "is for you to try a little harder, or this isn't going to work out."

Lucy swallowed. Nick had stood her up for lunch twice in one week. Her father had asked again about the insurance policy. She could no longer fit into her jeans.

"I want to make you happy," she told Dennis. "I've been distracted lately. Nerves, I guess. I'm sure everything will be better after the wedding."

He held out his hand to her. "Let's go inside," he said. "I'll calm you down."

He reached out and wound his fingers around her wrist, like a rope. She would have preferred to sit outside and watch the sun go down, but she still felt a strange listlessness come over her whenever he touched her skin, and she didn't resist. As he lay above her, she saw his face grow slick with sweat as her body wriggled closer to his. His will seemed to penetrate a dark part of her being that she hadn't yet reached, and she gave herself over to his pure insight, the evidence of her tingling limbs allowing her to believe that, for all their differences, instinctively they knew what they were doing.

On the dawn of the day before her thirty-first birthday, Lucy woke up with a terrible pain in her mouth. She packed her gums with aspirin, her taste buds contracting as the pills dissolved and the gritty bitter residue stuck to the back of her tongue. By midmorning her cheek was the size of an orange, and she could no longer assure herself that it would go away on its own.

"What do you think the problem is?" the receptionist asked her over the phone.

She knew she would sound crazy if she said the problem was symbolic. "It's an infected tooth."

"Can you come in at one o'clock?"

"I'll be there," she said with relief, although after hanging up the phone she had second thoughts. She didn't know anything about this dentist. She had picked his name out of the telephone book. Never before had she gone to a dentist who hadn't come recommended by people who were prepared to spend any amount of money to maintain their good health. Dennis had no suggestions. During the course of her search for someone who could help her, she learned that Dennis didn't have a dentist, a doctor, a lawyer, an accountant, a savings account, or any of the trappings of what she thought of as a reasonable adult life. She tried to reach Hugh for a recommendation, but he was out and she couldn't think of anyone else to call.

She found to her surprise that the dentist's office was clean and efficient, and that the dentist was young, handsome, and a graduate of the University of Pennsylvania dental school. She was ashamed that she had expected something squalid. The dentist seemed to read her mind on this point, explaining as he examined her that he had purposely forgone the route of profit and respectability in order to live near the ocean. He wanted palm trees in his yard. He wanted his future children to be able to go off on their bikes without his feeling that he had to follow them wherever they went, and he wanted sunsets.

But it was difficult, he said, to establish a practice in a small town. He hadn't taken a vacation in fourteen months.

She would have to take a heavy course of antibiotics, he said, then have a root canal after the inflammation went down. If that didn't work, she might have to lose a tooth.

As he wrote out the prescriptions, she watched his fine, thin fingers move across the pad and thought that she could have liked him if the timing had been right.

She could imagine standing next to him in front of a picture window, watching their children ride their bikes into the sunset.

If her tooth had blown up six weeks earlier, if she had walked into the dentist's office at the right moment, she might have ended up with him instead of Dennis. She could have been Mrs. Dentist rather than Mrs. Concession Stand.

Which made her wonder exactly who she thought she was.

She stayed inside all day on her birthday, but Nick never came over or called. Dennis lay on a rug he'd brought from the storage locker and watched her sullenly.

"I took tonight off so I could take you out," he said.

"It wasn't my idea to have an abscessed tooth."

Dennis laced his hands behind his head. "You're in love with him."

"You're wrong."

"You won't even walk down the sidewalk to pick up your birthday cards in the mailbox because you're afraid you might miss his phone call."

"He's my best friend. I don't think it's weird for me to want to see him on my birthday," Lucy said hotly.

"I think it's weird that you won't leave the house with your fiancé because you're waiting for this so-called best friend of yours to drop by."

"I happen to have a bad infection, you know. It might not be the wisest thing for me to go running around town."

"I do know. If it weren't for that, quite frankly, I wouldn't be hanging around."

"Don't do me any favors." She blew her nose into a paper towel.

During the silence that followed, Lucy tried to see things from Dennis's point of view.

She was taking Tylenol number 4, which contained 60 milligrams of codeine for the pain, and she'd been taking it all day.

Dennis went to the phone in the kitchen and spoke to someone in a low voice.

"You can stop waiting," he said when he got back. "Nick and Hugh went to Miami and they won't be back for a few days."

"He could at least call," she said in a quavering voice.

"Yes, he could and he should call, but he hasn't. Now can we go out to dinner?"

"If you'd like."

"What would you like to do?"

She thought for a moment. "I'd really like you to tell me about Vietnam."

"There's nothing to tell."

"Humor me. It's my birthday."

He leaned against the door jamb, intertwining his legs. "I went on a few patrols, I smoked a lot of weed, I counted the seconds until I could get away. You see? It's the usual. I've got nothing to tell you that you haven't read about."

"Did you see anyone get killed?"

"Yes I did. So did everybody."

"Did you kill anyone?"

"I don't know. I tried."

"All right," she said, "I won't push. But I think if we're going to be married you should be able to tell me everything. I feel like you're hiding something."

"Look, Lucy, if you're looking for a mystery, you're not going to find it here. I was drafted and sent over there just like thousands of other guys. I saw some combat and I survived. It's not my life. I don't make a big deal out of it. Why should you?"

"It interests me."

"It interests you because your class of people doesn't go to places like Vietnam. Your class of people won't even fight people who aren't white."

"That's not true. My father went to Korea."

"What was his rank?"

Her jaw throbbed. "He was a doctor. He worked in a MASH unit."

"Like Alan Alda?" Dennis rolled his eyes.

"Yes, I suppose. Yes, like Alan Alda."

ॐ

After she had her tooth pulled, Lucy lay in the dark apartment on Flagler Avenue and watched videos of feature films about the Vietnam War. She mixed Empirin with Percodan and managed to smoke cigarettes in spite of the pain in her jaw. She watched, in order, *The Green Berets, The Boys in Company C, Coming Home, Apocalypse Now, The Deer Hunter, Platoon, Hamburger Hill, Rambo III, Casualties of War,* and *Full Metal Jacket.* She watched *Apocalypse Now* three times, for reasons she promised herself she would one day decipher when she wasn't so drugged, although she knew even in her altered state that one of its attractions was that her father looked a lot like Marlon Brando, without the heft.

Dennis wandered in and out of the room when he wasn't working, handing her glasses filled with room-temperature liquids into which he always stuck a small paper umbrella and a flexible plastic straw. He had no interest in watching the movies with her, and she had no desire to discuss them with him. Every time he appeared in her sights, she saw the different aspects of his character as they might translate into action, depending on the circumstances, the situation, the heat, his health, his mood. Sometimes she saw the possibility of his being courageous, or even recklessly brave. Sometimes she imagined his being cruel, excusing his excesses in the name of being pushed too far, of fear, of interpreting orders.

"What are you looking at?" he asked when he caught her watching him.

She pointed to her mouth to indicate that it would hurt her to try to talk.

On the third afternoon after her operation, she was again watching *Apocalypse Now* when the front door opened and a man appeared in silhouette against a backdrop of the blazing sun. Dennis looked up from his accounting project and frowned.

"Is she making a big production of this?" Nick said, ostensibly to Dennis, but really to no one in particular. "Typical." He laughed, walking into the room. "Come on, Lucy, you've been lolling around here long enough. Your public is going to forget you exist unless you make an appearance."

"Don't make me laugh." She slurred her words; her cheeks felt thick and sloppy.

"I'm serious. You've got to get right back on that horse and say giddyap, or however the hell you pronounce it. You've got to get back to the beach. Now. Today."

Lucy sat up. "I'll go get my suit."

"That's the spirit," Nick said. He helped her to her feet and shot her a look that bespoke the seriousness of his mission, and she understood that he had not appeared in the white light of her doorway just to cheer her up.

"Do you really think you're up to it?" Dennis asked.

"She'll never know until she tries," Nick said.

"I'd like to try," said Lucy.

She walked into the bedroom on her rubbery legs. The wonderful drugs made her float. She floated into the bathroom, then back to the bedroom again. Her hand floated to the closet door. She found her bathing suit hanging on a hook beneath the battered ARVN helmet. Impulsively, she lifted the helmet and placed it on her head.

As the cool metal touched her scalp, she closed her eyes and saw as if on a projection screen in her own mind a story she couldn't remember having seen in any of her movies. There was a boy walking among a group of boys who were wading through streams and jumping from rocks in a lush wooded valley. It was summer. The sun hung directly overhead, and the boy felt the thick new hair that covered his lower abdomen mat as the heat penetrated his uniform. His rifle was heavy and strange and he wanted to put it down, just for a moment. He wanted to remove his clothes and lie in the cool water until it was all over, or until his nerve returned, whichever came first.

He wanted to go home and lay his head in his mother's lap. Suddenly he remembered a lifetime of small kindnesses that had been shown to him by his parents and friends in the village, and he wanted to embark on a pilgrimage to repay them all, one by one. It was odd: as a child, his dream was to be a soldier, to die a heroic death in the service of his country. Now that he had the chance to do so, his dream seemed empty and his country unreal. In the past few weeks, he had watched his comrades rush toward the guns in a frenzy. He had seen their faces grow full of betrayal and pain as their bodies collapsed.

There was nothing special about throwing yourself in front of bullets, the boy thought. Anyone could do that. It certainly wasn't enough to guarantee immortality, or even a hero's burial. No, if you were remembered, it wouldn't be for dying in battle. It would be for what you had done before. If you had never made your dog wait to eat, for example. If you had done good deeds. Your deeds alone would determine the quality of your life and the significance of your death.

The boy felt high and light as he pursued his thoughts. He looked around at his companions, the brave soldiers, and they seemed small and silly as they ran this way and that trying to protect themselves or distinguish themselves or simply do what they were told. He stood on a fallen tree trunk in order to gaze over the ranks of the ridiculous army. His back was turned when the flash broke through the woods.

The boy dropped, then snuggled into the earth as if the ground were his gentle mother. I never had a chance to tell her, he thought. I understood too late. He formed a prayer in his mind and raised his eyes to search the heavens, as he tried to figure out how to say good-bye. He blinked. When he opened his eyes again, there in front of him was the face of a big American hero, a face he'd seen in pictures and on the streets of his country for several years.

"Are you ready to go now?" the hero asked.

The last thing the boy felt before he died was the touch of the big hands on his brow, a wisp of fresh air on his crown.

Lucy shook her head slightly in an effort to clear it. Dennis took the helmet from her head as Nick handed her a glass of water. "Here, take another sip," he said.

"I think she's too out of it," Dennis said.

"It will be good for her," said Nick.

"I'll be fine. It will be good for me. You know how much I love the ocean," she said, as if her preferences and passions could make all practical considerations simply go away.

Nick parked the battered old station wagon in an empty spot in front of Hugh's house.

"I thought we were going to the beach," said Lucy.

"I only said that to secure your release. We can lie by the pool here."

"But I wanted to go to the beach. I don't want to see any-body."

She assumed Nick understood she meant Hugh. He laid his fingertips lightly on the steering wheel and stared ahead of him. Lucy rolled her head back and forth on top of the seat, feeling drunk. She watched a couple laden with leather suitcases walk into the hotel next to Hugh's house. The sidewalk, as always, was sprinkled with dead leaves, imparting the atmosphere and nos-talgia of a perpetual fall. Lucy's chest grew tight as a wave of homesickness swept over her. Usually she was homesick for a time or a sense of security that had never actually existed; now, however, she was specifically homesick for Hugh's.

"All right," said Nick finally. "I know where we'll go."

They didn't talk again until they'd settled themselves on the turquoise plastic chairs around the pool at the End of the World motel. Lucy recognized several of Dennis's friends in the crowd, their hands clasping the kinds of drinks that came complete with a maraschino cherry. Most of the women were topless, their breasts brown. Right next to Lucy, a man was rubbing suntan oil onto a woman's chest, swirling his hands in lazy circles over her ribs. He was careful not to touch her nipples, an omission that made the whole procedure seem less innocent than it otherwise looked. Lucy watched as the man's hands continued to move hypnotically. She willed him to touch the nipples; she found it embarrassing that he didn't. She was conscious of Nick also watching, which embarrassed her further. She was relieved when the woman flipped onto her stomach.

"Interesting place," she said. "I wouldn't think it was exactly your style."

Nick was examining the fine blond hair on his right leg. His shinbone was so delicate it was hard to believe it could bear his weight. Lucy watched as he pinched something off his leg, rubbed his skin briskly, then stretched out on the chair.

"The Theater by the Sea crowd comes here," he said.

"You don't mind the exposure, or is it just *my* boobs that you find hard to take?"

"I'm getting used to it. I like to think of it as an exercise in desensitization."

"Pig."

"Hey, I'm a member of a minority group. You're not allowed to call me names."

Lucy removed her T-shirt. Although she'd lost a few pounds since her root canal, she still felt fat in her old black bikini.

"Are you going to take off your top?" Nick asked.

"Do you want me to?"

He looked out to sea. "It's up to you."

"In that case, I think I'll pass. It's no fun if I can't torment you."

"And then there's the fact that you're too modest to take your clothes off in front of fifty people."

Lucy blushed. "Yes, there's that, too."

"Lucy, we have to talk."

For a moment they sat silently, although Lucy had the sensation of hearing all the thoughts he had in his mind, as if the conversation had already begun. "Go ahead," she said.

At first he spoke haltingly, for fear that what he had to say would hurt her. Gradually, though, his speech gained velocity as he pressed to convince her that he was telling the truth. He told her that everyone in town was talking behind her back, saying that Dennis wanted to marry her only for her money. And everyone said he was a flirt. Nick had seen him flirting with members of the acting troupe at the Theater by the Sea, and other people had seen him with Babe. Did she understand what he had said? He was still seeing Babe.

"Maybe he has business to tie up with her." Her mouth ached. The drugs were wearing off.

"Maybe," Nick said, his tone neutral.

Then he told her that Dennis had called Hugh the other day, claiming that Hugh owed him thirteen dollars from the time Dennis had bought ice for one of Hugh's parties. He insisted on being paid back right away.

"He doesn't have much money," Lucy said.

"Neither do I."

"He'll make money. We've talked a lot about expanding the business, opening a brownie store here and then eventually going national, like David's Cookies or Mrs. Field's. No one has done brownies yet."

"Maybe they have. Maybe brownies don't work. And anyway, do you really think 'Dennis the Menace' is a person with whom you could realistically go national?"

"What do you mean?"

"I mean, most kids have lemonade stands and dream of what they want to do when they grow up. Dennis seems to have gotten it the other way around."

Lucy felt a wave of heat and color crawl up her neck. "I'm aware of that," she said finally, "but I don't think you understand. Dennis does things for me that I need."

"Is that any reason to marry someone, because someone does things for you? You can pay for help, if help is all you want."

"I really don't think you're the one to lecture me about the process of selling oneself short," Lucy snapped.

"Ouch." Nick held his arms in front of his face, as if shielding himself from a blow.

"You have no right to criticize me. At least I offered you an alternative when I criticized you."

Nick lowered his arms. "The difference is, I have no alternative. You do."

"Bull."

"You could marry someone other than Dennis."

"Anyone who isn't you is Dennis to me."

"I know," Nick said quietly. "Anyone who isn't you is Hugh."

That night she slept at Hugh and Nick's house. She heard Dennis come into the room but she pretended to be asleep as he stared at her. Eventually she heard Nick whisper that she might as well stay over and Dennis agreed, saying he had to work anyway and it was better for her to be where someone could take care of her. After Dennis left, Nick grinned at her gleefully as if they'd gotten away with something, but it seemed to her that whatever she'd gotten away with was something she'd lost. Nick seemed childish to her in his thrill at having pulled a fast one on Dennis. He didn't understand what she meant when she told him it was not really like that. She didn't push it, though. It was easier to flow along on the wave of his happiness than to try to make herself clear. He brought a little television into the room and coaxed her to watch a movie with him. She was glad to do so, although she felt guilty and disloyal to Dennis whenever she laughed.

At some point Hugh made another of his miscalculated attempts to join in the fun, but Lucy had taken another pill and legitimately could not accommodate his mood. Nick simply didn't want to. He snapped the TV off and left the room. The next morning she learned that Nick had slept outside on one of the beige chaises by the pool, covered by a beach towel.

"I guess I'm going to have to go back," she said when Nick appeared with a breakfast tray.

"Why don't you stay here until you get better?" He placed the tray on her lap.

"Don't tempt me."

"It's my métier to be tempting. Don't you know that by now? I'm a devil."

"In the guise of a houseboy?"

"It's a tried-and-true disguise."

She took consecutive sips of orange juice and coffee, holding up a finger as she drank to indicate a pause in the conversation. "I don't think Hugh would be quite as willing for me to extend my stay."

"I thought of that. I think if you offer him a few of your Percodans he'll be happy."

Lucy giggled. "Ouch!" Her hand flew to her cheek. "Don't make me laugh."

"And if I let him do me every once in a while, he'll let you move in forever. He'll build you your own wing."

"You'd do that for me?"

"Maybe. If you're good."

"If I'm really good maybe you'll do it with me."

Nick blushed.

"Just joking," Lucy said.

They heard footsteps galumphing up the stairs.

"Hugh's at work," Nick whispered.

"It isn't Hugh."

Dennis appeared in the doorway, backlit by the skylights behind him so that his features were dark and indistinct. Lucy straightened up, smoothing the sheets at her sides, self-consciously aware as she did so that she was lying on the bed where she and Dennis had first come together. She remembered the sound of his — Babe's — dogs' toenails clicking on the wooden floor as they grew excited by the passion on the bed above them. It seemed long ago.

"I have to do some errands," Nick said. "You two kids have fun."

"Take the tray, will you? I'll eat later."

Nick picked up the tray. "Service with a smile." He bent over and looked at her conspiratorially. "See you later?"

She nodded. Dennis turned sideways to let Nick pass, then moved to sit at her side on the bed.

"How do you feel?" He touched her fingers.

"Better. Sore."

"I missed you last night."

"Well, it was probably good for me to just get some sleep."

"Celia Allen said she saw you yesterday at the End of the World."

"Yeah, that's Nick's new hangout. A place in the sun for the theater people."

"Did you have fun?"

"I guess."

He knelt onto the mattress, pressing his fingers to his temples. "God I have a wicked headache. I went out last night."

"With who?"

She was surprised to find that the thought of his being out without her had the power to make her jealous and regretful of her decision to stay with Nick.

"No one you know and no one you'd want to know, if you ask my opinion, although he wants to meet you. Old pal of mine, Jack McPhee."

"I've never heard of him."

"He doesn't live here. He just blows into town every once in a while for a little R and R. I let him sleep on the couch since you were over here. Do you have any aspirin?"

She handed him her bottle of Percodan. He took one without water.

"Is he still there?"

"He was when I left. Are you coming with me now?"

"Uh-huh."

She pulled her shorts up beneath the oversized T-shirt she wore as a nightgown, clothing herself modestly and chastely, as if she were getting dressed in front of Nick.

Jack McPhee was drinking when they returned to the apartment. Her first sight of him included a tequila bottle that obscured the bottom half of his face, but her obstructed view wasn't enough to prevent her from admiring his lean, outlaw handsomeness and the aura he had that was terminally dangerous to romantic women, the aura of a man misunderstood. Lucy held out her hand to him. He smirked as he shook it, suggesting they go out for a drink. She knew it would be prudent for her to be the one to drive, but Jack settled himself behind the wheel of Babe's car with such authority that she knew without having to be told that he'd driven under worse conditions in more expanded states of mind. Silently she deferred to his experience and popped into the back, allowing Dennis to ride shotgun.

Jack quizzed her about herself as they zipped across the island. He laughed sardonically at everything she said, as if he could read a deeper meaning into her bland factual statements that belied a cosmic humor obvious to him, hazy to everyone else. He did not laugh only at her; he laughed at everything. When the traffic light changed color, he laughed, as he did when they drove by joggers and bicyclists. He braked for a cat that ran in front of the car, which surprised her, as she figured him for the type who would chalk up imaginary points for running a cat down. Then he laughed as the cat changed its mind and retraced its steps.

"Poor bugger." He chuckled, idling the engine patiently as he waited for the animal to make itself safe.

"I'm surprised you didn't hit it," Dennis said edgily. Spoken aloud, the idea seemed ridiculous, although Lucy had wondered the same thing.

"Which tells me how much you know," said Jack McPhee.

Lucy blushed, not so much for either herself or Dennis but for her connection to him. She couldn't very well lead Jack McPhee to think she wasn't really with Dennis when she was wearing an engagement ring, but she could let Jack know that on an important level she knew the score, and furthermore, she knew that

Dennis didn't know. As she deliberately drew on a cloak of detachment, she caught Jack staring at her in the rearview mirror. When their eyes met, she looked at him boldly, trying to convey the inconsequentiality of her attachments, the purity of her intentions. To her embarrassment, he laughed.

Which showed her how much she knew.

From then on she kept her gaze fixed out the window until they pulled up outside a place she'd been by many times. It was called the Hot Spot, although it looked like a place about as far from hot as Lucy could imagine. She'd never seen a car near the place before they pulled up, not to say that the parking lot was ever empty, but the clientele were the type that tended to arrive in pickup trucks or motorcycles or by the hook of their own freewheeling thumbs. The building itself was a square, wood-planked box with no windows and not much of a door. Nick had told Lucy that there were murders in the Hot Spot all the time that were never reported in the papers. There were no rules against women going to the Hot Spot; they just knew they weren't wanted.

"Can I really go in here?" she asked Jack McPhee.

"With me you can."

She stole a glance at Dennis, who was doing his best to appear nonchalant, although she suspected he would rather have gone to one of the open, flowery restaurants they were used to. She was tempted to slip her hand into his, to make a connection that might put them both at ease, but she didn't dare make such a prosaic gesture in front of Jack. Instead, she did her best to appear confident yet detached, the posture she'd affected as a teen. It came back easily enough, like riding a bike.

The Hot Spot was as dark as she thought it would be except around the bar, where the rows of bottles were illuminated by lights that seemed to make them glow from the inside out. Jack ordered them each a strong amber-colored drink, the very mention of which had made the bartender raise a respectful eyebrow at their little trio, then lead them to a wooden table predictably decorated with the deep knife-cut ruts of a dozen carved initials. She quickly came to the conclusion that there was actually nothing to the Hot Spot. It wasn't a sacred place. If she rounded up thirty or forty girls to join her at the bar one night, they could lay claim to it as their own.

But of course, that was true for many things.

"So what brings you to the island, Jack?" she said conversationally, her tone just sarcastic enough to hint that she wasn't impressed by the phony he-man atmosphere that surrounded them.

Jack laughed, as if she had told a great joke.

"Really, I'd like to know. Are you on vacation?"

Dennis laughed, too.

"It depends how you look at it," Jack said. "Some might say I'm on a permanent vacation. Others might say I work all the time."

"Okay, so what do you do?" The novelty of Jack's inappropriate laughter was wearing off, and she was growing impatient with his cryptic replies. "Give it to me straight. I'm a big girl. I can take it, whatever it is."

Jack looked at her coolly. "Honey, no one can take it. Guys like me are paid to do the things that no one else can take."

Now Lucy laughed. Jack looked at her appreciatively.

"I usually get laid with that line," he said.

"You can't use lines on a New Yorker. We've heard them all before," Lucy shot back.

"I see." He placed his forearms on the table and leaned toward her. "How about this, then. I do what people pay me to do."

"Doesn't everybody?"

"Not exactly. Most people decide what they are willing to do and then they go out and find someone to pay them for doing something in that general range. The difference with me is that I don't make those kinds of decisions. I simply make myself available, and I don't make judgments about what I'm asked to do."

"I'm not sure I understand what you're talking about."

"Good," Dennis interjected. "Let's keep it that way."

"You don't have to protect me," Lucy said hotly.

"Yeah, Dennis, you don't have to protect her from me." Jack grinned.

Dennis glared at her, and she felt a brief flash of contempt for him for not being able to react to a challenge in any way more clever than the mute anger prompted by a quickening of the blood, a rise in his adrenaline level. She was not the type of girl who was flattered by violence on her behalf. She was not in the mood for a scene. "Let's change the subject," she said wearily.

He clenched his jaw. His lips thinned. "No, no, Lucy, you're right. I think you should know whose drinks you're drinking. Go ahead, Jack, tell her what you do."

Jack laughed sharply and tipped back in his chair. "Let her guess."

"She'll never guess."

"Won't she?" Jack looked at Lucy. "Won't you?"

Lucy gripped her cold glass. "Let me see. You're not a lawyer or a doctor or your hair wouldn't be so long."

"So far so good," Jack said.

"Your accent is different than Dennis's, so you probably know him from somewhere other than the old hometown."

"Good thinking."

"And you've as much as said you're a hired gun."

Jack raised his glass to her. "Bingo."

"Really?"

"Close enough." Jack grinned.

Lucy clinked his glass. "That's interesting."

"She's interested," Dennis said sarcastically. "My future wife who thinks it's wrong to take a dinner roll home from a restaurant decides she's interested in a man who will fight anybody's war as long as he gets paid to do the job."

"Well said." Jack applauded.

"Anytime." Dennis upended his drink. "So you like mercenaries, Lucy? I didn't know that. I wish I'd known that, but you never mentioned it. I didn't know there were a lot of mercenaries running around Philadelphia."

"Au contraire. Philadelphia is well known to be a very mercenary town," Jack said.

Dennis frowned. Lucy reached out and took his hand, squeezed it. After a stubborn moment, he squeezed back.

"Young love," Jack said. "Who can resist?"

Lucy forced herself not to let go of Dennis, although she suddenly felt foolish and resentful of his inability to keep up with the jokes, his need to be reassured.

"So how did you escape Philadelphia?" Jack asked.

"I got on a plane." Lucy felt flip. "So how do you become a mercenary?"

"You look in the back of *Soldier of Fortune* magazine," Dennis said, apparently bolstered up by his contact with her.

"Same as you," Jack said, ignoring Dennis. "You get on a plane. You land on an airstrip in any one of a dozen countries and you ask around."

"It's that easy?"

"If you call that easy."

"Do they take women?"

Dennis rolled his eyes. "Now see what you've done? The lemonade stand isn't going to be enough for her anymore."

Lucy nearly gasped at hearing her inner thoughts spoken aloud. She dropped Dennis's hand and turned to her drink.

"The point is, Deucy Lucy," said Jack, "the point is that there is no 'they.' 'They' don't take anybody. You take yourself there and you bring yourself back, and if you don't come back, there's no 'they' to send a telegram and a flag to your family. You're on your own. This is not the U.S. Army we're talking about."

Dennis stared at the ruts in the table.

"You just hit a sore nerve," said Lucy. "Dennis won't talk about the Army or the war."

"He won't or he can't?"

Lucy jerked her head up, startled.

"I'd say he can't tell you, because there really are no words to tell it. The kind of words you'd need to really describe what it was like don't exist, at least not in English, and you'd better be grateful for that. The only way to survive certain kinds of events is not to be too meticulous about naming them. If the only way you know to talk about the heat is to say it was hot, then you can draw an analogy in your mind to hot Iowa or this hot island, or some place on earth as we know it. When the worst thing people can hold in their minds is how hot it can get in Iowa, they'll be able to think that anything they encounter more awful than that isn't really real. They can ignore it until it goes away."

"You go crazy if you think about that stuff all the time," Dennis said to Lucy. "That's why Jack's crazy."

"He doesn't exactly seem crazy," Lucy said back to Dennis, not looking at Jack, "but it doesn't appear that he practices what he preaches, either."

"Too true." Jack laughed. He nodded at the bartender, who immediately began preparing another round of drinks.

"I'll bet Jack has names for all the unspeakable things," Lucy continued.

"Not names, exactly, but I think how I live is a way of calling attention to those things that makes them just as indismissible."

Lucy looked at him. "You are a witness."

"I wouldn't say that. A witness sets out to watch, and a witness has ideas about what he or she has seen. I do my best not to muddy the muddy waters with my own ideas. I take the tack of pure experience."

"You do, do you?" Lucy teased.

"So they say."

The bartender delivered three more drinks, and a little later, three more. Soon Dennis was out of the conversation completely, the alcohol having rendered him incapable of anything more than a grunt here and there, or occasionally a profound, self-aggrandizing sigh. Lucy, too, grew more and more quiet as Jack continued to talk, but her quiet was quick-witted, greedy, sometimes even an image or a leap ahead of the stories that wrapped around and around her like dark ribbons, binding her to Jack's vision. He told her what it was like to stop waiting for things to happen, to make them happen instead. He had gone to Vietnam in a cautious state of good faith, but when the pressure dropped on him as it had dropped onto all the characters in all the movies she'd watched, he discovered he had a different feeling about the pressure than did the other boys he knew.

"Rather than enduring it or wanting to run away from it or wanting to press right the hell back, I found that when I took a purposive walk back through the jungle of all the history I'd learned, when I added everything up, it turned out that I was the pressure. In my own body, stamped deep in the invisible genes and on this theoretical, ineffable soul were all the wars that had been fought, all the sources of conflict, all the impetuses for inventing killing weapons. In short, when I thought about it, I realized I was war. Vietnam was an opportunity for me to fulfill my potential. I did some things that were nice and some things that weren't so nice. It didn't really matter which manner of thing I did at the time, it only mattered in the end when I returned home and learned that everything I'd done over there, the nice and the unnice, were all called war."

He paused to drink deeply of the potent brown drink. She was quiet until he was ready to continue.

"So, having realized my true nature, when the war was over and I was free to lead my own life again, I began to hire myself out as war incarnate, a protean creature capable of adapting to any local tools of the trade, maintaining my energy and my cool by always keeping my eye on the vicious trajectory of history nipping at my heels, goading me on. One by one I shed all the teachings of my childhood and the inchoate, hopeful beliefs of my youth until I was nothing but a walking, talking example of the real.

"Now, if you'll excuse me for a moment?"

She nodded. He pushed his chair back and headed for the bathroom, leaving her alone with Dennis, which amounted to leaving her all alone. While he was gone, she tried to think about what he'd said, but his speech was obscured by the inner voice she'd heard that had murmured her own life story between his lines. Like Jack, she wished she could do something to make the world turn rather than feeling it was always turning on her. Yet the part of his story where he'd stepped out of the audience and become a player himself went by so quickly that she was left with the impression that, for Jack, change was merely a matter of changing his mind. For her, it wasn't as simple. On the surface of things, she was free to follow any path she chose as long as she allowed nothing to distract her from her dream. But what was her dream? She didn't feel free to dream it. In the back of her mind all the naysaying voices of her childhood chanted to her to play it safe, safer, safest.

She wanted to do something of consequence, but her ignorance seemed so vast that she wasn't even sure what such a thing might be. Was it running guns to the rebels? Was it being a good mother, a productive member of the community? She remembered all her impulses to do necessary, important things: open an orphanage in India; write about the half-lives of the people in South Africa; free animals from the laboratories in the university her parents had paid twenty thousand dollars for her to attend. She remembered lying on her bed at night imagining all the creatures in the world who were in pain, her mind spinning with the sorrow that circled the globe, yet what had she done about it? What was stopping her?

As she asked herself this question, she automatically looked at Dennis; she saw that what she loved about him was the distance he had put between himself and places like Philadelphia, things like nine-to-five jobs. Yet as she had attached herself to his version of freedom, she found herself less and less able to make any significant moves of her own. She suddenly realized that her whole life had been lived in a vicarious pursuit of freedom. She'd pursued her own ideals through boys who were living the life she wished to be living. When she wanted to be a poet, she loved thin, long-haired, neurasthenic boys who wrote poetry. When she wanted to be an activist, she loved fast-talking, first-generation immigrant sons who could extrapolate the tribulations of their own distant relatives into the pain of the world. When she'd grown tired of the struggle and decided it was enough to lead a decent, normal life, she'd attached herself to an advertising executive whose upper-middle-class values and aspirations were familiar to her. And finally, when she was weary of burning her own desires in the fire of Nick's denial of her physical being, she sought her freedom in Dennis's easy sexuality and his anti-Puritanical, unsymmetrical life. She had lived through men. She had focused all her energies through the vessels of life that were men. She had stood behind them, glowed for them, spurred them on by whispering advice in their ears, believed in them as she had never believed in herself, afraid to pursue her own life for fear of ridicule, loneliness, failure.

"What about women?" Lucy asked when Jack returned. "Did you shed your belief in us, or do we count as real?"

Jack laughed. "Good question, healthily narcissistic. I'm not sure how to answer that. If you're trying to find out if I believe in women as a tool to use for purposes of my own redemption, all I can tell you is that, in case you hadn't guessed, I'm not really a romantic guy. I don't tend to see women as other than men. My war doesn't extend that far."

"So you think women have war in them, too?"

"I don't see why not. The evolutionary information of the race is still passed on through both sexes, the last I heard."

"But historically we don't tend to fight wars."

"Not per se, but I think you'd have a hard time proving that women aren't implicated."

"So is that why men treat us as accessories, because we're accessories to their crimes?"

"Cute," said Jack.

"She's cute, all right," Dennis managed, his voice slushy.

"I don't feel cute," said Lucy.

She willed Jack to see how she did feel.

"But then, it doesn't matter what I think," he said.

"It doesn't?" she asked weakly.

"To be liberated is not to seek and achieve the recognition of others, but to step apart from them and not to be concerned."

"Is that a quote?" Dennis asked.

Jack laughed, and Lucy laughed with him, but she nevertheless understood what he was telling her. It suddenly became clear that what had been stopping her from doing the brave things that she imagined herself doing was her own need to feel safe and liked. Jack was willing for people to hate him. He was willing to get hurt, to be out of touch, and that was the difference between them. No one was stopping her from doing anything and going anywhere she wanted, if she was willing to take the risk. She could walk the worst streets in the world at three in the morning if she could accept the consequences. What Jack was saying was: you didn't have to buy in.

All afternoon she'd wanted to sleep with Jack, but even more than that, even more to the point, she realized that sleeping with him was a way to get close to her truer aim, which was to be free like him.

They drank all day. When they grew hungry and had had enough of the Hot Spot, they went to a Cuban restaurant where they ate a rich, fatty meal before finally going home. Lucy was drunk. When she lay down on the bed she knew she was as drunk as she'd ever been, her head spinning, her mind unable to hold fast to a single thought. She forced herself to get up and go to the kitchen, where she drank a quart of water, washing down a handful of aspirin and vitamin B complex. When she walked back through the living room, she stopped to stare at Jack, who had arranged himself on the sofa as if he were lying on the beach, the sun above him shining bright.

"Do you need a blanket?" Lucy asked.

"Back in the world of blanket" — Jack laughed — "and pretty women who want to cover you up."

Lucy smiled uncertainly. She wasn't sure if he wanted a blanket or not.

"Never mind," Jack said. "It's not really my policy to get too comfortable."

Lucy shifted from foot to foot, trying to stay alert. She gazed at the stripes of light cast on the floor by the slatted blinds. "When you go back to wherever you're going, I'd like to go with you," Lucy said to Jack.

Jack clasped his hands behind his head and turned to look at her. "Sorry," he said simply.

Lucy blushed.

"Anyway, I told you what to do. Just get off a plane and ask around. It doesn't take long to find trouble. It's not so different from how you found Dennis, when you think about it."

"It will be a stretch for me to see it that way."

"Hey, Lucy! Where are you?" Dennis called from the bedroom.

Jack laughed. "Go to bed. Don't think too much tonight."

She headed for the bedroom, where Dennis was sitting in the slipper chair by the far wall, naked, a canvas bag on his lap.

Lucy lay down.

"I have a surprise for you," Dennis said.

"What is it?" Lucy asked automatically. The room was spinning.

"See for yourself." Dennis sat beside her and emptied the contents of the bag onto the bed. There were several thin, carefully coiled ropes held in neat circles with garbage bag ties; two feathers, one yellow and blue, one brown, black, and white; something that looked like a dog leash split in two toward the end and tipped with tiny clothesline clips; and a long piece of hard rubber. She knew it was a dildo, although she'd never seen one.

"I don't feel well," she murmured.

"That's all right, sweetie. Just lay still."

She closed her eyes and watched a dark expanse wipe across the field of her inner vision. For quite some time she observed a series of whirling lights that spun lazily around, strange, mad stars that flung like sparks from their orbit images of a child's face, her expressions alternating from smiles to fear. She focused on the lines crossing the young brow, realizing with a shock that they were her own. She made an effort to trace the history of her child self, as Jack had traced the history of the world, to try to determine at what point she had lost sight of what the right thing was, yet every incident she brought to mind evaporated into a haze of melancholia before she could draw a lesson from it. The effort of remembering exhausted her, however, and when she roused, she found that her legs were asleep and her hands ached as if they had been hurting for quite some time. She opened her eyes and saw that she was naked and tied by her wrists and ankles to the bed.

"What are you doing?" she asked.

"Ssh, stop struggling. You don't have to struggle. Just enjoy yourself."

"I want to go to sleep."

"Go ahead."

She drifted off, vaguely aware of something hard between her legs. She drifted off. Sometime later she noticed that she was cold, but her body was strangely moist. Her dreams were jumbled and incomplete, peopled with everyone who'd made her feel insecure as a child. At one point she thought she saw Jack. When she awoke again, Dennis was snoring and her limbs were free. She grabbed her clothes and snuck out the back, where she dressed quickly, unlocked her bike, and pumped her quivering legs against the dewy steel, pedaling with all her might into the cool, clear morning past houses where easier sleepers lay peacefully asleep.

It wasn't exactly breaking in, she told herself as she crawled through Hugh's library window. It wasn't really criminal, because she was on close enough terms with the inhabitants to have a key if anyone had thought of it, and she wasn't planning to take anything.

Except Nick.

He opened his eyes as she stood in the bedroom doorway.

She beckoned him with her right hand, raising the index finger of her left to her lips.

Warily, he looked to his left, at Hugh, who stirred and heaved an eerie, prescient sigh. When he'd settled again, Nick slid gracefully to the edge of the bed and nodded at her, signaling her to wait downstairs for him. She tiptoed across the living room floor and gazed at the still pool. There was, she thought, something touching about a swimming pool early in the morning, when it was too cold to swim and the deck chairs were covered with dew. It seemed a good example of the quirkiness of human nature that one of the ideas people had invented with their ponderous brains was to build pools in their backyards, lakes that drained, blue jewels shimmering against the savanna and the sand. She was so deep in her thoughts that she nearly cried out when Nick laid a hand on her shoulder.

"Don't scare me," she hissed.

"What planet were you on?" he asked.

She shrugged. "Hangover thoughts. Nothing riveting."

They crept to their bikes and rode up the street toward the center of town.

"It's over," she said when they'd ridden a safe distance from the house.

"What happened?"

"You don't want to know."

Nick stared straight ahead, as if he were riding alone. "You were supposed to be at the house yesterday when I came home."

"You were supposed to be with me on my birthday," Lucy snapped.

They had the street to themselves, so they rode in the middle.

"I'm sorry," Lucy said. "Maybe you'll be able to return the suit you bought for the wedding."

Nick shrugged. "You never know when you'll need a blue suit. Anyway, Hugh paid for it."

Lucy resisted the urge to make a remark about this. "Can I stay with you until I leave?"

"Naturally."

"Do you want to come with me?"

"To New York?"

"Not necessarily New York. Just somewhere where we could live a real life. Somewhere where we could do real things, instead of just hanging around waiting for other people to do things to us."

Nick braked to a halt. Lucy circled back to meet him.

"You'd end up paying for me just like Hugh does."

"It would be different," Lucy said. "The point is, we have to stop being afraid."

"Not this again."

"What?"

"You've lectured me about this before, your theory being that we could get married and live happily ever after if I weren't so afraid."

There was a pause.

"Right?" he asked.

She didn't say anything. She had counted on Nick not to fight with her; he was letting her down.

"Right?" he repeated.

She fiddled with the front wheel of her bicycle, turning it from side to side. "Okay, right," she said wearily.

"Lucy, if you're serious about this, I think it would be a good thing if you stopped being afraid of me."

"What are you talking about?"

"You're afraid to accept me as I am. You're afraid to see the truth about me."

"Which is?"

"Which is that I am a homosexual. That's my life. I've been gay for as long as I can remember. I'm not attracted to women, and that has nothing to do with fear. What if you met the greatest woman in the world and you liked her more than anyone? Would the reason that you didn't spend your life with her be that you were afraid to?"

"Maybe," she said defensively.

"Be honest. The reason would be that your sexual orientation tends toward men, and you can't change that."

"Yeah, but I don't feel like my sexual orientation is a tragedy. You do."

"I don't think I ever said that, exactly."

"You implied it."

"Maybe I did."

"Maybe?"

"Okay, I did. Maybe I wasn't exactly honest about my relationship with Hugh."

"Oh, come on. You're not going to tell me you're in love with Hugh now?"

"I don't know. I've barely given him a chance. The important thing for you to understand is that I do have a relationship with him. I'm here because I choose to be. I'm not out to change my life, I just want it to be a little bigger. You act as though there's something tangible that's preventing me from being with you, but do you really think Hugh could stop me if I wanted to leave? The fact of the matter is I'm not with you, not because I can't be, but because it's not what I want. I'm not going to go with you, wherever you go."

"You acted like you wanted to be with me!"

"And you acted like you wanted to be with me, but you don't. You want to be with a straight guy who bears a resemblance to me."

Lucy's throat grew hard and full as she tried not to cry.

"I love you, Lucy. If it's any consolation, and it probably won't be, Hugh and I are doing a lot better these days, and I attribute that to you. You made me care about myself enough to ask for what I need. Lucy, he never knew. I treated him like a pathetic, dirty old man, so he acted like one. He's promised to let me work, and I'm going to. I'm going to take a job as a permanent producer for the Theater by the Sea. Who knows? Maybe I'll end up in New York someday myself."

"Great," she said bitterly. "We can have a drink at Sardi's."

"I do love you, Lucy."

She looked at the surface of the street. "I feel like I've never really loved anybody, like I made it all up."

Nick smiled. "You love me, I know you do. I just can't be your only love, that's all."

She could no longer not cry.

"Come on," Nick said, punching her lightly on the arm, "come on."

"I'll be alone."

"I doubt it. But better that than being tied to a lemonade stand."

Lucy laughed sharply. "You don't even know."

"I can guess. Come on, let's go get some breakfast. Wouldn't pancakes help?"

They decided to go to the Holiday Inn. They decided it was too far to ride their bikes to the Holiday Inn, that it would be wiser to go back to Nick and Hugh's house to get the station wagon. They headed home and were halfway there when they heard a car gun its engine and a horn blare staccato honks behind them.

"Turn left!" Nick said.

Lucy obeyed without looking back, whipping into a quiet side street. Nick pulled up beside her.

"Damn, they're still following us. Don't look back."

"What is it?"

"Gaybashers, probably. Keep going, but don't start a chase."

The car horn blared again, breaking the morning's peace.

"Hey, Lucy! Where do you think you're going?"

"It's Dennis," Lucy hissed. She began to ride faster.

"Get up on the sidewalk!" Nick yelled.

The car pulled up beside her. Jack was driving.

"It's over, Dennis," she said. "You must realize that. Now leave me alone."

"What do you mean it's over?"

"I mean, leave me alone. Get away. I never want to see you again."

"Oh, come on, Lucy, just because I got a little drunk . . ."

"I mean it."

The car fell behind her for a moment, then pulled up alongside again. Dennis's face was twisted and mean.

"You owe me fifty dollars, Lucy."

Jack raced the motor menacingly. Nick seemed to be dropping back toward her.

"I'll pay you," she yelled into the wind. "Leave us alone."

"I want my money now." Dennis's face was pinched into a leer. Jack raced the motor again.

"I don't have any money with me."

Dennis scowled. When the car swerved toward her again, she began to pedal faster. Nick was up on the sidewalk, but her bike was heavy and awkward and she didn't think she had the strength to make it jump the curb.

"Turn right at the corner!" Nick called.

She saw him sail into the intersection and she jerked her bike to the right. The car swished past, and she felt a rush of warm wind just before she heard the squeal of frantic, angry brakes, the rip of metal against metal, a tinkling of glass.

They've killed Nick, she thought. She was so sure of it that she felt foolish for not having seen it coming. Before she had time to lose her nerve, she turned back, not looking at anything except the road beneath her until she arrived at the scene, where a fat black boy lay writhing on the ground. Babe's car sat on top of a crumpled motorbike, the headlights smashed.

"Go for help!" Dennis yelled to Nick. "Call an ambulance!"

"Are you all right?" Nick called to Lucy.

She nodded.

Dennis pulled the key from the ignition of the motorbike as Lucy bent down over the moaning boy. A large piece of flesh had been cut from his leg and was lying on the road nearby. As she gazed at his wound, she saw the layers of his body; the black skin, the yellow fat, the ruddy blood and muscle, the white bone.

She touched his head. "He's clammy. He must be in shock."

"I want to go home," said the boy.

"I'm sorry," said Dennis. "It was an accident."

"Where's Jack?" Lucy asked flatly.

"He can't get involved in something like this," Dennis said.

"Oh? It would seem to me he was already involved." Lucy laid her fingers on the boy's wrist. He barely had a pulse.

"Shit!" Dennis said. "What was a kid like this doing around here at this hour of the morning, anyway?"

"It's a free country, Dennis. Or hadn't you heard?"

Until the ambulance and the police arrived, she did what she could for the boy. Nick and Hugh pulled up as the police were questioning Dennis, and they were questioned, too. The paramedics told her that the boy would be all right, although he might lose the use of his leg. They lifted him onto a gurney and drove him away.

Someone tapped her on the shoulder.

"Did you see what happened, miss?" asked a policeman. "Did you see who was driving the car?"

Behind the policeman, Dennis signaled her to blame the accident on the boy.

"Did you see whose fault it was?" the policeman asked.

"I told you, he pulled out in front of me," Dennis said.

Lucy looked into the policeman's eyes and saw in them that if she handled herself in a certain way, he would make things easy on her, that if she gave the right answers she could probably be on a plane to New Zealand or the Central African Republic or even Philadelphia that afternoon. She closed her eyes and pressed her fingers to her temples as her mind's eye filled with images of all the boys she'd known and loved, or thought she loved, kissed, made love with, left, been jilted by, lied to, confided in, all of them marching over the crest of a green hill, going away.

She opened her eyes.

Nick was leaning against Hugh, Dennis against Babe's car.

"I didn't actually witness the accident," she said to the officer, "but the responsibility lies with me."